ABOUT THE AUTHOR

Doug Johnstone is a writer, musician and arts journalist based in Edinburgh. He has a PhD in nuclear physics. He is also a singer and multi-instrumentalist in a band, Northern Alliance, who are part of the Fence Collective. He is married and has a son. *Tombstoning* is his first novel.

Tombstoning

DOUG JOHNSTONE

PENGUIN BOOKS

PENGUIN BOOKS

Published by the Penguin Group
Penguin Books Ltd, 80 Strand, London WC2R 0RL, England
Penguin Group (USA) Inc., 375 Hudson Street, New York, New York 10014, USA
Penguin Group (Canada), 90 Eglinton Avenue East, Suite 700, Toronto, Ontario, Canada M4P 2Y3
(a division of Pearson Penguin Canada Inc.)
Penguin Ireland, 25 St Stephen's Green, Dublin 2, Ireland
(a division of Penguin Books Ltd)
Penguin Group (Australia), 250 Camberwell Road,
Camberwell, Victoria 3124, Australia (a division of Pearson Australia Group Pty Ltd)
Penguin Books India Pvt Ltd, 11 Community Centre,
Panchsheel Park, New Delhi – 110 017, India
Penguin Group (NZ), cnr Airborne and Rosedale Roads, Albany,
Auckland 1310, New Zealand (a division of Pearson New Zealand Ltd)
Penguin Books (South Africa) (Pty) Ltd, 24 Sturdee Avenue,
Rosebank, Johannesburg 2196, South Africa

Penguin Books Ltd, Registered Offices: 80 Strand, London WC2R 0RL, England

www.penguin.com

First published in Penguin Books 2006
1

Copyright © Doug Johnstone, 2006
All rights reserved

The moral right of the author has been asserted

Set in 11/13 pt PostScript Monotype Dante
Typeset by Rowland Phototypesetting Ltd, Bury St Edmunds, Suffolk
Printed in England by Clays Ltd, St Ives plc

ISBN-13: 978–0–141–02757–9
ISBN-10: 0–141–02757–6

For Andrew and Eleanor, Trish and Aidan

'The past is never dead. It's not even past.'

William Faulkner

I

The Antiquary

It all started with an email.

David stumbled into work just before ten, his short hair pointing several ways at once, his jeans a gritty grey-blue, with a whiff of last night's booze about him. As he swiped his card by the front door two removal men emerged, shuffling their way out with a battered pool table. There goes the last of the games room, thought David. It figured.

Still Waters was a thrusting, vibrant web-design company. At least it had been, almost, when the company launched five years earlier. Now that the dotcom dream had well and truly dissolved they were laying people off, frantically exaggerating to clients in a desperate attempt to win contracts, and sheepishly flogging all the superfluous, gimmicky crap they'd initially bought to attract graduates. The Playstation was long gone, as was the table football, and now the pool table was going the same way. David was surprised it had taken so long. After all, they'd already given nearly a dozen employees the bullet. Naturally, there were half a dozen directors still on the payroll, clocking up miles on the company Mercs and spending the afternoons at lunch or on one of Edinburgh's more exclusive golf courses. But further down the food chain they were reduced to a handful of designers, programmers and developers, all so disenchanted with pay-cuts, increased hours and lack of recognition that there might've been a mutiny on the directors' hands, if anyone could've been arsed.

David shrugged past the removal men into his cubbyhole corner of the office, keeping his head down to avoid being seen.

Still Waters occupied the first two floors of a crumbly old stone building hidden down a cobbled alleyway off the main drag of Stockbridge. The walls were thick, the windows small and the ceilings low. Nestled between bohemian antique sellers and the poshest charity shops in the country, Still Waters was within a few yards of umpteen restaurants, cafés, delis, bistros and boozers, the last of which David and his disgruntled colleagues made good use of whenever they could sneak out.

David was probably still a bit pissed from last night. Nothing special, just a few pints after work followed by cracking open the bottle of Lagavulin when he got back to the flat. He would probably have to knock that whisky nightcap thing on the head, even if it was excellent fifteen-year-old stuff.

He fixed himself a coffee, fired up the PC and settled in for a day of surfing, with the occasional work-related moment thrown in to keep folk off his back. Christ only knew how long the company would stay afloat. David was surprised that he hadn't been amongst those already booted out. He could do the work, it was a piece of piss to be honest, but he just so badly couldn't be bothered exerting himself for a company that was about to go tits up anyway. Today's hangover wasn't exactly helping. At the moment he was supposed to be working on a site for some ridiculous motivational guru, Frank Lavine, whose command of office buzzwords, feelgood gobbledegook and doublespeak was something to behold. David was tempted to stick some made-up, meaningless platitudes in there, see if old Frank noticed the difference.

He started wading through his emails. Twenty-four in the inbox since he'd left at five last night, including all the usual spam and junk – cock enlargement, Viagra, Prozac, lap-dancing clubs, buy yourself a degree, online mortgages – did anyone ever fall for this shite?

Then he saw it, that name, sitting amongst all the drivel. Nicola Cruickshank. A coincidence? There must be loads of Nicola Cruickshanks in the world, it wouldn't necessarily be from her. He clicked it open and as he read down he felt a tightening in his gut that couldn't solely be put down to his hangover.

From: nicola.cruickshank@historicscotland.co.uk
Subject: hullo you
Date: 8 August 2003 9:15:37 GMT
To: david.lindsay@stillwaters.co.uk

David,

Is this you? I'm pretty sure it is, because I saw your profile on the Still Waters website and it sounds like you. Anyway, hullo, how's it going? Long time no see and all that crap. Oh yeah, this is Nicola, as in Cruickshank, dunno if you remember me from all those years ago at Keptie High? Can't really believe that was 15 years ago, it seems like hardly any time. Then again it also seems like a lifetime ago, so who knows? I'm rambling.

How's life? Hope you're doing well, life's been good and that you haven't gotten fat and bald. Actually, scratch that, because if you are fat and bald then that last comment was insanely insensitive. I'm not helping by going on about it now, am I? I really don't know when to shut up in emails. But anyway, I hope you're well, irrespective of your current waistline and hair, or lack thereof.

And so to the point. I've been roped in by some of the illustrious ladies of our year at school to help organize a class reunion. I don't really have much to do with it, to be honest, but one of them rang me up and asked if I wouldn't mind trying to get in touch with a few people. When they mentioned your name I'll admit that my interest was piqued. So what the hell have you been up to for the last 15 years? Are you married? Kids? Are you even still male? (These days, anything can happen, you know, I'm not casting aspersions on your manhood or anything – look, here I am talking drivel again.)

Anyway, the reunion is organized for next Saturday, that's the

16th of August, in – believe it or not – Bally's. I know, it'll be bloody terrible probably but, well, I'm going and it would be nice if you could make it. I believe Bally's is now officially called the Waterfront or something, but everyone still calls it Bally's.

It would be great if you could come, but if you don't fancy it I understand. Either way, it would be good to hear from you. Feel free to give me a phone anytime you like if, for example, you think you need a bit more persuading about this whole Arbroath thing. Or just for a chat. It would honestly be great to talk to you.

Right, I've taken up way more of your time than I meant to so I'll leave it at that. Take care, and I hope you get in touch.

See ya,
Nicola xxx
mob: 07970 132 265

****

Nicola Cruickshank
Historic Scotland – Safeguarding Scotland's Built Heritage

****

His head was spinning. Nicola Cruickshank. He hadn't thought about her for years, but for what seemed like a lifetime he had fancied her at school, never getting up the bottle to go for it. He had always put it off and put it off, waiting for the right time, which inevitably never came. All through their drunken, hormone-addled sixth year they had flirted and danced around the issue, without ever getting anywhere. He waited and waited and waited for the right time and then . . . well, then there was the accident. And nothing was ever the same again.

He had never been back, not in fifteen years. That was helped in no small part by the fact that his parents had absconded to France, retiring to do up a barn in Limoges ten years before it was a trendy thing to do. Just as well, he would've struggled to go back to Arbroath, back to the place where his best friend had

4

died. And now, here was a call from someone he was besotted with at the time, asking him to do just that. Jesus.

David drifted through the day. His hangover gradually receded, but the buzz of Nicola stayed at the forefront of his mind. He re-read the email umpteen times, even printing it off to take with him into the bogs where he read it twice before having a quick snooze, his cheek pressed against the cold ceramic of the cistern.

He noticed that her message had managed to tell him virtually nothing about herself. She still had the same surname, so did that mean she wasn't married? He didn't suppose it meant anything much these days. She worked for Historic Scotland, wasn't that in Salisbury Place? Only about five minutes from his Rankeillor Street flat in the Southside of the city. How long had she been in the same city as him? She had gone to Glasgow Uni, he remembered that much, but then a degree only took four years, what the hell had she been doing for the other eleven?

He couldn't stop thinking about her during the afternoon meeting, when they were informed that if productivity didn't improve there would be more layoffs. He wasn't being paranoid, there really were pointed looks in his direction at the mention of this, but the two pints at lunchtime helped him to ignore that.

By five o'clock he was thinking about Nicola more than ever.

Nicola had clicked 'send' then had a tiny panic attack. Why had she written to him first thing in the bloody morning, before coffee? Was she nuts? She re-read what she'd sent and cringed – it was even more rambling than her usual emails, and that was saying something. She didn't have much demanding work today, just filing and processing, so she could've left it until she was a tad more coherent. Then again, she *had* been putting it off for ages, so at least now it was done.

David Lindsay. No one from Arbroath had heard anything from him for fifteen years, not since the accident and then the funeral afterwards. After she'd been called up about the reunion

5

it had taken about half an hour of googling to find out that he designed web pages for a company in Stockbridge – quite a flashy and well-to-do one, judging by their website and list of clients. So he was still in Edinburgh after all this time, living in the same city as her for the last four years.

She didn't have a problem with Arbroath, but she much preferred her life in Edinburgh, and her job at Historic Scotland was just about perfect, allowing her to get stuck in to history, architecture and archaeology without any of the pompous stuffiness of academia. The office was fine, if a little gossipy for her liking, and she worked on site a fair bit, which always made her feel like she was doing a proper job, not just penpushing.

As for her life outside work, that was dominated by Amy. She had been a grumpy little madam this morning when Nicola walked her to Sciennes Primary. Just like her mum, she was definitely not a morning person. Nicola pictured the two of them at the school gates, straggly haired, bleary eyed and buttoned up all wrong, two generations of the same family both struggling with the concept of an early rise. Sometimes it scared the shit out of her, how much Amy took after her, then at other times Amy seemed like an alien from another planet, with all these weird ideas of her own. Such is parenthood, Nicola thought with a sigh.

She tried to remember what David looked like. Tall, definitely – at least as tall as her, and pretty cute in a gangly, unformed kind of way. Plenty of buzz and chat and daft ideas, she remembered, mostly fuelled by booze, but he was still pretty good company to be with. She had fancied him, she supposed, although thinking about things in such terms now at the age of thirty-four seemed more than a little ridiculous. They had kissed, hadn't they? A couple of times at parties or down at Bally's or something, but she couldn't really remember. She hadn't taken it any further. They were all heading off to uni by the end of the summer anyway, that was the plan. She was going to Glasgow, he was off to Edinburgh, not exactly much of a distance away, but when you'd grown up in Arbroath such places seemed like a different universe. And besides, he hadn't really said anything about fancying her. God, listen to yourself, she thought, talking about fancying each other, it's as if all this reunion chat is making you regress into a former life.

She wondered what he would make of her email. What did she make of it herself? It didn't matter anyway, it was out there, in the ether, winging its way to his inbox and that was that. She had issued the invitation to the reunion as instructed, so it was up to him now what he did about it.

Nicola was looking forward to the reunion, just out of amiable curiosity more than anything else. She was back in Arbroath quite a lot, letting Amy spend time with Granny and Grandpa and all that, but she rarely went out when she was back, and she hadn't seen most of the folk from their class in years. She heard plenty of gossip from her folks; in a town that small it was inevitable that everyone seemed to know everyone else's business. She wasn't sentimental; would never have logged on to Friends Reunited expecting an unchanged world. But now there was this reunion, she was genuinely interested in how everyone's lives had turned out. Hers had been gently adventurous, and she had Amy to show for it, so there must be dozens of other mini-adventures out there waiting to be discovered. David had blue eyes, she suddenly remembered, really cute blue eyes. She shook her head a little to clear the thought, and got up to make that coffee.

David turned into St Stephen Street in the muggy afternoon heat and descended into the subterranean gloom of the Antiquary. Spook and Alice from work were already in, and Spook was at the bar so he put in his order and headed towards Alice amid the burnished oak scruffiness of the pub. Alice was an irrepressibly chirpy English web designer, ten years younger than David, who managed to be relentlessly upbeat despite the perilous state the company was in. The fact that she did so without getting on anyone's nerves was something of a miracle. Spook, on the other hand, was a dishevelled slacker goon who was obviously completely uninterested in his job, an attitude David had some sympathy with.

He couldn't shake the image of Nicola from his mind. He'd already googled her, but rooting around the Historic Scotland website hadn't come up with anything. He pictured her standing outside Boots, next to the steeple in the centre of Arbroath, that last New Year there. She was wrapped up in a massive red duffel coat and woolly hat and they had their Hogmanay kiss, which kind of extended itself into a snog. He didn't know how long they snogged for (in fact, he couldn't recall much more about that evening) but he did remember that they were interrupted by someone getting thrown through Boots' window by opportunist looters, and they all had to scarper quick. He and Nicola had been drunk. At least, he had been drunk, and assumed she was too. Anyway, that was the closest he'd got to her. He had completely forgotten about it until this morning. Parts of his brain not used in fifteen years were getting powered up and made to process information. How could one little email manage that?

Spook and Alice got talking about work, but David wasn't listening. They were joined by a couple more of the company's bottom feeders, keen as ever to slag off the directors and the owner, safe in the knowledge that at least the next forty-eight hours were work-free and theirs to fuck up whichever way they chose.

David still wasn't listening. He was thinking of the time he and Nicola had sat beside a fire on Elliot Beach, huddled together on a blanket against the North Sea chill. Several others were sitting around drinking and a few couples had sneaked off to the sand dunes for more privacy. Two brave idiots were skinny-dipping. They hadn't even kissed then, David just enjoying the proximity to her, feeling her long, fair hair against his cheek, looking at that beautiful, slightly crooked nose of hers that she wiggled when she was amused like that woman out of *Bewitched*, and gazing at the long bony elegance of her neck.

But one memory leads to another and another, and once he was on Elliot Beach he was straight away thinking of Colin, how the two of them used to walk Colin's Irish setters in the afternoons along there, fooling the dogs into the water after imaginary sticks and arguing about the problems with Arbroath FC; excited about how Colin was going to make a difference when he joined the club.

And once Colin was in his mind, it was a small step to the funeral a few weeks later, up at the Western Cemetery. Standing there, utterly numb, in a borrowed suit several sizes too big, his school shoes and his dad's black tie, wondering how the fuck such things could be allowed to happen.

This is why he hadn't thought about the past, why he hadn't been back to Arbroath, this knot in his stomach even now, fifteen years later, thinking about the wasted life, the wasted opportunities, the stupid, pointless waste of it all. He hadn't consciously thought about Colin for years before today, but now the memories filled his mind. The oddly curly black hair that framed a face which seemed to make every girl (and every girl's mum) in town swoon, with a disarming little smile and a glint in his dark eyes that said he knew he was good-looking but wasn't going to abuse that fact. The way he was also the strongest and fastest person David had known, yet you only saw that on the football pitch. He was also bloody smart academically and could've gone to uni, but kept quiet about it. The way he was so effortlessly good-natured was something that used to simultaneously produce awe and irritation in David. How could someone be so nice all the time? But he was, he was nice all the time, but never sickeningly so. And he'd been dead now for fifteen years.

There was a calendar behind the bar, flaunting a bland picture of Highland beauty. David realized with a start that it was the eighth of August, which meant it was fifteen years and two days since what would've been Colin's eighteenth birthday. That meant fifteen years and three days since his funeral. For the first few years the anniversary had produced a sense of foreboding in him, an uneasy tension, but somehow, somewhere along the line, he had forgotten about it. This year it had zipped by through the week and he'd been utterly oblivious.

And now there was this invitation from Nicola. He had the printout of the email in his back pocket, pretending to himself that he'd accidentally left it there when he came out the bog earlier in the day, but he knew he wanted that contact with her, that reminder of her, close to him this weekend. His mind was now racing with memories of Arbroath and school, the pubs and parties, fights and snogs that made up the final few months of life there. He sensed a rush of energy, and it felt like the inside of his skin was itchy. His teeth seemed to throb and his throat was dry. How could the dim and distant past affect him like this?

He finished the dregs of his pint and got another round in. These days he was very definitely on weaker cooking lager. For years he had pummelled his body with executive – Stella, Kronenbourg, Staropramen – but now his body was rebelling. His hangovers got worse and he seemed to get more drunk, despite drinking less.

He returned to the table. The rest of them were still sniping at Still Waters, picking over the debris of the latest botched job – a half-arsed site for a charity that was delivered over budget, past deadline and with only half the functionality they'd promised – and what it might mean for the future. All their coats were already on shaky pegs, and they were speculating who would be next out the door. This wasn't exactly what David had pictured when he'd done his computer science degree all those years ago. Back then it was as if computers had barely even been invented, and if ever there had been an opportunity of getting in on the ground floor it was then. After his degree and a couple of years kicking around doing fuck all – working in pubs, mostly – he'd done a Mickey Mouse web-design post-grad at Napier, just when the internet was getting going. The millions were there for the making, as Amazon, Ebay and Google had subsequently proven, but none of that success had come David's way.

He was also on his own. His friends in Edinburgh were either people he'd known since university or random mates he'd picked up on the way. With precious few exceptions they were all either married, engaged or in long-term relationships. Several of them now had kids. He had been shocked the first time he'd had to hold a friend's baby. They'd let him hold on to their child? What the hell were they thinking? But him, he had no one. Sure there had been women, although not nearly as many as maybe he would like to think when he totted it all up, but for whatever reason (and he couldn't really think of any, now that he tried to) none of them had stuck around very long. And of course, he had never kept in touch with schoolmates. Christ, what was that Lemonheads' song he listened to all the time back in his student days? Something about a ship without a rudder. That just about nailed his life at the moment.

He dipped in and out of the conversation around the table, gazing absent-mindedly at a dark and dusty portrait hanging over the empty fireplace in front of him. The guy in the painting looked like a right stuffed shirt, from maybe two hundred years ago, and his eyes gazed impassively back at David.

Just then Spook suggested they fire up into town, maybe the Basement, make a night of it. David couldn't face it. He'd had a few pints and, sure, he wanted to get hammered, but not with these people and not in the Basement, which, anyway, he'd been going to for so long it made him feel like a fucking granddad. He scooped the last of his pint and, shaking his head at the protestations from the motley assortment around the table, got up from his stool, doing a John Wayne dismount, and headed for the door.

It was shockingly bright outside the Antiquary, and David squinted reflexively into the sun, raising his hand to shield his eyes. The mugginess of earlier had burnt off, and the Scottish summer sun was doing its best to burn pale northern skin into the evening. David was a bit unsteady, having had a few pints on an empty stomach. He decided he couldn't be arsed with the bus home, and flagged a passing taxi.

'Rankeillor Street, mate,' he said as he keeled into the back, ignoring the signs to put his seatbelt on. It was only then he remembered with a groan that it was the first weekend of the festival, and the traffic across the centre of town would be a fucking nightmare. He was in for a long, bumpy and expensive ride.

So what about this class reunion? he thought. Of course, he wouldn't go. He couldn't, not after all these years. It sounded from Nicola's email that all these people had kept in touch with each other over the last decade and a half – she'd said that the organizers phoned her up, hadn't she? – how the hell was he supposed to fit into all that?

Who else would be there? He found himself struggling to match names and faces from his class. He wondered what it was like for those people who had never left Arbroath, wandering around town repeatedly encountering faces, places, street names, buildings, parks from the past – it must be like walking through a history book, or a graveyard where through some freakish twist you can see all the ghosts, the decomposing corpses risen again to wander forever, never finding peace.

Then again, he had his history in Edinburgh, he had lived here almost as long as he had in Arbroath. That sudden thought shocked him. He worked it out – in three more years he would've spent half his life in this city. But those were adult years, grown-up years, even if they hadn't really felt like it. The Arbroath years, they were rammed full of all that formative childhood crap, the stuff that supposedly made you who you were, not that David subscribed to that point of view. You made up who you were in the present, moment to moment, and that could change any time you liked. When he moved to Edinburgh he'd changed from David to Dave, not such a big leap, dropping a syllable from your name, but it signified everything, a new start, a new person, a newborn life, with no history, no past, no baggage. A clean slate.

Who was he kidding? He had carried Colin's death around with him for years. He had never talked about it. Ever. To anyone. Why not? Truth be told, what was the point? The past was a foreign country, or whatever that saying was. Damn right it was. He had basically started a whole new life in Edinburgh back in 1988, and had never looked back.

Until now.

He wondered again who would be there at the reunion that he might know. What about the other two from the ADS? The ADS – it seemed so puerile now. The Arbroath Drinking Society had been named as a piss-take of the Arbroath Soccer Society – the equally pretentious name that the footy casuals had given themselves. The casual violence surrounding football had seemed all-pervasive at the time, and their wee joke at the arseholes that perpetrated it was intended to make a point, something which was now lost.

There were four of them in the ADS. Himself, Colin, Gary Spink and Neil Cargill. They were best of friends in fourth year at school, when they'd formed the drinking club, and it had lasted as a benevolent clique for two years. By the time they left school, though, the four of them were drifting apart, but they still clung to a last childish emblem of camaraderie, more out of convenience and an embarrassment about admitting that their lives were going in different directions. Colin was about to embark on a career as a professional footballer with Arbroath FC; David was off to uni; Neil, with nothing better on offer, had signed up for a life of military discipline in the Marines and was heading for basic training at the end of the summer; and Gary, well, Gary was stuck in Arbroath with the prospect of working for a bank, building society or worse.

Then Colin had died. After the funeral David had left town

early, speeding over to France to help his folks renovate their barn. From there he had gone directly to Edinburgh, and had never since spoken to anyone from Arbroath.

Until now.

He just couldn't go to the reunion, he thought as the taxi pulled into his street and he started rummaging for notes and cash. But then he thought of Nicola again. Jesus, Nicola Cruickshank, he said out loud, shaking his head. He paid the taxi driver and stumbled out the cab into his home.

David's flat was a typical bachelor affair – two black leather sofas and a large flat-screen TV in the living room, generic film posters from his past (*Trainspotting, Reservoir Dogs*) lining the hall, and a messy bedroom dominated by a massive king-size bed. Among the debris in the living room were CDs, DVDs, magazines, empty lager cans and a couple of large pizza boxes. David finished another lager and surfed channels, cursing with each flick the banal choice of Friday-night television.

He should've stayed out. What use was sitting here on the weekend, alone, doing fuck all? No use, that's what. But then he thought of the rest of them in the Basement, and he felt a shiver of repulsion at that prospect too. He mentally surfed through his other friends in town, but couldn't come up with anyone he wanted to talk to, let along meet up with. Where did that leave him? Back here on his own, that's where.

He made for the drinks cabinet, a classy wooden globe, and poured himself a house measure of Lagavulin. As he sat back down, the sofa gave a sigh under his weight. He took the email printout from his pocket and read it again.

A school reunion was not an attractive prospect, that was for sure, but Nicola Cruickshank? That was a different story. He dug his mobile out his pocket and thought about phoning her for the next fifteen minutes, his body enduring little ripples of nervous excitement each time he went to dial, then stopped. Eventually he downed what was left in his glass, poured himself a bigger one, sat down with his mobile in his hand and dialled the number at the bottom of the printout.

Who the hell was that now?

Nicola had not long got Amy to bed after the usual lengthy struggle of wills between parent and child, and before that she'd had her mum on the phone for over half an hour. Bless her mum and everything, but she didn't half go in for pointless gossip. She had just poured herself a second large glass of wine when the mobile went off. She fished it out of her bag and checked the screen. She didn't recognize the number. Probably some arsehole trying to sell her something, she thought as she pressed 'reply'.

'Hello? Is that Nicola? Nicola Cruickshank?'

It didn't sound like a call centre eejit.

'That's me.'

'This is Dave, Dave Lindsay. Erm . . . from Arbroath, I suppose.'

Nicola laughed out loud and followed it with a little squeal, much to her own amused disgust.

'David Lindsay. How the hell are you?'

'I'm good, thanks, a wee bit tipsy, truth be told. How the hell are you back?'

'Pretty good, pretty good.' Nicola found herself laughing again. 'Well, I suppose the appropriate cliché is long time no see, isn't it? I'm guessing that you are the David Lindsay who works for Still Waters, then, and that you got my rambling email today?'

'I am indeed the Dave Lindsay of Still Waters fame, although for how much longer, Christ only knows. And I did get your email, yes, although it wasn't really rambling at all, it was . . . it was nice to hear from you after so long. Listen Nicola . . . I . . . I suppose I don't really know why I phoned, except that you mentioned in your email that I was welcome to call any time, so, well, here I am phoning you. I hope it's not a bad time or anything . . . is it?'

'No, it's fine, I'm glad you called. So, what do you think then?'

There was a silence down the line, followed by what sounded to Nicola like glugging.

'Think about what,' said David cautiously.

'The reunion.'

'Oh yeah, the reunion. I don't really think it's my bag, if you know what I mean. I've never even been back there, not once in fifteen years, not since . . .'

'Don't be soft,' said Nicola, deliberately filling the gap David had left at the end of his sentence. 'It's the same for everyone, David. I don't suppose anyone's seen anyone else for years, but that's kind of the point, I guess. Everyone's in the same boat. Come along, it'll be a laugh. And even if it's shit, it'll be a shit laugh, if you know what I mean.'

'All the same . . .'

There was that glugging noise again.

'What are you drinking?' said Nicola.

'What?'

'What are you drinking? I can hear you slugging away on something.'

'Oh, whisky. Lagavulin.'

'An Islay, very nice.'

'You know about whisky?'

'I know about a lot of things, none of it very useful. I'm on the Chenin Blanc myself. Are you at home?'

'Yeah, and you?'

'Afraid so. All on my lonesome. How sad is that, sitting at home drinking alone watching shite telly on a Friday night.'

'Snap.'

'So, listen David Lindsay from Arbroath,' said Nicola, 'are you sure about the reunion? You can't be persuaded to come along, keep me company amongst the scary freaks that all our ex-classmates will have turned into?'

'How do you know I've not turned into a scary freak?'

Nicola laughed, wiggled her nose a little and took a swig of wine.

'That's a very good question. I suppose I don't. But then the same goes for me. Maybe we're the scary freaks, and everyone else has turned out normal. Shall we go to the reunion and find out?'

'I really don't think so.'

'Tell you what, why don't we meet up, and I'll have a go at talking you round in person?'

Nicola was surprised at the idea which leapt from her mouth before it had even properly formed in her brain. There was a long pause at the other end of the line. Did he want to meet up with her? Did she want to meet up with him?

'Why not?' she heard coming down the line at her. 'Where and when did you have in mind?'

She had to think on her feet, she hadn't expected this at all.

'What are you up to tomorrow afternoon?'

'Nothing yet.'

'OK, I've got a few hours spare while Amy's at a friend's birthday party, so how about if you meet me outside the Museum of Scotland on Chambers Street at two o'clock. How does that sound?'

'Cool.' Then a pause. 'Who's Amy?'

'Oh shit, didn't I say already? Amy's my daughter.'

'You have a daughter?'

'Very well deduced from my last statement. Yes, I have a daughter. A gorgeous little eight-year-old who is equal parts sweet angel and stroppy bitch. Do you have any kids?'

'No.'

'Well, I guess we can do all this chat tomorrow,' said Nicola. 'If you still want to meet.'

'Sure, why wouldn't I?'

'Just checking. Right, two o'clock outside the museum. I'll see you there?'

'OK. Have a nice evening, sitting in drinking on your own.'

'Right back at you. See you tomorrow.'

'Yeah. See you.'

Nicola pressed 'end call'. What just happened? Had she just organized a bloody date? No, it was just two old school friends meeting for a chat. After fifteen years? OK, that seemed slightly odd, to just arrange to meet like that after so long, but where was the harm in it? She re-ran the conversation in her head, what she could remember of it. He didn't have kids, but she didn't know if he was married or not. Mind you, now she came to think about it, she hadn't explained her situation (or lack of one) with Amy's dad either. So they were quits on that score. What did it matter anyway, she wasn't looking for anything out of this, just to meet up with someone she knew and quite liked at school to swap stories about how their lives had turned out.

He had seemed . . . well, she didn't really know how he seemed on the phone. Cheery? A bit pissed? Maybe he was really drunk and he wouldn't remember the conversation in the morning. She would go to the museum, see if he turned up. She loved that place anyway, ever since they'd tacked it on to the old Royal Museum a few years back. Of course you couldn't keep the whole history of a country in one turreted building, but it was a good start, and she liked the peace, the airiness and the dignity of the ancient past that the place seemed to hold, despite being new.

Yes, she would go to the museum tomorrow, and see what happened. What the hell harm could it do?

2

A Declaration

Christ, I'm not as fit as I used to be, David thought as he puffed his way up Chambers Street. He was ten minutes late and he was working up a sweat in the close August heat. He had worn two layers, a T-shirt over a long-sleeved top, assuming it would be cold out, but the day had thrown him a curve ball and was almost relentlessly bright and sticky. The arse of his jeans was wet with sweat and his feet were hotting up in his Golas.

He looked ahead at the museum but couldn't see anyone waiting. Shit, she's already left, he thought; either that or she decided not to come at all. He couldn't blame her, it had seemed surprising when she suggested it in the first place. Maybe she'd been drunk last night, and had forgotten the conversation. No, she had an eight-year-old daughter, she wouldn't be sitting loaded in the house with her, would she? Why not, he supposed – there were no rules about that sort of thing, were there?

After he'd put the phone down he'd had another few whiskies, but the memory of the chat was still strong in his mind. Her voice sounded more grown-up than he remembered. She still did that thing where it sounded like she was about to laugh after every single sentence, but not in an annoying way, more like she just found any situation thoroughly entertaining.

He got to the museum's entrance and there was definitely no one there. He was knackered. Is this what happens to your body in your thirties, he thought, you start getting worn out just from walking fast? He had to start getting fit again, soon. He'd said that to himself so many times over the last three years that he now just ignored himself, knowing it would never happen. He was standing with his hands on his knees, getting his breath back when he looked up. There she was.

His throat felt tight as he looked at her. Goddamn it, she looked fine. She was beautiful. Her hair was a little shorter, more stylish maybe, but still a bit all over the place. Her wide smile and clear, hazel eyes were as welcoming as he remembered and that nose, that kooky little nose just killed him. She was wearing a pair of sleek black trousers and a flimsy fawn blouse, and seemed taller somehow. He remembered her as being pretty but always slightly uncomfortable with that fact. She had definitely grown into her looks, she fitted her features better and seemed so at ease with herself, confident.

Her smile grew wider as she approached him, and he felt himself responding with an idiotic grin. He awkwardly stuck out a hand and she laughed, grabbed him and kissed him on both cheeks before standing back and giving him the once-over, her hands still on his shoulders.

'You haven't changed a bit, is the correct cliché, I believe,' she said, and her nose went for a wiggle. David felt the knot in his stomach disappearing and knew they were going to get along just fine.

'That cliché applies much more to yourself, I suspect,' David said, 'except you actually look younger and better than you did fifteen years ago. Whereas I'm just the same, except with two stone of weight added on somewhere.'

'Well, you were always too skinny at school,' she said. 'I can't believe it, David Lindsay from Arbroath, as I live and breathe. How about that?'

'Actually, most folk call me Dave these days.'

'I think I'll stick with David. It's more grown-up. And weren't you David in school?'

'Yeah, I changed it when I came to Edinburgh.'

'Ah, the old "drop a syllable" routine. Never succumbed to it myself. Day one of "throwing off the shackles of the past" and all that. I think I'll stick with David, how would that be?'

'That would be just fine.'

'Good stuff. So what now, David? Fancy a trawl through thousands of years of Scottish history?'

'Not really, to be honest. It seems like such a nice day maybe we could just find a beer garden or something . . .'

'Nonsense. Apart from anything else, I'll burn to a bloody crisp in this sun, my pasty face can't handle it. And anyway, I love this building and all the old stuff they've got in there. You didn't do history at school, did you?'

'No.'

'Well, then I can be your informal guide through the corridors of time' – she was putting on a booming voice-over voice – 'through thousands of years of bloodthirsty mayhem and savage carnage.' She returned to her normal voice with a laugh. 'Eat yer heart out, Simon Schama. Come on, I won't lecture you too much, and I promise to go for a pint later on. How's that?'

David couldn't give a damn about the last five thousand years of Scottish history, but he sure as hell wanted to spend the next few hours with Nicola Cruickshank. He motioned towards the museum's squat, sandy turret of an entrance.

'After you, madam. Is age before beauty the appropriate cliché?'

'Watch it, I'm only a few months older than you,' said Nicola, punching him on the arm and laughing to herself. David watched her go inside with wide eyes, a big smile and feeling for all the world like he was eighteen years old again.

The air was cool inside and it was so dark compared to the glare of the street that it took David a couple of minutes to see things clearly. Gangs of rucksacked foreign schoolkids filled the airy space with shrill chatter, while tired-looking families trudged around the main concourse. Nicola was a few yards ahead of him already, heading past a crumbly sandstone cross into a section marked Kingdom of the Scots. She turned back, beamed that smile at him and waved her hand in encouragement.

David wasn't hot on museums. He didn't really see the point in all that ancient history, and the exhibits always seemed so dry, dusty and disconnected with anything remotely like a real life that someone might actually have lived. Maybe he just didn't have the leap of imagination necessary to fully appreciate what all this old crap was meant to signify. But for the sake of hanging out with Nicola he could easily stomach a few lumps of old rock and metal, the odd statue or bit of broken pottery. He could see her at the first spotlit display. My god, she was beautiful. He walked into the first room keeping his eyes on her all the way.

Nicola was studiously examining a tiny metallic trinket box in the display cabinet, but she was thinking about David. She knew he was watching her. When you were a woman with years of experience of catching men's eyes, you knew when someone was watching you, you could just sense it. She didn't often appreciate it, but she liked the feeling today because she knew that he was comparing her school self with herself now, and she reckoned that modern Nicola won hands down. She couldn't figure out why exactly, but she just felt like more of a human being than that awkward, gawky kid she had been all those years before.

She'd made a joke about it, but David really hadn't changed. Well, OK, physically he had filled out a little, she could see that around his face, but that really was a good thing in her book; she'd always thought he had a kind of haunted look about him when he was younger, like there wasn't quite enough flesh under the skin stretched tight across his cheeks. He had shorter hair and it was a mess, but it was a cool mess. He was dressing younger than his age, a T-shirt over a long-sleeved top, skater-boy jeans and trainers, but then there was nothing wrong with that as long as you didn't look ridiculous. And David didn't look ridiculous. Far from it. He looked pretty damn cute. She wasn't getting carried away or anything. But he was cute.

'The Monymusk reliquary,' said David, reading the blurb. 'Associated with St Columba and Robert the Bruce. It's tiny. What does it do?'

'You keep ancient relics in it.'

'Relics?'

'Bones. Of saints. This one was small so they could wear it round their necks. They paraded it in front of the troops at Bannockburn, so they say.'

'Who says?'

'Historians.'

'Ah, them.'

'It sounds like you don't hold much truck with the word of historians. And before you say anything, bear in mind that I've got an honours degree in history and archaeology from Glasgow Uni.'

'I was just about to say that historians are great, and always right.'

'Nah, you're right, they're a bunch of speculative bastards. Especially all the high-profile television ones.' She looked away from the strange shiny box in front of them and around the room. 'Recognize anything in here?'

David looked around. In front of them was a small sign which said 'Scotland Defined'. That seemed like quite a claim, he thought, but he let it pass. On either side the walls were covered in large quotations, done in fancy script, and he realized straight away that they were quotations from the Declaration of Arbroath. They had, of course, done it to fucking death at school, seeing as how it was the town's main claim to fame. The Scottish nobility's letter to the Pope backing Robert the Bruce as king, asking the Pope to recognize Scotland as an independent nation and asking if he'd mind having a go at the English for hammering the crap out of us. Written, signed and sealed in Arbroath Abbey in 1320. The primary school history lessons were trickling back now. He read the two inscriptions, one about not cowing down to the English while a hundred of us are still kicking around, the other about fighting for freedom. It was all very *Braveheart*.

'Ah, I get it,' he said. 'A not-so-subtle piece of subliminal advertising for the school reunion, is that it? Surround me with messages from the past about the importance of Arbroath in our history?'

'Nah, I just thought it would be a cheeky laugh to bring you here,' she said. 'My own declaration of Arbroath. Or something. Actually it didn't occur to me until after I put the phone down last night. But it fits quite nicely, don't you think?'

She turned and looked at him. Her eyes were a very attractive shade of brown. They were smiling at each other now, both caught in a moment, wondering what was really going on here. Nicola moved first, breaking eye contact and heading through into the next room of the museum in a casual saunter that felt slightly on the forced side.

David followed on, feeling a bit like a dog on a lead, but happily wagging his tail. They wandered around the rest of the floor, swapping comments on the bits and bobs in glass cases, the stone sculptures, the old swords, armour, coins, trinkets, spears and a multitude of other pieces of the pointless past. He paid scant attention to the exhibits, his thoughts constantly returning to Nicola. What were they doing here? Why had she asked him? Why had he agreed to come?

He made an effort to concentrate at a display of Robert the Bruce stuff, reading the accompanying blurb which said that everything in the case was either 'a facsimile of the original', 'rumoured to have belonged to Robert the Bruce' or 'found at Bannockburn, but possibly a later forgery'. Christ, the stuff in here wasn't even the original old crap, it was less ancient copies of old crap. A thought suddenly struck him.

'Is the Declaration of Arbroath here?' he said.

'No, it's in Register House on Charlotte Square.'

'Why?'

'Who knows? Historian politics? It's a backbiting business, the study of Scottish history. Not quite as bloodthirsty as the history itself, but not without its battles.'

By this time they had worked their way around the ground floor. The restrained air of the place, the relentlessly studious vibe, was beginning to tire him. He looked up from the open-plan concourse and the building seemed to go up forever, shafts of daylight splitting the dusty air at irregular intervals.

'How many floors has this place got?'

'Six.'

'Jesus. You're joking.'

Nicola looked at David's face. She'd realized straight away that he wasn't at all interested in the museum and its exhibits, and she'd kept on slowly heading round the place to wind him up, see how long he could put on a brave face just to stay with her. She was testing him and she knew it was a bit puerile, but she had enjoyed doing it all the same. She laughed, looking at his hangdog expression, and took his arm, turning him towards the exit.

'OK, David Lindsay from Arbroath, no more history for today. You've earned your pint.'

'Too right I have,' said David, relieved to be leaving, exhilarated to be arm in arm with this woman and damn well looking forward to the first pint of the day.

Sandy Bell's was that rarest of things, a traditional pub still going strong in the centre of town. The tiny space was dominated by a large ornate gantry lined with dozens of single malt bottles. Half a dozen crumpled old men lined the bar. A young couple sat in the corner in front of the toilets playing guitar and fiddle gently, the melodies and rhythms intertwining with the thick fog of cigarette smoke that danced in the sunlight filtering through the windows. Nicola and David were squeezed into the table at the front of the bar, both nursing pints of lager, and they could just see the arse end of the museum across the road. They clinked glasses together in a cheers and drank.

'So,' said David with a deliberately ironic air of clunky formality. 'Nicola Cruickshank. From Arbroath. Tell me about your life for the last fifteen years.'

She gave him a sideways look. 'The concise version, or the ultra-concise one?'

'Concise version, please.'

'Left school, four years at Glasgow, backpacked round the world, worked in Australia, came home, discovered I was pregnant, had Amy, worked at Arbroath Abbey, moved to Edinburgh.'

She had been counting off the points on her fingers with a smile, and now returned to her pint.

'Wow, what the hell is the ultra-concise version like?'

'Graduated, travelled, Amy, job.'

'Fair enough. So . . . a daughter, eh?'

'Yes, indeed. I assume you're wondering about the father? Well, I haven't seen him since before Amy was born. He's Australian, we had a thing going over there for a while, nothing even remotely serious, then we split up and I came back to Scotland. Two weeks after I got off the plane I discovered I was two months pregnant. That was 1995. He knows about her, I post pictures and he sends stuff on birthdays and Christmas, but he's about as interested in us as we are in him, to be honest. He's also six years younger than me, barely more than a baby himself when I got pregnant, and on the other side of the world, so I can't really blame him for not taking more of an interest.'

They both took another swig of lager as a plaintive violin line meandered around the room.

'I guess that must've been tricky, bringing a daughter up yourself.'

'I had the family. My folks were great about it, they couldn't get enough of her. Still can't. After a year or two I managed to get a job at the abbey, doing the tourist guide stint. I suppose I was slumming it with a degree and everything, but it was a decent enough job. Plus I got a foot in the door at Historic Scotland, and now I work at the headquarters at Salisbury Place, inspecting and categorizing listed buildings and that sort of malarkey. It's a job I really enjoy, and it's good to be out of Arbroath.'

She swigged the remains of her pint and squeezed out from behind the table to get the round in.

'Same again?'

'Yeah, cheers.'

David watched her as she went to the bar and couldn't help noticing her figure. She was as slim as she'd always been, but she still had curves where women were supposed to have curves. He wondered how his own body had changed over the last fifteen years. It didn't look as good as hers, that's for sure. When Nicola turned back with the pints he self-consciously turned away to look down at his empty pint glass. Nicola noticed, smiled and squeezed back into her seat.

'So,' she said, drawling the word in a parody of his earlier opening gambit. 'David Lindsay. From Arbroath. A potted history, if you please.'

'I'm afraid mine isn't nearly so interesting. If I count them on my fingers like you I'll probably only get to about three.'

'Quit stalling and make with the info.'

'OK. Left school, came to Edinburgh to do computer science, graduated with a 2:2, worked in pubs for a couple of years, did a post-grad at Napier in web design, worked through a string of gradually less impressive and less exciting jobs over the last' – he counted in his head – 'Jesus, eight years. I've been doing this shit for eight years.'

'And now?'

'And now what?'

'What about this place you're at now – what is it, Run Deep?'

'Still Waters, I like what you've done there. Nah, it's a shithole, and a failing one at that. The arse has fallen out the web-design market, everyone and their bloody dog can do it nowadays. I suspect the dole queue beckons soon, to be honest.'

'Really? Sorry to hear that. Although it doesn't sound as if you particularly like the job anyway.'

'No, I don't suppose I do, but it pays the bills.'

'That is surely the saddest phrase in the English language – "it pays the bills".'

'I know what you mean. But it does.'

David took a breather and a few slugs of lager. Just the mention of his mundane, depressing work was enough to get him down. Nicola couldn't help noticing.

'Anyway, enough talk about work,' she said. 'This is a Saturday after all. Instead, let me apply some peer pressure on you about this school reunion. Give me your hand.'

David offered up his arm and Nicola grabbed his wrist and started twisting.

'Chinese burn, Chinese burn,' she said. 'Are you gonna come to this bloody thing?'

David drew his arm away laughing.

'I don't know. It makes me feel a bit queasy even thinking about it.'

'Come on. I know we've only just re-met after fifteen years, but we're getting along OK, aren't we?'

'Sure.'

'Well, it'll be the same with everyone else, won't it?'

'I don't know about that.'

'Why not?'

'Well . . . I don't know.'

'Not good enough.'

'The trouble is, you've obviously kept in touch with people from back there over the years. I haven't. Not only have I not kept in touch, I haven't even set foot in the place since . . .'

'Since Colin died?'

David was jolted by the mention of it.

'Yeah.'

Nicola had a look that was part sympathy, part exasperation.

'Really, David, that's all ancient history. I mean it was fifteen years ago. No one will ever know whether it was an accident or suicide and . . .'

'It was an accident,' said David automatically.

Nicola stopped in her tracks. She reached out and took his hand across the table.

'It doesn't matter. It really doesn't matter. These things happen all the time. OK, so it was an accident – if there's one thing

28

teenagers are prone to, it's accidents. So he fell off the cliffs. It's sad, it's a fucking waste, of course it is, but it was so long ago now that surely you can't still be upset about it.'

'That's not the problem,' said David, enjoying the touch of her skin on his. 'I mean, initially that was my problem with the place, I suppose. The fact that I associated Arbroath with Colin's death. But it's become more ingrained than that. Don't you see, even the physical act of returning seems totally alien to me. I'm not sitting around here pining for Colin. I long ago reached the conclusion that this sort of shite just happens every day and people have to get on with it. I used to remember the anniversary of the accident every year, but I haven't for the last five years at least. That's not the point. The point is a plain and simple one, I haven't kept in touch with the people or the place, and I don't see any point in doing it now.'

'OK then, what about all our other mates from the time? What about Gary and Neil, for example? The three of you and Colin were pretty close back then. Wouldn't you like to know what they've been up to for the last decade and a half?'

'That's just the thing – I haven't bothered until now, so why start?'

'But if you never bother about what's gone before, how can you know who you are? Everything that happens to us over the years makes us into what we are today. Don't you think?'

David didn't really want to tell her that he didn't think that, that people reinvented themselves successfully every day all around the world. He was enjoying holding her hand too much. He looked her in the eye and he could see real compassion in there. She seemed to care about him, although why she should, since they hadn't spoken a word in years before yesterday, was a bit beyond him. It felt good, though, having someone looking out for him. He hadn't had that feeling for a long while.

'Look, we can go together,' said Nicola, relaxing a little and letting go of his hand. David didn't want the contact to stop, but he didn't know how to keep it going so he just grabbed his pint and started drinking while she talked. 'We can be the sarky, cool pair at the back slagging everyone else off for being boring bastards, how about that? We can get stupidly drunk and carry on like a pair of idiots, and if we offend everyone then fuck it, we don't have to ever see any of them ever again. Christ, I could do with a serious piss-up, I haven't been hammered in a long, long time. These things happen when you're a responsible parent and you've got kiddies' parties and school uniforms and packed lunches and trips to see *Shrek* followed by your tea at Pizza Hut to worry about. But up in Arbroath next weekend I'll have my folks looking after Amy. So go on, how about it?'

David had been half-listening, thinking about what she'd said earlier about ignoring your past. He was over Colin's death years ago, but the vacuum left in his life was still there, the space where a background should've been. Part of him thanked his parents for moving away, giving him an excuse to never go back, but part of him also blamed them for not giving him the option, ever, of returning to the place where he'd grown up, played football, ridden his bike, got drunk in the park and briefly, all too briefly, snogged Nicola Cruickshank outside Boots one Hogmanay.

'I'll go.'

'Really?'

'Why the hell not, eh?'

He wasn't at all sure why he was saying this, but his half-drunk instinct had brought him this far – to a smoky pub on a summer day across a table from a beautiful woman with her head screwed on tight – so he could trust it a little further. He finished his pint and got up.

'Same again?'

Nicola nodded. He got them in and came back to the table. Nicola was grinning from ear to ear.

'What?' he said.

'Nothing. Just looking forward to going to this bloody thing now.'

'Me too.'

'Really?' She sounded dubious. David laughed.

'No, not really. But if you promise to hold my hand if it gets too scary, I'm sure I'll manage.'

'Cross my heart and hope to die.' She raised her glass and they clinked them together again. 'To the Keptie High School class of '88 reunion!'

'Jesus. There's still time to change my mind, if you keep up that enthusiastic, cheerleading shit.'

'Don't knock it, mister. I'd look great in a ra-ra skirt and pom-poms, even now.'

'I don't doubt it.'

They both took a drink, David thinking about Nicola in a cheerleader outfit, Nicola smiling at him over her pint, fully aware of that fact.

After their third pint it was time for Nicola to pick up Amy from her mate's party. They were getting on so well David badly wanted to stay out with her but he realized that couldn't happen and offered to walk Nicola up the road.

'Where's the party?' he said.

'Livingstone Place, just across the Meadows. It's one street along from our own flat, in Gladstone Terrace.'

'Really? I'm just down the road in Rankeillor Street.'

'Small world.'

'How long did you say you've been in Edinburgh?'

'Four years.'

'And we've never seen each other.'

'Hardly that surprising unless you spend your time loitering outside Sciennes Primary School, or my work. I scarcely get anywhere else these days.'

They were walking through the Meadows, the large park spread across the area south of the university. The sun was still blazing away in the early evening, and the grass was covered with semi-clad students, tourists and festival-goers, all soaking up rare and valuable rays. Groups of lads kicked footballs about and frisbees got flung far and wide. They walked past some hippies practising firestick juggling, and accepted flyers from some androgynous oriental types for the Ladyboys of Bangkok spectacular. The festival was getting properly going, thought David as he took another handful of flyers from some posh twat for a student revue show in a cave somewhere. He put all the flyers in the next bin. He really hated the fucking festival. They reached the bottom of Livingstone Place and stood kind of awkwardly loitering, like they were at the end of a first date.

'I'm just going to pick up Amy then head home, do you want to meet her?' said Nicola, fully expecting David to say no. Why would he want to meet her daughter, just because they'd spent a few hours together after fifteen years of silence?

'Yeah, why not?' he said.

'Really? That's cool. I could do with the back-up, to be honest. Lots of Amy's pals seem to have really posh parents, and they all look down on me, single mum and all that. Stuck-up twats. Mind you, if I turn up stinking of booze with a strange man, I don't suppose that's gonna endear me to the members of the PTA, now, is it?'

Nicola rang the bell of the main-door flat and a dumpy woman in glasses and a turtleneck answered. She reminded David of that girl from *Scooby Doo*, not the sexy one, but the one who was always losing her glasses, and who always worked it out in the end.

'Cassandra,' said Nicola, turning on the charm, 'how's everything going?'

'Oh, mayhem, as you might expect. Come on in and watch your step, Melissa's junk is everywhere.'

They followed her down the hall, Nicola turning to whisper to David. 'Ever been in a room full of eight-year-old girls before?'

'Not that I remember, which means either no or I was very drunk.'

She made a face as they entered the living room. David looked around but the carnage didn't seem that bad. There was a blur of fast-moving pink bodies scooting around the large bay-windowed room, and a noise a bit like a gannet colony in mating season, but he'd been at parties dafter than this.

David hung about in the background as Nicola extricated Amy from proceedings. It seemed quite easy, Amy apparently not at all bothered to be leaving. David spotted which one was Amy straight away. She had inherited her mother's looks, her smile not quite so wide but her eyes bigger and deeper brown, and goddamn it, she had the family nose, that wee squint kink that he liked so much in Nicola. She stood out from the crowd by virtue of the fact she was the only one not in regulation pink; instead she sported a cornflower blue summer dress with yellow shoes and matching Alice band and bangles. She was also the only one not running around in that daft stomping gait that children have; instead she seemed light on her feet.

'Amy meet David; David meet Amy,' said Nicola, gently touching Amy's back as she guided her towards the door.

'Hello, Amy,' said David, trying to sound as normal as possible. Had he ever spoken to an eight-year-old girl before? Not since he was eight himself, probably.

'Have you been drinking with Mum?' said Amy, using her big eyes on David.

'Yes, I have,' said David with a laugh.

'You smell of beer, Mum,' said Amy.

'That's what happens when you go out with strange men, dear. I hope you don't find that out for yourself for a very long time.'

Amy rolled her eyes and looked at David as if to say, 'See what I have to put up with'. She turned and waved goodbye to the pink flurry of the room, which briefly stopped to wave and shout back, then she headed out the door. Nicola looked at David, smiled and shook her head slightly. Amy, at the front door now, shouted 'Come on!', and David and Nicola made their way down the hall and out the door sniggering like a pair of kids themselves.

At the end of the next street David and Nicola did that moon-ing-around thing again, as if on a date, this time with Amy hanging around looking bored next to them.

'Can we go, Mum? I want to see *X Factor*,' said Amy, swinging off her mum's arm.

'Hold your horses.' Nicola turned to David. 'So, I guess I'll see you next Saturday, then. Unless you bottle it, in which case I'll never speak to you again.'

'What, not for another fifteen years?' He had said it as a joke, but the thought of it sent a tiny shiver down his spine.

'Exactly. That'll teach you.'

'Maybe I could call you through the week?' He held her gaze for longer than was necessary, and she held it right back.

'Yeah, you could do that.'

They looked at each other for a few more seconds smiling, then David leaned in and gave her a quick kiss on the cheek.

'OK, I'll see you.' He looked down at Amy, who was scuffing her yellow shoes on the edge of the kerb. 'Nice meeting you, Amy.'

'Yeah,' Amy replied, noncommittally.

With that David reluctantly turned and walked away towards the edge of the Meadows and his own flat beyond.

'How was the party, then, madam?' Nicola asked, taking Amy's hand and turning up Gladstone Terrace towards home.

'All right, I suppose,' said Amy. 'But Melissa thinks she's better than everyone else, and her mum made us play stupid games for little kids.'

'Right,' said Nicola. 'Let's get a pizza in and you can tell me all about it.' She waited a moment then said, 'What did you think of David?'

Amy thought for a moment.

'Dunno,' she said. 'All right.' She thought for another few seconds. 'He had cool trainers.'

'Right,' said Nicola. 'Cool trainers.'

A few hundred yards away David let himself into his flat and opened a beer from the fridge. He thought about Nicola and he thought about Arbroath. He would go there to spend more time with her, it was as simple as that. He wished he was with her right now, but he knew enough not to rush into anything. It was Saturday night, but he didn't feel like going out. He finished his beer and opened another, took the phone off the hook and sat thinking about Nicola some more.

3

Return to Arbroath

On Sunday morning David changed his mind about going, then changed it back. He pottered around the house thinking about Nicola and Amy, then Colin and the past, doing nothing and deliberately letting his mind churn over what had happened and what might happen. Why was he attracted to Nicola now? She was beautiful, and she seemed to be interested in him – wasn't that one of the main criteria for being attracted to someone, that they were attracted to you as well? Of course there was the past, the whole idea that by hooking up with Nicola again he might be reclaiming his past and all that psychobabble bullshit, but he didn't really believe that. It was a here and now question – he was here and now and so was she, and they got on, so why not try and get together? He kept seeing her face, over and over again, looking over her shoulder in the museum, smiling at him in Sandy's, looking with unfathomable love at her daughter. Damn, it was a nice face.

But then this reunion was another story. Couldn't he try and hook up with Nicola without this dreaded trudge into the murky swamp of the past? Probably, but then he *had* said he would go, for whatever reasons, and she seemed pretty set on the idea, so what the hell. Then again, like he'd explained to her, he had no connection emotionally or physically with Arbroath now, with this place of his childhood. So why bother?

He talked himself in and out of going for the next two days, then received a flirty email from her, taking the piss out of him gently (she had rightly assumed that he was swithering) and suggesting he call her if he was having any doubts. He phoned her that night.

'Hello?'

'Oh, hi, Amy? This is Dave, your, em, mum's friend. Is she around?' He really was going to have to get used to communicating with an eight-year-old girl if this was going to go anywhere. He heard her calling for Nicola playfully, then there was a long wait. He was dreaming when she finally picked up.

'David?'

'Hi.'

'You got my email then.'

'Yeah. You were right, I was beginning to reconsider the whole Arbroath thing this weekend.'

Her voice was full of laughter down the line.

'Ha! I knew it. That's what happens when you spend time away from my wily, womanly charms. So what can I say to persuade you? What's the equivalent of a Chinese burn down the phone? Why the second thoughts?'

David didn't know why. The same stuff as before, really, everything he'd said in the pub to her. He told her so, but she was having none of it.

'That's all just crap up here, and I am now tapping the side of my head with my finger like a woodpecker, since you can't see me,' said Nicola. 'Psychological mumbo-jumbo claptrap of the highest order. If you really seriously don't want to go then fine, I don't suppose there's anything I can really do to persuade you, but I bet you anything once you're there you'll have a good time.'

'It's the logistics of it as well, Nicola,' said David. 'I mean, where the hell would I even stay? Everyone else can probably stay with their folks, not me.'

'That's no excuse. If it wasn't so crowded at my folks' you could've stayed there. Tell you what, why don't you leave it to me – I'll book you a B&B or something, take the hassle out of the whole thing.'

'I can do that myself, it's just . . .'

'I won't hear another word. That's decided. I'll book you something for Friday and Saturday nights. I'll email you the details once it's done. Any other objections? Do you want me to sort out travel and meals while I'm at it? Help pick out your wardrobe for the weekend?'

David laughed despite himself. 'Really, I can't let you go to the bother of . . .'

'I told you, it's decided. Next topic of conversation?'

Nicola came off the phone wondering why she had just rail-roaded him into going. Why did she care so much if David was there? She couldn't really understand his reticence about going, to her it was just a weekend away from the usual humdrum stuff of life, a chance to see what the hell the people from her past had been up to, and an excuse to catch up with her family. But now, she supposed, it was something else as well. Since meeting David at the weekend she had been thinking about him a lot. He still seemed young and naive. He'd never had to grow up in the way that she had with Amy. Somehow this reunion was part of it all, she wanted him to see that the past wasn't a scary place, it was just the past, and she wanted him to grow up a little, so that he could maybe, just maybe, fit a little better into her life. But she was also drawn to that naivety, that thing that she didn't have any more, the idea of living only in the present. Because you couldn't do that, not with a daughter and a future to think of. Was she jealous of him in a way? Probably, she thought. But a good kind of jealous, she told herself. Whatever the hell that meant.

David got an email the next day at lunchtime with B&B details. Fairport House, 66 Nolt Loan Road, owned by a Mrs Swankie, charging £20 a night. It was a few doors down from the house he'd grown up in. Nicola had obviously booked this place as a joke, or a reminder or something. It was a street of century-old semis opposite the Keptie Pond, a place where he'd had count-less childhood adventures, falling through ice, chasing swans, upturning boats, discovering glue-sniffers, losing footballs, falling off his bike, fighting other kids and all the rest. If anywhere was going to open the floodgates of memories it was this street. Great, thought David, but part of him was also pleased that Nicola had gone to the trouble of sorting him out with somewhere, surely that meant something. Or was he totally getting ahead of himself? Yes, he thought, he absolutely was, but he couldn't help himself and he found that as the days went on he was trying less and less to stop himself doing so.

She phoned him on Thursday night.

'All set for tomorrow, then?'

'What makes you think I'm going?'

'Well you haven't told me otherwise, and you'd bloody better be, because otherwise I'm due the money on that bloody B&B.'

'Yeah, OK, I'm going. Thanks for sorting that out, by the way.'

'Not a problem. Can't vouch for the place, could be a doily-filled, lacy shitehole, but you'd be surprised how little tourist accommodation there is in Arbroath. Or maybe you wouldn't, since you grew up there and you know what it's like.'

'Nolt Loan Road as well.'

'Yes, I thought that was a nice touch. Trip down memory lane, etc. All very obvious, but there you go. If you will leave your arrangements in my hands, that's what you get.'

'Do you want a lift up the road?'

'Me and Amy are getting the train after she finishes school. She's still at the age where the train is exciting, although she won't admit that any more, of course.'

'Of course.'

'When are you heading up?'

'Hadn't really thought about it yet.'

'Well, I'll give you a phone at this B&B, say, early evening? We can meet up and go out for a proper drink this time, what with me having a houseful of babysitters. Get ourselves in the mood for the big do on Saturday. Fancy it?'

'Sure. I'll speak to you then.'

And that was it, done and dusted. He was going to Arbroath for a school reunion after fifteen years away, and he was doing it to be with her.

It was the kind of beautiful, clear summer evening that hardly ever happens in Scotland, but when it does it reminds you why you bother to hang around. A fat, orange sun cast long shadows down the Firth of Forth as David crossed the bridge, thankful to be out of the throb of Edinburgh traffic and heading into open spaces. He kept his window down after paying the toll, enjoying the sea breeze in his face. Radio One played their latest inane drivel but he didn't mind, enjoying the numbness of not having to think while he listened.

The road through Fife was pleasantly monotonous. Rolling crop fields were interspersed with small bursts of trees, and occasionally a tractor or harvester could be spotted kicking up dust in the distance. When he hit Dundee, he took the riverside route, preferring to keep the Tay at his side. The tide was out and sandbanks glistened in the slanting sunlight.

After Dundee, David didn't recognize the road at all. Diggers, trucks and all sorts of roadworks vehicles scuttled back and forth amid a maze of traffic cones. One large sign declared that they were converting the road to Arbroath into a dual carriageway, scheduled completion date 2007. They had been talking about that since he was a boy, and it looked like they were finally getting around to it. The going was slow and dusty as he sat behind a lorry kicking up dry dirt everywhere.

The trance of driving left his mind free to wander, and he started to think about Colin. He was a natural sportsman – one of those irritating kids who was good at every sport they tried. He probably could've become a professional at golf, tennis or even athletics, but had chosen football, something he had an innate gift for. When playing in the school team Colin had to dumb things down a bit so as not to make the sides too uneven, relegating himself to a peripheral role as left back or sometimes going in goal, but even then he was the best keeper the school had seen in Christ knows how long. His real position was centre of midfield, though, controlling the game, and he seemed to have an instinct for passing and movement well beyond his years. That talent seemed immense next to the duffers and hackers, David and his classmates, but whether Colin had enough to make it professionally only time would've told. Except he never got time.

A couple of professional clubs had tried to tempt him away from school at sixteen, then again in fifth year, but Colin was no idiot and he'd hung around until the end of sixth year, getting a pretty decent handful of qualifications, just in case the football didn't work out. By the summer of '88 he had signed to Arbroath FC as a starting point, and he was due to start pre-season training with the club that August. He never made it that far.

Back then, football violence was commonplace, and although it was a small club, Arbroath punched above its weight, literally, in terms of hooliganism, with running battles around the streets of the town every other Saturday a regular occurrence. The four of them in the ADS never got involved in any of that – what was the point? It was all about the drinking for them, massive amounts of drinking on a very regular basis, something David had never really shaken off over the years. It was a stupid macho game, seeing who could get the most drunk the quickest, and it inevitably ended in puking disaster, but that never seemed to stop them. It was as if some unseen force was driving them on to drink larger and larger amounts.

But pretty soon they learned to handle it. They got used to each other drunk as hell and they looked out for each other. This was at the age of sixteen, when the four of them seemed to have plenty in common. Two years later, in their final year at school, the drinking was the only thing that kept them together. They knew the ADS wouldn't last, but it was one last summer blowout, and it was a riot.

That July of 1988 was one long party. David and Neil had a joint birthday party, David's eighteenth but Neil's nineteenth since he'd been held back a year earlier in school. Neil was a year and a day older than David. Neil had been born on the very day that Apollo 11 landed on the moon, and he had been named after Neil Armstrong (his middle name was Armstrong, much to everyone's amusement except his). Their birthday party had followed the usual pattern – insane levels of drinking early on, unsuccessful attempts to get off with a few girls, drunken camaraderie around the streets in the early hours of the morning, then getting to bed long after dawn. It was just one of many piss-ups that summer, but a week later one of those piss-ups ended with Colin's death, and they never went out together in Arbroath again.

It was the last Saturday of July and they'd done the usual, down the West Port to a few pubs, then Tropics to check out the talent. When Tropics shut they headed along the front to Bally's (formerly Smokies, people were still getting used to the name change), which was the same schtick except open till three. At chucking-out time they headed to Victoria Park, then the cliffs, one of the few places they could hang out without hassle from patrolling police. Sometimes they would light a fire, more often they would have a carry-out and would continue drinking as wide boys sped up and down the promenade in Ford Escorts showing off to girls.

Throughout July they had started joking in a fake macho way about jumping off the cliffs. They weren't the biggest cliffs in the world, between a hundred and two hundred feet depending where you were, but they were high enough to kill you if you fell from them. The red sandstone was crumbling all along the five-mile stretch of clifftop walk from Arbroath to the tiny fishing village of Auchmithie – not that the ADS ever went walkies, they usually hung about the Arbroath end, drinking from cans of lager and bottles of cider and throwing things over the edge into the sea. If the tide was in, spray would sometimes shoot up and soak them, and when the tide was out, small shingly beaches and ominously dark little caves were exposed at the bottom of the cliff face. That night the sky was already starting to lighten a little in the east, the black cloudless expanse invaded by outstretching lavender and lilac fingers. As they staggered around the cliffs, their teenage years and drunken bodies made them utterly oblivious to the danger of falling. They joked about cliff-jumping. They dared each other. The tide was in and the sea appeared in benign mood, gently sloshing against tufts of grass at the cliff base, pushing plastic oil drums and other bits of flotsam gently against the massive expanse of rock. But they were only joking. Not even if you were completely paralytic would you consider something as idiotic as that, and for all their puerile teenage humour and their often idiotic banter, none of them was that stupid.

As the sky continued to lighten the four of them drifted away from the cliffs, heading back into town, to their beds, ready to spend the whole of Sunday recovering. They split at the bottom of the High Street, David and Gary heading west, Neil and Colin going north, waving sloppy goodbyes to each other, half arranging to meet up the next night for a quiet Sunday pint. The gulls were out in force, squawking and diving for carry-out food scattered up the High Street. It was the last time David ever saw Colin. When he got home he crawled into bed, fantasizing about a girl he'd been chatting up that night (was it Nicola? He couldn't remember now) and already thinking about a fry-up for breakfast.

He was woken at eleven by a phone call. It was the police telling him that Colin had been found dead at the bottom of the cliffs. He was hungover and still drunk, and he didn't really get it at first. Yes, they'd been to the cliffs, he told the officer, but they'd all left and gone home, and Colin was fine. No, he didn't know what time that was, but it was getting light. Yes, they had joked about jumping off, but it was just a joke, and no, Colin hadn't seemed depressed, what the hell was he implying? Suicide? No fucking way. David was probably his best friend, but he was friendly with everyone, charming, clever, fit, funny, happy – all the other positive things you could think of. It was not suicide. David couldn't make sense of it. What the hell was Colin doing back there after they'd left? He just couldn't get his head round it.

He phoned Neil, who sounded even more hungover and shocked than he did. Neil confirmed they'd just headed home, and he'd said goodbye to Colin five minutes after they'd left David and Gary. It didn't make any sense. It just didn't add up. He couldn't work it out at all. He hung up, went back to bed and lay there for a very long time, his head pounding, his mind whirring in confusion and his body shaking from the hangover and the shock.

There was an inquiry into the incident which came back with death by misadventure, whatever that was supposed to mean. Colin had a high level of alcohol in his blood, but the same would've been true of any of the four of them, of anyone between the ages of fourteen and forty in the whole bloody town on any given Saturday night. David couldn't understand it – he just wasn't drunk enough to have fallen accidentally, but there was also no way he would've jumped, and nobody would've pushed him, the thought was fucking absurd. And what was he doing there? Maybe he'd left something there, or lost something, and he'd gone back to look for it, or he couldn't sleep and had gone for a walk, a piece of the clifftop giving way under him. You were always hearing scare stories about bits of the cliffs crumbling away, sandstone was notorious for eroding at a fair rate in the onslaught of the sea's force, so maybe that was it, maybe it was just a stupid accident that could've happened to anyone.

David was still puzzling over this and still somehow in shock by the end of the week, and Colin's funeral. It was the first funeral David had ever been to and with almost unbearably poignant timing it was the day before what would've been Colin's eighteenth birthday. You couldn't make this shit up, thought David as he trudged the short distance past Keptie High to the Western Cemetery. It was a stupidly hot day, utterly incongruous with the atmosphere of the town, as if the heavens couldn't believe that this sort of thing could happen and had refused to play ball

44

by providing the appropriate rain and wind and cold. David was sweating as he walked up the hill, feeling like a different person in a borrowed suit, borrowed black tie and school shoes that hadn't been out the cupboard in a month.

This was the eighties, before Britain had a culture of mass-media mourning, and with school out for the summer there was no public grieving, no counselling sessions for friends, no appearances sobbing on local television. There was a big turn-out at the funeral, though. Colin had been a bright hope in the town, a charismatic presence, an athlete, an academic and a charmer of each generation.

The Western was a well-groomed cemetery with evenly spaced graves, wide walkways and huge monkey puzzle trees. It sat on the edge of town, overlooking tattie fields through a thin wire fence. Colin's grave was at the back, amongst the more modest modern plots, and David walked up alone, noticing a line of neat Marines' graves, all young men, not much older than David, who had died in the Falklands War. The idea of all those once youthful bodies lying decomposed under the turf shocked him. Poor bastards. Enjoy life while you can, he thought, because you're a long time dead. The thought didn't cheer him up any.

At the graveside he met up with Gary and a few other class-mates, most looking like little kids playing a dressing-up game, trying to look upset, trying to wear a seriousness that they simply didn't have the life experience to actually feel yet. It felt so unreal, the sun beating down between the tree shadows, cars zipping past beyond the fields, the sombre religious intoning from some-one who didn't even know Colin – 'a life cut down in its prime', for God's sake. David noticed Neil wasn't here. He had considered not coming himself, so he understood.

He looked at Gary, who seemed in worse shape than he was. He wanted to say something, something meaningful that might help both of them make sense of what was a nonsensical situation. A few days ago they'd all been blind drunk together, and now one of them was in a box, having earth shovelled over him. He suddenly couldn't stand to look at Gary anymore. He wanted to be alone and very, very drunk; he wanted to crawl into his own little hole and hide.

He went to the wake to show face, but only stayed briefly. There was such a colossal distance between his generation and his parents' that he couldn't think of anything to say to Colin's lost-looking mum and dad. His own parents were there, offering bland, formulaic condolences, and all the older mourners seemed like automatons, offering the appropriate programmed responses to stimuli. David just wanted to get out of there and start drinking properly.

He spent the rest of the day drifting from pub to pub, going to places that were not his usual haunts, just so he could be alone and unknown. But there was no such thing in Arbroath, and too many vaguely recognized well-wishers kept making comments about Colin that were simply strings of platitudes and clichés hung out to dry. He was thrown out of two pubs for being loud and abusive, then picked a fight with a large stranger outside Fatty's chippy, just so that he could be hit and feel the reality of pain in his body. He staggered home, blood dripping from his nose on to his white shirt, and vowed never to go out in this stupid fucking town ever again.

Yet here he was, driving past the old golf clubhouse that was now a guesthouse perched on the hilltop edge of town. He negotiated a new roundabout on the road in, drove past a new statue which seemed to have two people in monks' outfits waving a parchment in the air, and headed up the hill towards his B&B.

As he turned into Nolt Loan Road and caught sight of the Keptie Pond his mind was deluged with lighter childhood memories. The water tower stood imperiously over the pond like a tinpot baron's castle, while the island in the middle of the pond was still packed with trees and ducks and swans. There had been some new landscaping around the edges, he noticed, and new signposts warning about thin ice, and forbidding ball games, and reminding dog walkers about picking up dogshit as they went.

The hut where you used to hire boats from was gone, as were the boats. But despite all the small changes, this was definitely still the same place, still the street that he grew up in, still the place he had spent the most time in his life. And now he was back.

4

The Cliffs

'Please, call me Gillian.'

She pronounced it with a hard 'G', but that was about the only thing hard about Gillian Swankie, thought David. She was a short, voluptuous woman somewhere in her forties with an easy-going, bright red smile and a body made of flamboyant curves. She greeted David at the door with a strangely intimate handshake and a brace of air kisses, making him reel a little. She was certainly attractive, although she wore too much make-up. She was nothing like the lonely old widow he had imagined. The inside of the house didn't match up to his expectations either – there were no toy dolls, lace curtains, frilly cushions, flowery patterned wallpaper or carpets. Instead the place was done out in neutral show-home colours, with exposed floorboards covered by simple rugs. There were no pictures of graduating children (she was probably too young for that, right enough) or tiny grandchildren – a staple of most B&Bs he'd stayed in around the country, the owners turning their now-empty family home into a pension-boosting money-spinner, the men taking a back seat, the women enjoying the company of strangers to fill the mothering void in their lives. But the Fairport felt different. Gillian with a hard 'G' seemed altogether younger, more vivacious and more dangerous than his image of a B&B owner, and although she was Mrs Swankie he couldn't picture her as a doting wife. Was she alone or married or divorced? Did she have kids? What business was it of his what the hell she'd done with her life?

'We don't get many single visitors through Fairport, are you here on business?'

'Not exactly,' was all David could think of to say. She looked at him and a crafty smile came across her comfortable, worn-in, handsome face. She seemed to know something David didn't. She turned to head up the stairs and David followed, his eyes trained on her impressively large arse which swung from side to side as she pulled on the banister. 'I'll show you to your room,' she said, looking over her shoulder. David glanced up with a start, shifting his eyes from her arse to her face a moment too late. Rumbled.

The room was standard issue, no-nonsense B&B – small telly mounted on the wall in a corner, plain double bed, small en suite toilet and shower and a tray next to the bed with a kettle, sachets of instant coffee, biscuits and two cups. Genuine Scottish hospitality. He got the spiel about breakfast (served until a surprisingly late eleven o'clock) and the front door (stayed unlocked through the night) from Gillian, who locked eyes with him throughout, smiling in a knowing way. Were the two of them alone in the house?

Gillian left and he got settled in, but a couple of minutes later he heard a phone ring and she called up to him. It must be Nicola, he thought, why hadn't she tried his mobile? He went downstairs and picked up the receiver.

'Alright, droopy drawers, ready for some reunion action?'

'David?' It was a male voice and he recognized it.

'Yeah?'

'It's Gary. Spink. From school.'

The first thing David thought was how the fuck does he know I'm here? Some sort of small-town telepathy thing going on? Jungle drums? An announcement in the *Arbroath Herald*?

'Hey, Gary. How the hell are you? Long time no see, and all that.'

'I'm fine.' He didn't sound fine, thought David. He sounded nervy, or timid, or something similar. But then he'd always been a little shy of life, thought David, always acting as if something was about to jump out from behind a tree and scare seven shades

49

of shite out of him. Maybe sometime in the last fifteen years, something had done just that.

'How did you know I was staying here?'

'I ran into Sonia the other day and she mentioned it.' Sonia? Who the hell was she? And how did she know who, and where, he was? 'Listen,' he still sounded nervous and David imagined him twisting the phone cord around a fidgeting finger. 'Do you fancy maybe going out for a pint tonight? Catch up on old times and all that? Just thought it would be an idea before the reunion proper tomorrow.'

He had to think quick. He was waiting for Nicola to phone, and the prospect of hooking up with her tonight, just the two of them, blew everything else out the water.

'I was thinking I might just take it easy tonight, Gary, to be honest. You know, chill out. Keep the powder dry for tomorrow night and all that. You understand.'

'Sure. It was just an idea. Well, listen, if you're not busy tomorrow during the day, how about we go to the football? We're playing Montrose at home. If you fancy it?'

Gary sounded so pathetic on the phone David felt sorry for him, then guilty for feeling sorry. He thought, well I don't even know this guy from fucking Adam anymore, I haven't spoken to him in fifteen years. But then he was bouncing him tonight in favour of a woman who, a week ago, he hadn't spoken to in just as long. Why the hell not go to the footy the next day? If nothing else, he could do with a few afternoon pints, might as well get a head start if this reunion was going to be at all bearable.

'Sure, Gary, why not?' He could hear the boyish relief down the phone, and something else, a more desperate sensation he couldn't quite put his finger on.

'Great,' said Gary. 'Want to meet in Tutties? Say about one o'clock?'

'Cool. I'll see you there.'

'See you there.'

David put the phone down. Another voice from the past, he thought, but then why be surprised by that? He was, after all, in the town he grew up in for a stupid school reunion.

The phone rang as he was still standing there, and he picked it up instinctively.

'Hello?'

'Is that you, David?'

Nicola.

'Hi there, gorgeous. What's wrong with trying my mobile?'

'Tried it. Straight on to answer machine.'

'Maybe I'm not getting a reception here.'

'Maybe. It's a terrible backwater, after all.'

'Sure is.'

'You made it then, didn't bottle out?'

'You thought I'd bottle out?'

'Didn't you?'

'It did cross my mind.'

'So now you're here, how is it?'

'Strange. Just had Gary Spink on the phone.'

'Really? Saying what?'

'I'm meeting him for the footy tomorrow.'

'So you're still free tonight? How about we go out and get drunk, as previously discussed.'

'Funny, I was thinking exactly the same thing. When and where did you have in mind?'

'Well, I thought we could pay the Lochlands an overdue visit, but before that, how about you take me for a drive?'

'A drive?' David could sense something funny. 'What sort of drive?'

'You know, a drive. In your car,' said Nicola. 'Brrrm, brrrm. I'm doing that steering wheel thing with my hands. Internationally accepted gesture for driving.'

'Where to?'

'You're a right suspicious sod, aren't you? Just around. Around and about. Maybe we'll do handbrake turns in the Viewfield

Hotel car park, maybe we'll drive down to the harbour and I'll push you in.'

'Or maybe we'll drive out to the cliffs where Colin fell?'

There was a slight beat of a pause.

'Maybe that'll happen,' said Nicola, and David heard a slyness in her voice that was irresistible. 'Anything's possible.'

He didn't hesitate.

'Will I come pick you up?'

'I thought you'd never ask,' said Nicola, the slyness replaced by a bubbly chirrup, no less irresistible. 'You remember the house? 10 St Vigeans Road. I'll see you in, what, ten minutes?'

'Make it five,' said David.

His head spun slightly as he put down the phone, but he took the stairs two at a time back up to his room to get the car keys, and was out the front door in twenty seconds flat.

Such a beautiful setting on such a peaceful evening, it was hard to accept a life being snuffed out in this place. The sandstone of the cliffs seemed to glow in the late evening sunlight, as if the rock was resonating with the sun's wavelengths, giving off its own light and heat in response. The North Sea seemed a different creature to the notorious icy beast that had claimed so many lives through the years, more like a gently purring cat at the heels of the land, ingratiating itself with little friendly lapping sounds. Nicola and David gazed out at the enormity of the sea, hypnotized by the white noise shush of the green-brown water.

'Next stop Norway,' said Nicola. David didn't seem to hear, or was lost in his thoughts. Eventually he emerged from the trance he was in.

'What?'

'It's something my dad always says looking out to sea. "Next stop Norway", as if it was swimmable or something. As if you could just wander in like Reggie Perrin, and by teatime you'd be ensconced in a cottage on the banks of a fjord, feasting on a smorgasbord with some Nordic family decked out in big woolly jumpers. I really like that idea, making the massive, faceless sea seem small and personal.'

Nicola wondered why she'd brought David here – to the cliffs, to Arbroath at all. He'd looked a little shocked as they'd driven around town for a while, as if every corner they turned was unveiling new, horrific memories for him. Of course she knew that those memories weren't horrific, he wasn't a traumatized man for Christ's sake, it's just that the memories hadn't been visited in a long, long time, without the visceral presence of the actual places to unearth them. For her the town was an organic entity, changing and developing, for better or worse, but for him it was maybe a place trapped in amber, buried in time, locked instantaneously in a moment, like Pompeii. It was a ridiculous way to look at a town, she thought, and he needed to stop looking at Arbroath, and his past, that way.

She turned her back on the sea and looked again at the small memorial stone. 'In memory of Colin Anderson, who died here July 31st, 1988.' It was a simple enough inscription on a three-foot, rough-hewn stone, the grey granite grain of it somehow out of place amongst all this sandstone. The rock under their feet seemed alive with possibilities, while the memorial stone re-minded Nicola only of pallid death. Maybe it had been a mistake to come here, she thought. What was to be gained? She looked out over the fields inland from the cliffs, the low potato plants still green in the ground, a couple of months yet before they could be picked. The rows of fields seemed to go on for miles, somehow further than the sea she had been looking at, because of the parallel lines drawing her eye to infinity.

'Whose are the flowers, do you think?' David was looking at the stone. A bunch of wilted carnations, dirty white and jaundiced yellow, lay at the foot of the stone, kept in place by a rock.

'Probably his mum and dad's,' said Nicola. 'Can't imagine anyone else coming up here to place flowers after all this time. Although you'd think they would've done that at his tombstone, rather than here. I can't imagine being here would be too comfortable for them.'

'What about us?' said David. 'What are we doing here?' He didn't sound angry, just a little sad.

'I thought it would be good for you,' said Nicola. 'I don't think I was right, was I?'

'It's fine, really,' said David. He looked across at Nicola and her face showed lines of worry – caused by him, he realized with a start, and he felt briefly ashamed. This wasn't how the evening was supposed to go. Without thinking he put his arm around her and pulled her closer to him, the pair of them still facing the stone, which seemed dwarfed by its awesome natural surroundings, an insignificant token.

David could feel the shape of Nicola's hip against his, and the gentle warmth of the fading sunlight on his back, both sensations giving him a tingle down his spine that he liked a lot.

'There's a card with the flowers,' said Nicola, pulling away from him to reach it. 'Colin, I'll never forget,' is all it said.

'No signature,' said Nicola. 'Isn't that a little odd? Don't people always sign these things? Don't they want others to know who left the flowers?'

'Check you out, cynic girl. It doesn't matter who left them, they know who they are, and presumably that's all that matters.'

'It doesn't look like a mum or dad's handwriting, either,' Nicola continued. 'It's a real scrawl. It almost looks like a young boy's writing or something.' She held the card closer to her face, then passed it over to David.

For a second David thought he recognized the handwriting, but the moment passed. That sort of thing wasn't something he'd ever been good at – it was always more of a girl thing, wasn't it, like spotting wedding rings on fingers – and he let the thought go from his head. She was right about one thing though, even David could see that it was no elderly mother or father's writing, it was way too messy for that. Older generations always had better handwriting. But what did it matter? So someone was remembering Colin apart from his own folks, well, good. He bent and put the card carefully back in with the flowers.

'This is hardly the thrilling, drunken evening of debauchery you promised me,' he said, smiling.

'You're absolutely right,' said Nicola, deciding that enough was enough. 'Let's get the hell away from here and hit the Lochlands.' She put her arm around him and playfully pulled him up, away from the stone. 'Let the debauchery commence,' she yelled, startling a crow into flight from the adjacent field, making them both jump, then laugh. They began running down the hill, using gravity to take them away from the past.

The Lochlands was heaving, and to David's dismay they were greeted with a rowdy cheer from a table round the corner when they pushed in the small door, abandoning the last of the day's sunlight for the smoky rammy of the place. Somebody obviously knew they were coming. This was supposed to be just the two of them, him and Nicola. He tried to catch Nicola's eye as she headed for the table, smiling and dragging David along with her.

'Look who I found,' she said to the table. There were half a dozen people squeezed into the corner, and every face was one that David immediately recognized, and yet he couldn't think of a single name to go with any of the faces. This was a fucking nightmare. He wasn't ready for all this shit.

'The long-lost David Lindsay, everybody. David, you remember Alison, Carol, Debbie' – she paused briefly to allow head nods down one side of the table – 'Steve, Anne and Derek.' There was some more nodding, smiles all round. Everyone looked fatter than they used to, their faces saggier, their hair shorter in the case of the girls (fuck, not girls, women, very definitely women), or gone in the case of the guy nearest him (was that Steve?) and the other guy, who surely didn't wear specs before. He felt like he was drowning and his throat was dry. He pulled his arm away from Nicola's hand, which was still gently anchoring him in reality.

'What do you want to drink?' he said to her.

'Pint of lager, cheers.'

He was at the bar in a shot, cursing, his face tripping him. He looked around at the Lochlands; it hadn't changed a bit. There was football memorabilia covering the walls, framed photos of old Scotland World Cup squads peeking shamefully out from the corners they were tucked away in, signed shirts and scarves for a host of teams mounted everywhere. Two televisions in opposite corners of the room showed football and cricket from somewhere nameless around the world. He saw other faces that he recognized amongst the gangs of men and women sitting at the scatter of tables or crowding round the bar, the puggy, the jukebox. The faces seemed fainter than they should be, as if they were ghosts or faded photographs. He recognized the barman, now with grey around his temples; the same fucking barman that used to serve the lot of them when they were all under age, he was still here. The thought seemed somehow obscene. He ordered the pints and turned from the bar. Nicola was at his side. She looked him in the eye for the first time since they'd come in, and her knowing expression was hard to resist.

'I thought it was going to be just the two of us.'

'I never actually said that,' she said. 'I maybe just let you think that without correcting you. Look, you're here for a reunion, so you might as well start reunioning, or whatever the correct verb is.'

'It's just that I wasn't really psyched up for it yet,' he said, realizing that his voice was getting whiny, hating the sound of it. 'I mean, if you'd told me . . .'

'If I'd told you, you probably wouldn't have come, would you?'

'I don't know why I did come. I mean the whole thing.'

Nicola stood back a little to take him in better. She understood, but also felt a little exasperated. He'd replied to her initial email, he'd met up with her, he'd agreed to come along to the reunion, even allowed himself to be taken to the cliffs, so why the hell was he moaning now?

'Look, David, I don't know why you're pissed off, or even if you are really pissed off, because if you are, then I'm not sure why you're even here. This is a bloody holiday, OK? Think of it like that. It's a weekend away from the usual shit, something a bit different, just in a place where you happened to grow up. There is booze aplenty and there are friendly people to chat to, what more do you want?'

He digested her outburst while the shouts, laughs and murmurs of the crowd enveloped them.

'You're right,' he conceded when the pints came and he handed over a fiver. 'Of course, you're right. I'm an arsehole, OK? Let's get fucking pished then, eh? And let's get to know these miserable old schoolmates of ours all over again.'

'Good,' said Nicola, and she leaned over and unexpectedly gave him a peck on the cheek. 'Now if we're going to do this properly, I better get some shooters to go with these pints.'

'Shhh,' said Nicola, giggling and trying to put a finger to his lips. 'You'll wake my parents.'

'What are we, fucking seventeen?'

'Shhh, and watch the fucking swearing.'

'What fucking swearing?'

They stood in St Vigeans Road, an ordinary line of sandstone terraced houses that sloped up to the town's Cairnie Hill. It was a two-minute walk from the Lochlands that had taken them at least half an hour, including a detour to MacDonald Park to play on the roundabout and swings.

When the Lochlands' chucking-out time came, the rest of the group around the table had decided to head down the West Port, maybe to Tropics (which was now called Rumours or something equally cheesy, the names changed but the places remained the same) to get a couple more drinks. Nicola had excused herself, saying she had to be up early to spend time with Amy, and David offered to walk her home. Their departure was met with catcalls and good-natured whistling, which neither of them minded.

They had spent four hours drinking fast and talking shite to the people at the table. The conversation was stilted to begin with, especially for David, as he tried to remember the childhood lives of the people around him, and as he continually rehashed his mundane story of the past fifteen years. But as the evening went on and tongues loosened with alcohol, the chat picked up. The eight of them started the fun, scab-picking exercise of reminiscing about 'the good old days', days scarily stacked with all sorts of potential, potential that had, for the most part, remained unfulfilled.

The crowd was much more amiable than David would've thought. Before tonight his impressions of them were as school-children, with all the spiteful, self-centred, confused, jealous, wilful, half-formed attitudes that entailed. He remembered some of the things he'd done and said in 1988 and felt ashamed, so why should he judge the people around him on events, moments, snapshots in his brain from then?

Somebody at the table mentioned their relief that everyone had turned out to have normal lives, normal jobs, normal fucked-up relationships. Nobody had become an astronaut, and nobody was a paedophile. Nicola had pointed out that astronauts and paedophiles almost never go to school reunions, it's the regular ones that show up. Which was a very fair point, thought David, as he watched her effortlessly dip in and out of conversations with those around her. There she was chatting to Alison about her forthcoming wedding to someone high up at Standard Life; there she was listening attentively as Debbie told her about husband number two; and there she was swapping kid stories with Derek, whose eldest daughter was the same age as Amy. It was all so easy, thought David, this reunion malarkey.

For all he'd had to drink, he was still sober enough to realize, as they stood outside the Lochlands and Nicola announced she was heading home, that this was his chance. When you're drunk things seem both more and less clear, somehow.

For Nicola's part, well, of course she had engineered it, and she had hoped that he would offer to walk her home and not head on to the next pub. And it had worked. She didn't know where the hell any of this was going, if it was going anywhere at all, but despite his occasional grumpiness, David was funny, clever and cute. That was more than enough to be going on with for now.

Standing half-drunk outside her mum and dad's house with a man, she was reminded of countless dates, drunken walks home, snogs with various boys (very definitely boys back then), all of whom had drifted into an ether of the past that was comforting but unimportant background noise to her life today.

She looked at David and realized that they had their arms around each other. How had that happened? Had she done it first? Did it matter who had done it first? She was happy it had happened. She decided to kiss him, and so she did, long and deep and probably more forcefully than she would've if she'd been sober, her tongue playing with his in his mouth after a few seconds. She felt his hands moving over her back and her arse, and she moved her hands in similar fashion, pulling his thin body closer to her. She couldn't remember the last time she'd kissed like this, with tongues flicking, hands sweeping, a slight movement of her pelvis towards his, and all in the street, at night, under a streetlight throwing gleaming yellow rays over their entwined bodies. It was like she was seventeen all over again, except that she knew so much more about life, relationships, feelings and men than she could've ever dreamt of back then.

After a long time they separated a little, still with their arms around each other, leaning back slightly and bouncing a knowing smile to each other.

'I don't think I've kissed like that since I was at school,' said David with a laugh in his voice.

'I know what you mean,' said Nicola. She could feel the

hardening in his trousers through his jeans and hers, and was pleased that she could still arouse a man with a kiss. 'I'd better head in,' she said, wanting to stay, but feeling that something might be lost or spoiled if this went on too long.

David looked slightly crestfallen, but quickly covered it with a smile.

'Sure, whatever you think.'

'I'm thirty-four, but that doesn't stop my parents sticky-beaking in whenever possible. They're probably waiting up for me to come in.'

'I think that's pretty cool.' David thought briefly of his own parents in their converted French barn.

'Yeah, I suppose it is in a way.'

They kissed again, intended as a quick goodnight kiss, but it stretched out longer and longer, neither one really wanting to let go. Eventually Nicola did, finishing with a handful of little feather kisses on his lips that David thought were even better than the snogging. She broke away from his arms and got her key out for the front door.

'I guess I'll see you tomorrow, then,' she said.

'I guess you will. I'll call you during the day, we can sort something out for tomorrow night.'

'You do that.'

'I will.'

'You better.'

'Goodnight.'

'Sweet dreams.'

He watched her go in, giving a little wave as she did, and turned to head back to the B&B. He wanted to punch the air, so he did. He wanted to yell out with joy, but he managed to stop himself. He wanted another drink, and he certainly didn't want to sleep; his mind fizzed. He remembered the bottle of Ardbeg he'd brought with him in his bag. Within ten minutes he was sitting alone on a bench by the Keptie Pond, staring at the syrupy surface of the water, swigging from the bottle of Ardbeg, and grinning from ear to ear. What the fuck had he been worrying about, coming back here? Everything was turning out absolutely fucking perfectly. He sat drinking whisky and thinking of Nicola, happier than he'd been in a long time.

5

Tutties Neuk

Tutties Neuk had been bought over recently, but a comprehensive facelift hadn't stopped the dregs of Arbroath FC's fan base popping in for their traditional few pints before the match across the road at Gayfield. The pub now advertised the fact that it served food, but when David entered the mobbed, hazy bar, full of nervous energy and the familiar comfort of a pre-match ritual carried out for countless years, there was no sign of anyone taking anything other than liquid refreshment.

The tables were given over to old-timers nursing pints and nips, chain-smoking with sickly yellow fingers, their dedication to the cause respected by the younger ones who stood around in footy tops and scarves, with close-cropped hair, downing pints and glancing up at the English premiership match on the television in the corner. The three middle-aged women behind the bar glided effortlessly and efficiently between each other, providing pints and banter as required.

David had missed breakfast. Still buzzing a little from the extended whisky nightcap, he had tottered gently out the door of the Fairport, avoiding any contact with Gillian with a hard 'G'. A blast of sun-soaked fresh air sobered him up and the memory of holding Nicola outside her folks' house put a wide smile on his face. He'd strolled past the railway, through the High Common and down the hill to Tutties, an ancient, pebble-dashed, whitewashed building sitting exposed next to the main Dundee Road, which carved through the town turning north.

So here he was, in the pub again. Could be worse, he thought. He had a quick look for Gary, not at all sure that he would recognize him, then headed to the bar and got a pint in. After a couple of big gulps he felt a tap on his shoulder.

Gary Spink had not taken the years well. He had always been a frail kind of figure, but these days he looked positively apologetic about still drawing breath from the atmosphere. He was small, several inches shorter than David, and seemed even smaller by virtue of a slouch which was a long way towards becoming an old man's hunch. He wore dirty trainers, worn-out jeans, a lumberjack shirt and a cheap-looking Toronto Blue Jays baseball cap. He had a scratchy, half-hearted goatee which made his face look dirty, something compounded by greying, lopsided teeth in a thin-lipped smile. He removed the cap and ran a bony hand through his thinning hair before replacing it. He had a downtrodden air and a weasly way of moving. It wasn't a good look.

'David,' he said in a gentle voice, almost a whisper. 'You're looking well.'

'You too,' said David. 'Pint?'

'Lager, cheers.'

They found a table in the corner, next to the newly painted gents toilets, and sat down. David tried to dredge up what he could about Gary's life from his memory. Hadn't he stayed in Arbroath, working for a bank or something? He had been good with numbers at school, as well as something else, but David couldn't remember what. He had always been the put-upon character out of the four of them in the ADS, and behind his back they had called him Snarf, after the comedy character from *Thundercats*. Thinking about it now, David realized the way the three of them treated Gary back then was a gentle, latent kind of bullying – never treating him as an equal to themselves, always taking advantage of his demure nature. It was pathetic really, but wasn't it just the way all boys are growing up? Taking advantage if they can? He felt a pang of guilt in his stomach and took a swig of lager.

'So, how's it going?' he said.

'Good,' said Gary, sipping gently at his pint and lighting up a fag. He offered across the table but David waved the pack away. 'It's good to see you again. After all this time, eh? Quite something.'

'Yeah, suppose.'

'So what have you been up to?'

David was already sick of recapping the last fifteen years of his life, but he had honed it to a nippy forty seconds of bare facts, and he gave the spiel to Gary.

'What about yourself?'

'Oh, you know, nothing too exciting. You can't get up to anything too exciting in this place. I'm still working for the Royal Bank. Slow progress up the career ladder, all that shite.'

'No wife? Kids?'

'Well.' Gary looked sheepish. 'There is a wife. Kind of.'

David looked at him. 'What the hell is that supposed to mean? Spill it.'

'Five years ago I saved up enough money and holidays to take an extended trip to the Far East. Three months I was over there. Anyway, I met someone while I was out, a Cambodian girl called Lee. Well, long story short, we got married while we were there and she came back to Arbroath with me.'

'That must've got the town gossips going.'

'Not as much as a month after we got back, when she emptied my bank account and disappeared. I've never seen or heard from her since.'

Fuck's sake. David felt sorry for Gary, but almost spluttered his pint nevertheless. It was such a clichéd story: emotionally stunted Westerner gets taken for a ride by shyster looking for a free ticket into Britain. But the cliché of it didn't stop it hurting, he supposed, and he could see it still rankled with Gary that he'd been fished in so gullibly.

'I know, I know,' said Gary. 'Don't think I haven't heard it a million times before, especially from my mum. The folks around here think I'm a fucking joke, I'm used to that. Gary Spink – gullible arsehole. But, well . . .'

He seemed to give up on what he was saying, ending with a shrug and a sip of his pint.

'Fuck this town,' said David, warming to Gary all of a sudden. Fifteen years ago, when he was part of this town, David had treated Gary shabbily, when he was supposed to have been his friend. It was too late, but maybe he could at least make up for it in some way by taking Gary's side against this place now.

Gary was nervously removing his cap and swiping at his strands of hair, and David realized what a good idea it had been to leave when he did. This town had worn Gary down – he looked at least forty, rather than the thirty-four he actually was. He had smoked three fags since they'd sat down, each one devoured with a hunger born of depressing addiction. He wasn't enjoying them, he was just smoking them because he had to.

'You did the right thing, leaving Arbroath,' said Gary, as if reading David's thoughts. 'This place is fucking useless, it sucks the life out of you, so it does.'

'Why don't you leave, then?'

Gary's face lightened, his features seeming to come into focus as the fag smoke cleared. 'Funny you should say that. I'm planning on doing exactly that.'

'Yeah?'

'Well, you remember I was always good at art back in school?' Art, that was it, thought David. 'I never really got a portfolio together, but I'm doing it now, painting and drawing, and I'm going to apply to art college as soon as I've got enough decent stuff to show.'

It didn't sound the most convincing plan David had ever heard, and considering Gary had spent fifteen years penpushing in a small town, he suspected this was a pie in the sky plan that would never come to anything. But then, what the hell did he know about Gary's life?

'Sounds great,' he said, waving his empty glass. 'Another pint?'

'I'll get them,' said Gary, and shuffled off towards the bar.

David felt exposed without Gary's puny frame between him

and the pub, and he was eliciting stares from the other punters in the place. He kept his eyes on the television until Gary returned. Another snippet of Gary's life came to him as he started his second pint.

'How's your sister doing?'

Gary had a sister, a very cute sister a couple of years younger than them, one of the main reasons that the rest of them had hung about with Gary, truth be told. Despite being two years older than his sister, Gary had always seemed like the runt of the litter as far as the Spinks were concerned. Susan was outgoing, vivacious, always smiling and happy and finding the good in people. She was brainy too, David remembered, one of the brightest in her year. Naturally she'd got all the attention, with her attractive yet unthreatening looks, her effortless charm and her exam results. It couldn't have been easy for Gary, living in the shadow of a younger sister all those years, but he never seemed to resent Susan's assumed status as the successful one in the family.

'She's in Prague. Did languages at Glasgow Uni and has been travelling ever since. Amsterdam, Sicily, Lisbon – all over the place. Now she's working for the British Embassy in Prague, something pretty high up. Handy for the odd holiday. She definitely had the right idea, getting out of here.'

'I'm sure you'll do the same. What sort of stuff are you drawing?'

'Dunno, whatever comes into my head. Kind of fantasy graphic stuff, I suppose.' Gary clammed up, unwilling or unable to talk about something so close to him. The word 'fantasy' didn't exactly fill David with confidence for Gary's chances of art college, but you never know, he thought. Better change the subject.

'How's the folks?'

'Fine, fine. Still working. Mum's a cleaner at the school and Dad's now a security guard up at the hospital. Works nights. I still live with them, did I tell you?' David raised his eyebrows. 'I know, it's pathetic. I was going to get my own place, but . . . well I don't know . . . stuff kept getting in the way.'

David waved this away. 'You don't have to explain anything to me,' he said. 'Live where you like. Besides, if you're getting out of here, what does it matter?'

'Exactly.'

'Here's to getting the fuck out of Arbroath, then.'

'Cheers.'

They clunked pints and finished off what was left in the bottom of the glasses. David got up to get another round in, and Gary gently but firmly held on to his arm.

'You know, it's good to see you again,' he said, suddenly serious. David felt awkward standing there, looking down at Gary's wonky teeth and scrotey beard.

'It's good to be here,' he said, because he felt he ought to say something.

Every other square inch of Scotland was basking in unlikely summer heat but, despite the unbroken sunshine, Gayfield Park was somehow still cold, windy and wet. The most exposed football ground in the country, the rickety old maroon and white stadium sat precariously on the edge of the sea, just a few hundred yards down the coast from the harbour which reputedly used to shine the beacon that the team's nickname, the Red Lichties, derived from. They were close enough to the waterfront for the salty fish smell to reach their nostrils and the occasional sea spray from the waves to gradually soak them through to their skins. The wind whipped in off the North Sea relatively calmly, but it was still enough to cancel out any warmth from an unconcerned sun that sat so high in the sky it looked as if it was set for life up there.

The mince on show before their eyes wasn't helping, David thought. The Scottish premier league that he watched on television was dire stuff, but this was a hundred times worse. It had been so long since he'd been exposed to third division football that he was almost shaking with the shock of how rank it was. It seemed barely any higher up the skill ladder than a park kick-about, both Arbroath and Montrose teams (deadly local Angus rivals) consisting of a mish-mash of hapless young kids in ridiculous fin haircuts or mullets, and old warhorses thickening around the middle and never shy about leading with the studs up in a way that, years of experience told them, would make maximum carnage of the opponents' legs.

Still, it was entertaining in its singular dreadfulness, and the relatively good weather had led to a healthy crowd of around four hundred home fans and the same again of travelling support, both sets of supporters enjoying swearing at the tops of their voices at everyone and everything imaginable, occasionally to a jaunty little tune.

Gary and David were standing on the crumbling terrace beside a rusting, ramshackle metal stanchion and soaking up the atmosphere. Sadly, Montrose had gone into an early lead after a dodgy offside decision and the old-timers and kids alike were letting their feelings be known to the poor bastard in the black. Arbroath's bright young hope of a centre forward had the unlikely surname of Brazil, the irony of which was not lost on both sets of supporters, both sides giving him pelters every time he skied a ball high and wide, either into the sea at one side or onto the main road at the other. It had been a long time since David had stood on a terrace at a match like this, and he found the experience incredibly comforting – the smell of piss, the air full of profanity, the occasional witty one-liner from someone who looked like they couldn't even tie their shoelaces. This was the real heart of Scottish football, he thought to himself.

Watching the football made David think sentimentally about Colin. He'd been on the club's books when he died. It was impossible not to think of that. Of course anything could happen in a football career. Colin could've been injured early on and dropped out of the game, or maybe the drink and small-town hero worship would've got to him. Maybe he just wouldn't have been able to cut it, or he might've ended up like one of these hatchet men on the park at the moment, gradually drifting further back in the side until he was the two-footed stopper at the centre of defence. Or he could've signed for a bigger club, then a bigger one, his ambitions taking him to the premier league, such as it was, and maybe international honours, whatever that was worth in the current climate, with the dire state of the national team. Ifs and buts. David knew it was pointless speculating, but he momentarily enjoyed the pointlessness of it, drowning in a soporific sea of possibilities.

'Reckon Colin would've done better than this shower of shite?' he said. He noticed a tightening of Gary's jaw.

'Couldn't have done much worse.'

There was a pause. Gary didn't seem too comfortable with the subject but David continued anyway, the booze having made him chatty.

'Do you ever think about him? About what happened at the cliffs?'

There was another pause as Gary studiously followed the match even though action had stopped for an injury in the middle of the park. Eventually he spoke.

'Sometimes. Not so much these days.'

'I know what you mean. I was the same, until this reunion came along. I mean, no offence, but I hadn't really thought about anyone from Arbroath for a while until I heard about the reunion. I thought maybe it would've been different for you, staying here. I thought there might've been more jogging of your memory about Colin.' Another long pause. 'Well, has there been?'

Gary slowly turned to David and he had a glassy look in his eyes, as if his mind were somewhere else. 'No, not really. It's best not to think about these things. Accidents happen, that's all there is to it. Talking about it now isn't going to bring Colin back, is it? In the end, it doesn't matter if he fell, jumped or was pushed. He's dead, and all the wondering in the world about what happened that night isn't going to change that fact.'

'He fell,' said David pointedly.

Gary seemed to come out of his trance, and fixed a surprisingly clear eye on David.

'You don't know that for sure, do you? No one will ever know that for sure.'

'*I* know.'

Gary shook his head, almost imperceptibly, then turned back towards the game.

'No. You don't.'

The half-time whistle blew, and a rush of Arbroath fans headed for the exits, piling across the road to Tutties for a traditional half-time pint. David and Gary joined the throng, got their pints in and stood against the outside wall of the pub, soaking up the sunshine as cars swished past on the Dundee Road. Another hustle back across the road and they were there for the second half. It was probably the only ground in the country where a half-time pint was possible, something the Arbroath fans were immensely proud of. Despite still losing 1–0 they sang more vocally than before, Gary and David joining in with a slapdash rendition of 'There's Ducks on Keptie Pond'. As if to repay their support, Brazil raced into the box from the left-hand side and latched onto a loose ball to put Arbroath equal. Gary, David and the rest of the fans leapt and shouted and cheered until they were hoarse, bouncing and taunting the Montrose lot. Six pints down and back on level terms, David thought – could be worse.

As the jubilation died down, he noticed for the first time that most of the advertising hoardings around the ground were blank except for a couple of local pub signs and a large recruitment board for the Royal Marines. It made him think instantly of Neil.

'Ever see Neil Cargill these days?' he said.

A look that David couldn't quite pin down seemed to flash across Gary's face before he quickly regained his composure, thrusting his hands deep into his pockets as he eventually spoke.

'Not really. I've bumped into him once or twice in pubs over the years. But I think he keeps himself to himself, pretty much.'

'I take it he did join the Marines, all those years ago.'

Gary seemed to sigh, as if already tired of the subject.

'Yeah, he did. Fought in the first Gulf War, apparently. At one point he was a copper as well, I think. Not sure what he does now. I heard he lived out Auchmithie way, for a while. Bit of a recluse.'

'Really? Doesn't sound like Neil,' said David.

Gary turned and fixed his gaze on David for a second time.

'People do change, you know. Just because you haven't thought about us for fifteen years doesn't mean we've been frozen in time.'

David was surprised by Gary's tone, which was bitter yet firm, as if that was the end of the topic. He looked at Gary, who was back watching the football again. Maybe he had misjudged him, thought David. He realized now he'd felt a condescending sympathy for Gary earlier in the pub, something which was misplaced. Gary, Neil, Nicola, Colin, the whole fucking town and the whole situation, it was worth a lot more than his condescension, which was pretty much all he'd been giving it so far. He had considered himself above all this, observing the town's inhabitants as if from a great height, pissing on them righteously. What did he have to be so righteous about?

He turned back to watch the football. As he did, Brazil skied another shot miles over their heads and out the ground, and David joined in the lusty hoots of derision around him, smiling as he did so.

Back in Tutties the mood was light-hearted and boisterous. After all, the sun was shining outside and Arbroath hadn't been beaten by those Montrose bastards from up the road. David and Gary got another round in and snaffled the table next to the puggy. A teenager was compulsively firing pound coins into the machine, but getting nothing back.

'David, isn't it? David Lindsay?'

They turned from watching the depressed kid at the puggy

and saw Mr Bowman, their old maths teacher. Mr Bowman had been one of the cooler teachers when they'd been at school, and he'd been in the teachers' five-a-side team that they'd played against in sixth year. He must've been about mid-thirties back then, which meant he was pushing fifty now. The five-a-sides was meant to be a relaxed lunchtime kickabout but gradually took on a terrible, competitive seriousness, the teachers trying (and mostly failing) to prove they still had it in them to beat this handful of cheeky upstart kids. It was an open secret that Mr Bowman had a budding drink problem back then, and he was clearly in a shambolic state now. The man's eyes were a watery scarlet colour, as if a vodka–blood mixture would pour out the sockets at any moment, and his nose was a similar colour, the pigment leeching across his cheeks to his ears. His hair was thin, straggly and ash grey, and he wore mismatched suit trousers and jacket, both of which had green and brown stains all over them. He swayed that sway of the habitual drunk, moving his arms in an involuntary, syncopated way to balance the movements his unsteady legs were producing in his helpless torso.

David was surprised he had recognized him. But years of drinking practice had clearly imbued Mr Bowman with the capacity not only to cope with his alcoholic state but to positively revel in it, to the extent that if you took the booze away from him he might not survive the traumatic separation.

'And Gary Spink, isn't it?'

Despite being bloodshot, his eyes were keenly focussed, while his speech was clear and, by Christ, he was good at the names-to-faces game. David tried to do a quick calculation in his head of the number of pupils Mr Bowman must've had over the years, but he'd taken a fair pint himself and gave up almost as soon as he started.

'Mr Bowman, how's it going?' he said.

'Call me Jack, please. Mind if I take a seat?' He didn't wait for an answer, and slumped with expert lack of grace onto a spare stool at their table. The table wobbled a little as he nudged it, and a heavy glass ashtray rattled as he banged his pint down.

'It's quite a coincidence, meeting you two here,' he said.

'Oh yeah?' said Gary, finding his voice. 'How so?'

'I was just thinking about Colin – Colin Anderson – and that whole terrible business at the cliffs all those years ago.'

Jesus Christ, thought David, was this going to come up every time he met anyone?

'It could happen all over again, you see.'

'What?' David couldn't see at all. 'What are you talking about?'

Jack fished a rolled-up newspaper out his back pocket and slowly unfolded it on the table. It was the local weekly rag which rarely had any news in it. When he had it flat, he twirled the paper towards the pair of them and stuck a chubby, greasy finger on the page.

The headline read 'Tombstoning Teenagers Risk Lives for Kicks', and as David and Gary read down, they exchanged a look of disbelief which left them gaping at the paper slack-jawed. A craze had started amongst teenage boys, the article said, for jumping off the Arbroath cliffs into the sea at high tide. There had been several incidents witnessed by people walking their dogs and such like, kids apparently chucking themselves straight off the cliff face and falling up to two hundred feet into the water below. A spokesman for the coastguard said that in the office they had nicknamed it 'tombstoning' because it was 'one of the fastest ways of killing yourself'. There was more to the story, padding about the various incidents and quotes from gormless witnesses. As Gary scanned the paper, David looked up at Jack. The combination of umpteen pints and a quick change of focus made him feel very drunk, and he leant his hand against the table firmly to get his balance back.

'Fucking idiots,' he said.

'My thoughts precisely,' said Jack. 'But it really is taking off, if you'll pardon the pun. There have been quite a few sightings of kids doing this, and although no one's been formally identified,

I'm sure several of them are in our current fifth and sixth years.'

'It's like the Darwin awards, isn't it?' said Gary. 'A fantastically stupid way to die.'

'Well, no one's died yet, thank God, but it will surely only be a matter of time.'

'Wait a minute,' said David. 'This has nothing to do with Colin. He fell. And he was on his own and drunk, so it's hardly the same thing, is it?'

'Nevertheless, it is connected,' said Jack. 'I believe the craze has grown up around the legend of Colin's death. God only knows how or why, but the boys today revere Colin for some reason, see him as a tragically fated local hero.'

'Bullshit,' said Gary. 'How do you know, if you don't know who's doing it?'

'Graffiti. The last few months have seen graffiti appearing all over the place relating to Colin's death. "Colin Anderson R. I. P., died a hero" had to be wiped off a wall at the school. References to "The Tombstoners" are scratched into walls and desks all over the place. And I believe there was similar stuff up at his gravestone and the memorial at the cliffs too, which the council had to remove sharpish.'

'That's insane,' said David. 'Colin didn't jump and he wasn't a fucking hero. He didn't have a death wish and he wasn't a fucking adrenalin junkie.' He was getting angry now and shouting, and people were starting to look over in the direction of their table, all except the kid at the puggy, still plugging in the quids. 'He was just a mate and his death was a stupid accident.'

'I know that,' said Jack, swigging his pint. 'And you both know that, but it seems these boys don't know that. Who knows how these things start, but I fear it'll take someone dying for it to stop, and maybe not even then.'

'Can't you speak to them?' said Gary.

'Why would they listen to teachers?' Jack took another large swig from his pint and a sly look came over his face. 'Maybe if one of *you* came to school to speak to the fifth and sixth years, you know, as a friend of Colin's, to explain that he didn't jump. That might help the situation.'

David and Gary suddenly both felt fished in. Jack had clearly thought of the idea as soon as he'd seen them, and had been leading up to it from the start. The crafty alky bastard, thought David. Well, he won't get me hooked.

'Unfortunately, I don't know if I'll be back in Arbroath again after this weekend,' he said. 'I'm only back for the school reunion tonight, then I'm heading back to Edinburgh.'

Gary got a look of panic in his eyes. Both Jack and David turned to look at him as he spluttered a little into his beer.

'I'm n-n-not very good at public speaking,' he said, stuttering as if to prove his point. 'Plus I'm not very good with kids either. And I don't really know what happened with Colin, so I really don't know if . . .'

'Fine, if you don't want to,' said Jack. 'But it could make all the difference to some poor young bastard.'

No pressure, thought David as he sat drinking his pint and feeling relieved. He looked at Gary and felt sorry for him, but rather him than me, he thought.

Gary crumbled under the pressure and agreed to try and speak to some of the older kids sometime in the next week. Jack unearthed a pen from somewhere in his jacket and wrote Gary's number down on the margin of the newspaper. He had got what he wanted but didn't seem in any hurry to leave.

'Either of you lads ever see Neil Cargill these days? You used to hang about with him, didn't you? The four of you, in your own wee gang.'

'Never seen him,' said David.

'Not in years,' said Gary.

'Did you say you were here for a class reunion?' said Jack.

'Yeah, just down the road at Bally's,' said David.

'I think it's called the Waterfront now,' said Gary into his pint.

'I'm still getting over the name change from Smokies,' said Jack, chuckling to himself. 'That's what happens when you live in a place like Arbroath as long as I have, the pubs all change their names so frequently that there's no point in trying to keep up.'

'That happens in Edinburgh too, right enough,' said David.

'Do you think Neil will be at the reunion?' asked Jack.

'Doubt it,' said Gary. 'Haven't seen him around in ages, don't know what he's been up to.'

'Shame,' said Jack. 'It's always good for old friends to catch up, relive old times.'

'You think?' said David.

'Of course,' said Jack. 'Don't you?'

David had doubts but said nothing. He tried to picture what Neil Cargill would look like now. He was always the most direct, no-bullshit, no-nonsense member of the ADS when they'd hung out together, something matched by his physique – stocky, barrel torso; short, powerful legs; and a dark, serious face that turned veiny when he got agitated. He had never been any good academically and that, combined with dyslexia diagnosed too late, had meant that he'd re-sat a year at primary school. He was a year older than the rest of them, yet he was still in remedial English. He'd had a much older brother Craig who at the age of eighteen, when Neil was only eleven, had somehow managed to wrap his car around a tree on the back road to Arbirlot on a clear spring evening. The police estimated he must've been doing over ninety miles an hour. He died instantly. Neil had carried that weight around with him, occasionally falling into sombre moods only to snap out of them with bursts of aggressive excitement at nothing in particular.

Despite all that, Neil had been a good friend to the other three, always reliable and willing to back them up in a stand-off, which was pretty handy because he was one of the hardest kids in town when it came to fist fighting. And despite being short he definitely looked his extra year, easily swanning into offies, pubs and Breakers' snooker hall confidently at the front, getting the round in and covering for the rest of them. Driven by a need to impress his parents – who were much older than David's, Colin's or Gary's folks, and who were burdened by the same desperate sadness over Craig's death that Neil carried – he'd set his heart on joining the Marines from secondary school onwards. The Condor base just outside Arbroath was home to the 45 Commando Unit, and they did a lot of recruiting from the local schools, but it was made pretty clear that only the fittest and hardest need even bother applying for the Marines, the rest could fuck off to the regular army or fuck off entirely. Neil had no problems with fitness or hardness, but he did struggle with the basic literacy and numeracy requirements, until finally, with the help of a rather hippyish dyslexia specialist that he paid for out of his own Saturday job wages, he passed the Marines' entrance exam in June of 1988. Basic training started two months later, so Neil had spent the summer relaxing and drinking.

So had the Marines worked out? Were his parents proud? Hadn't Gary said he'd joined the police? There were so many holes in David's knowledge of the past, of the collective past of this town, there wasn't a hope in hell of him ever catching up, even if he wanted to. He wondered if Neil would come along tonight, and thought it would be good if he did.

He looked at his watch.

'Shit, it's coming on seven o'clock,' he said, quickly arsing the rest of his pint and nudging Gary. 'We better get a bend on. I've gotta get back to the B&B and get something to eat before I head back out.'

'We could just stay out,' said Gary. 'It's only just down the road to Bally's.'

It was tempting, but David had had seven or eight pints and nothing to eat, and he needed to freshen up and get his shit together for meeting Nicola. Christ, he hadn't thought about Nicola for hours. He tried to picture their kiss from last night, but it seemed blurry and murky already in his memory, as if viewed from the bottom of the Keptie Pond. He hoped he'd get the opportunity to refresh that memory tonight.

Both David and Gary got up to leave, Jack waving his pint glass at them nonchalantly as they pushed their stools back. 'I'll give you a phone through the week, Gary,' he said. 'Sort out the details for this talk at the school.' Gary looked pained at the reminder, but smiled thinly anyway.

'Cheers Jack, nice meeting you again,' said David.

'Aye, and all the best to you too, David. Enjoy yourselves tonight, the pair of you. Don't do anything I wouldn't do.'

They pushed through the smoky babble of the pub and out the door, into the fresh air of a beautifully sunny Scottish evening. David felt the sun on his face and couldn't believe how good the weather had been recently. He patted Gary on the shoulder and arranged to meet him in an hour and a half in Bally's along with the other dregs of Keptie High School's class of '88. The thought didn't fill him with dread, and as he walked purposefully up to the High Common he even started to hum a nondescript tune.

Reunion

Nicola downed another double gin and tonic and looked around. This had been a mistake. Not the idea of a reunion as such, but the sticky-floored venue they'd chosen was a massive miscalculation. Within ten seconds of entering the place she'd almost been puked on by a rubber-limbed boy with curly hair and the baggiest jeans she'd ever seen.

Bally's was packed with kids old enough to be her offspring. Nicola knew it was a cliché to think that, but she couldn't help it. It was the nightclub that time forgot. Nicola hadn't seen the likes since they stopped showing *The Hitman and Her*, that ridiculous late-night celebration of the old-school, small-town disco mentality hosted by Pete Waterman and Michaela Strachan in the late 80s. These days Waterman was doing a television documentary about trains and Strachan was presenting wildlife programmes. Nicola felt similarly out of touch with her past in the face of the flashing lights, mirrorball, dry ice (dry ice, for Christ's sake, she thought) and wrought iron and perspex that filled the large cattle-market dancefloor and sheltered booths arranged around it on two levels.

The reunion had hired out the 'executive suite' area of the club, which was little more than a handful of booths cordoned off with one of those old-style barriers – twisted rope tied between small stands. A squat, burly guy in a black pilot jacket stood guard over the entrance. They did have a section of the bar to themselves, which meant that at least they didn't have to jockey for position and beers with the rest of the scum, avoiding the resultant arse-pinching and lewd comments that would entail.

Nicola was taking full advantage of the bar. She ordered another double gin and tonic and looked at the people filling the executive suite. There were about twenty-five here already, and they were expecting the same again to arrive. In the Lochlands last night there had been half a dozen friendly faces, swapping stories in a laid-back easy-going atmosphere. The current setting, with the shrieking kids half her age and the collection of thirty-something failures with droopy faces, seemed desperately unappealing.

As she was getting a goodnight kiss from Amy, the phone had rung. It was David. It was obvious straight away that he was reasonably drunk, which didn't surprise or bother her. She knew he'd been at the football in the afternoon, and she drank the best part of a bottle of wine with her tea, partly to keep up with him and partly, she surprised herself by thinking, because she was a bit nervous. Nervous about the reunion, and a bit nervous of meeting up with him again after last night. It was just a kiss, that's all it was at the moment, but it was a damn nice kiss, and she probably wouldn't mind a few more like that.

He said he was running late and she'd agreed to meet him here, telling herself that it was ridiculous to need someone else for support. She was regretting that decision. She had wandered in and found the segregated reunion area, had her name ticked off by the bouncer and headed straight to the bar, only turning to see who else was in once she had a drink in her hand. Now she spotted a couple of people from the Lochlands last night, and just as she was about to make her way over, Kirsty suddenly appeared in front of her.

At school Kirsty Boyd had always had the airs of an American prom queen. She'd been short and trim, with big teeth and bigger hair. Tonight the haircut was more restrained (and about ten times more expensive, judging by the highlights running through it) but her figure was just the same, as was the plastic smile spread across her face, hiding a venomous tongue and a more poisonous mind. Kirsty had been the driving force behind this whole reunion, and Nicola suspected that she'd done it entirely to show off her own currently affluent situation and apparently perfect family life.

Kirsty was married to a square-jawed man who had made his money in construction and now owned the controlling share of a Scottish premier league football club, making him the youngest football director in the country. She lived a few miles out of town in a custom-built house with far too many bedrooms, all en suite, situated perfectly amid mature woodland, with a sea view, a jacuzzi, an indoor pool and a playroom with an enormous drinks cabinet. She had two small children that the nanny took care of while she was off doing charity work or fucking her fitness instructor. It was half *Footballers' Wives*, half *Stepford Wives*, and it was all awful. Nicola wasn't jealous of Kirsty, she was just wary of her presence and her motivations. She had seen Kirsty backbiting and scheming too many times, both at school and when she lived in Arbroath with Amy. She mirrored Kirsty's fake smile and took a drink.

'Nicola, hi! How are you?'

Air kiss, air kiss.

'Good, thanks, Kirsty, and you?'

'Oh, fantastic. Isn't it great seeing everyone together again like this? Everyone keeps thanking me for organizing it, but you know it wouldn't have happened without everyone turning up. I'm just glad that so many people responded to my idea of having it.'

She took a delicate sip of what appeared to be a glass of white wine. It was the first time Nicola had ever seen anyone drinking wine in Bally's. Why had she arranged for the reunion to be here? Unless she had some kind of ulterior motive that Nicola couldn't fathom.

'And how are you, Nicola? How's single parenthood treating you?'

'Oh, you know, pretty damn good, I guess.'

'I know it's old fashioned to think so, but I have to say it's so brave of you to bring up little Amy on your own. I mean, it can't have been easy with her dad on the other side of the world and not interested in the pair of you.'

'We do OK, thanks,' said Nicola through gritted teeth.

'And how is Amy? Enjoying school?'

'Yeah, getting on great. Causing trouble, as per usual, but no more than any other kid.'

'My two are absolute angels at the moment. They're no trouble at all, they behave themselves so well I really don't know where they get it from because Ian and I can both be so naughty if we want to be.'

Jesus Christ, thought Nicola, please let me get out of this conversation and back to the bar.

'Did you come down on your own?'

'Erm, well . . .' said Nicola, looking round.

'How brave, but then you always were a brave one, weren't you? Dashing round the world like that for an adventure and coming back with a baby! Why don't you come over and have a gossip with the ladies. We're just over here.'

Nicola felt a hand on her back lightly but firmly pushing her towards Kirsty's little coven of sycophants, the girls who had never managed or wanted to escape from the thrall of Kirsty's influence. Anita Milne, Lesley Masson and Claire Pollock were virtually indistinguishable from each other, their highlighted, shoulder-length hair, neat designer outfits and buffed appearance pathetically mirroring Kirsty's. Nicola would rather speak to just about anybody else than this lot, but she could feel herself getting sucked towards them.

'All right, ladies, how's it going?'

Nicola suddenly felt Kirsty's hand fall away as David's presence split them up, and he stood swaying slightly in between them. Kirsty was quick to react.

'David Lindsay! How are you?'

She made to air kiss him, but David ducked nimbly out the way. The resultant awkward physicality of Kirsty as she tried to right herself made Nicola smirk.

'My, we haven't seen you around these parts since – when would it have been? – well, since Colin's funeral, I suppose.'

'Straight to the point, Kirsty, just like I remember,' said David. 'I'm fine, thank you for asking. And I haven't been here since then, you are absolutely correct. But it's great to be back. You are looking fantastic, if I may say so, Kirsty. How do you get your hair to do that?'

David waved a hand towards Kirsty's head, and a brief look of panic crossed her face as she thought he was actually going to run his fingers through her hair. She regained her composure and ignored his comment. Her gaze focussed on David's other hand, which was lingering on Nicola's back as the three of them stood there, like a polite Mexican stand-off. Eventually David spoke.

'If you don't mind, Kirsty, and despite the fact that you're looking fantastic – did I say that already? Well, you can't hear that sort of thing often enough, that's what I always say – anyway, if you don't mind, Kirsty, I have some urgent business to discuss with Nicola. I have to get her as drunk as me. So if you'll excuse us, you fantastic-looking woman, I'm going to take her over there' – he pointed generally over his shoulder to nothing in particular – 'and buy her drinks. It's been great meeting you again. Save a dance for me later on, will you?'

With that David grabbed Nicola's hand and headed towards the bar. Kirsty watched them go with a sly look in her eyes, and turned to go and spread the gossip she thought she knew.

'You're drunk,' said Nicola.

'Absolutely correct, but actually I'm not nearly as drunk as I was pretending to be just then. I thought you needed rescuing from scary, plastic features over there.'

'You were right about that.'

'And I wasn't lying. I do intend to get you more drunk.'

'Good, because I fully intend to allow myself to be made more drunk.'

'Then life is sweet. What have I missed round here?'

Nicola looked around her at the horror of Bally's. If she wasn't mistaken that was Atomic Kitten playing. She could see Kirsty and her cabal in close consultation.

'Fuck all. Let's get a drink in.'

Three shooters and Nicola was just about all caught up with David in the drunk stakes. The pair of them had started schmoozing around a few other people at the reunion, including some of the crew from the Lochlands the previous night, swapping small talk as they drifted around, separate but keeping a close watch on each other's movements. They fell into different conversations but their communal two-way booze round kept them loosely tethered to each other, deliberately so.

David was talking football with Gary and a couple of other guys that he hadn't known too well at school. One of them was nicknamed Plunge at school – David never knew why – but now introduced himself as Dean. The other guy was called Jonathan something, David forgot what, and his chin still stuck out like Bruce Forsyth. David's only memory of Jonathan was seeing him running about at Andy MacDougall's house party with a kitchen knife, screaming at the top of his voice that he was going to circumcise himself. They got the knife off him pretty quickly. That was the same party where Andy himself got locked in the bog and had to jump out the first-floor window. Strange night, David vaguely recalled.

He felt a slap on the back and turned to see the leering, perspiring face of Mike Clarkson. Clarkson had been a royal pain in the arse at school, a hardnut who bullied the hell out of the no-marks and nobodies. He wasn't tough enough to be in the big league, but he had enough balls to bully most people at school, and enough pals to back him up if necessary. David's friendship with Neil had made him less of a target for Mike, but he was still the subject of plenty of verbal from the guy, as was just about everyone else in their year. And here he was now, that same over-confident swagger to him, the same cautious eyes and tensed neck muscles, the same button-down collared shirt and crew-cut hair, the same pathetic need to get one over on everyone in the basest way possible. There might be plenty of good reasons for coming to a school reunion, but Mike Clarkson sure as shit wasn't one of them.

'David, how's it hanging?'

'Mike.'

'Haven't seen you round these parts for years,' said Mike. 'Since Colin died, eh? Nasty business that, right enough. Don't blame you for buggering off, I suppose, having your best friend commit suicide.'

'He didn't commit suicide,' said David with a sigh. 'It was an accident.'

'Well, that's one way of looking at it, I suppose. The inquiry would say that, wouldn't it? No point in making his folks more unhappy about it than they already were.'

'It was an accident, Mike.'

'There were folk that suggested he was pushed as well. I suppose that could've happened. How would anyone know? We all know what the cliffs are like, it would be easy as fuck to trick someone up there, shove them over and that would be that.'

'No one tricked anyone, or pushed anyone,' said Gary.

'Maybe someone who was jealous of him,' Mike continued. 'Jealous of everything he had that they didn't. It's possible, you can't deny that.'

'Like Gary said, no one pushed anyone, Mike,' said David.

'When you suddenly disappeared after the funeral, David, there were rumours that you'd had something to do with it. I never paid those rumours any fucking mind. That would be ridiculous, I used to say, David wouldn't have had anything to do with Colin's death.'

'That's touching, Mike, really.'

'And anyway, he most probably just topped himself, didn't he? People do it all the time. The suicide rate amongst blokes in this country is through the fucking roof. Of course, there is another possibility. Maybe he jumped off for a thrill and fucked it up. Kids have started doing that, you know, they're calling it tombstoning.'

'Yeah, we heard,' said Gary. 'But that's not what Colin did.'

'We'll never know, will we? It's a right fucking mystery. Must've been hard for you though, David, living with the death of your best mate, your bosom buddy, your special little friend that you went everywhere with.'

'Are you trying to say something?' said David.

'Like what?' Mike couldn't pull off a pretend innocent look without smirking.

'Like that me and Colin were gay.'

'I never said that, did I?' He turned to the others. 'Did I say that? Did I?' He waited for an answer, and after a few seconds of silence turned back to David. 'I never fucking said that, OK? And even if you were, what fucking difference would it make? Unless it was having a dirty, hidden secret that made Colin top himself. Couldn't stand living the lie any more and all that shit.'

'You're a fucking joke,' said David, and the air chilled.

'What did you say?'

'You heard me.'

They stared blankly at each other as the beat of some cheesy dancefloor-filler throbbed all around them, their faces close enough to smell the booze on each other's breath. Eventually Mike broke the spell, chuckling to himself and downing what was left of his bottle of Sol.

'Watch yourself, David, you cheeky cunt,' he said, pointing with his bottle hand. 'Just watch yourself.'

He turned and sauntered towards the bar and the vacuum he left was filled with slightly nervous exhalations. Jonathan and Plunge had been hiding wide-eyed behind their pints, hoping Mike would ignore them. Gary glared at Mike's back as he walked away, muttering 'fucking prick' under his breath. David just shook his head and smiled at the ridiculousness of it all.

*

Nicola was washing her hands in the toilets when Kirsty and her entourage swanned in. This was not a coincidence.

'Nicola!' Kirsty declared it as if surprised to see her. 'Great timing, we're just about to have a cheeky wee line of Uncle Charlie, why don't you join us?'

She pulled out a wrap, unfolded it and started chopping out lines of white powder as Anita watched the toilet door and the other two pretended to relax at either side of her. It was like being back in the school bogs, thought Nicola. She hadn't snorted anything in years. She had been quite partial to a bit of speed in her student days, and tried various things while travelling, but all that had stopped with Amy. But then here was Kirsty with a couple of kids younger than Amy, and a couple of grams in her pocket. Nicola had never really taken to coke anyway, its price always seemed way out of proportion to the effect. It was the narcotic equivalent of a Prada bag, a rather tacky and ultimately pointless demonstration of wealth in the face of those that didn't have it.

'I'm all right, thanks.'

'Very wise, I'm sure,' said Kirsty. 'You're so responsible.'

'No, I just don't like coke.'

'But I did notice there was something you did like out there,' continued Kirsty, getting out a note and rolling it. 'Or rather someone.' She took a blast, then the other nostril, then did the sniffing thing so as not to lose the coke snot. She passed the note to Claire. 'I couldn't help seeing that you and David Lindsay seem to be getting on well.'

Nicola sighed. 'He's OK. We're just friends.'

'It looked like you thought he was more than OK earlier on. Anything we should know about?'

'What, in your official position as town gossip, you mean?'

'Nicola Cruickshank, there's no need to be like that, I was only asking. I don't know what you see in him, myself, he's hardly catch of the day, is he? But then I suppose as a single mum you can't be too choosy about which men you let into your life.'

'Now, Kirsty, that is just plain rude.'

'Not at all, dear, I'm sorry if you took offence. I didn't mean anything by it.'

'Didn't you?'

'I didn't as it happens. You're being very hostile, you know that? I don't know why you're being so defensive, unless you've got something to hide.'

'Whatever, Kirsty. It doesn't really matter what I say, does it? You're going to assume that me and David have a thing going, aren't you?'

'And would I be wrong if I assumed that?'

Nicola sighed again and thought about leaving, but something kept her there. By this time the note had been passed round all four girls and back to Kirsty. There was still a line cut out in front of them and Kirsty offered the note to Nicola.

'Sure I can't tempt you?'

'I told you, Kirsty, I'm not a fan of coke. Turns people into gobby, arrogant arseholes, as far as I can tell.'

'Now who's being rude?' said Kirsty with a smile, before quickly ducking down to hoover up the last line and sniffling. 'And how does David feel about Amy? He does *know* about her, doesn't he?'

Nicola let out a small snort of a laugh. 'Sorry to disappoint you, Kirsty, but yes, he does know about her.'

'And they get on OK? I mean, it's such a lot to take on, someone else's daughter. I suppose you both living in Edinburgh makes things easier.'

'Kirsty, I haven't said there's anything going on, have I?'

'Well, isn't there?'

Nicola shook her head. What was the point?

'There is nothing going on between me and David. Is that clear enough for you?'

'I think the lady protests too much, what do you think, girls?'

'Oh for fuck's sake,' said Nicola, tired of the exchange. She pushed herself up from the sink she was leaning against. 'If you're quite finished slagging off me and my . . .'

'Yes?' said Kirsty. 'Your what?'

'My *friend*,' said Nicola, deliberately. 'Then I'll get out your way.'

She pushed past Kirsty, then Anita at the door, letting the throb of the dance music briefly enter the toilets as she swung out. She headed off towards David, who was within spilling distance of the bar and talking to a little goblin of a man she recognized as Gary Spink.

'Nicola, you remember Gary, right?'

'Hi Gary, long time no see.'

'You're looking great, Nicola.'

'Thanks. Are you the man responsible for getting muggins here shapeless this afternoon?'

'Well, it was a quiet pint really, but you know how these things can escalate.'

'I do indeed. I'm away to get a round in, what are you both having?'

She went to the bar, and David felt a mixture of pride and irritation as he watched Gary's gaze follow her arse.

'She's looking great, isn't she?' said Gary. 'She seemed pretty friendly with you. Something going on there I should know about?'

'That would be telling.'

'Because if not, I might have a go at chatting her up myself.'

'In that case, yes, there is something going on.'

'I knew it. You look good together.'

'We're not actually together, you understand. Well, we might be. I don't know, really.'

'Don't worry, I'll leave you to it. I wouldn't have a chance with her anyway.'

By the time Nicola returned, Jonathan and Plunge had some-how drifted back into orbit around them, and introductions were duly done. Nicola turned to Gary.

'You were another of the ADS, weren't you?'

'For my sins.'

'Have you kept in contact with Neil?'

'Haven't seen him in years, don't know what he's up to.'

Plunge piped up. 'I thought I saw him earlier.'

The rest of them seemed to notice Plunge for the first time.

'Really?' said Gary. 'Here? I thought he was a bit of a recluse these days. Are you sure it was him?'

'We're talking about Neil Cargill? Joined the Marines? Yeah, I'm sure I saw him earlier. It wasn't in the reunion bit, he was over the other side of the club, on his own. He's a stocky fucker, with tattoos? I'm sure it was him.'

Plunge turned to point to where he had seen Neil. To the right of the DJ booth was a dark area, where the lights seemed not to reach into the corner, but there was no one there. They all craned their necks in comedy unison, like meerkats on the lookout, to see further into the dark recesses of Bally's, the swarm of drunkards around them making it impossible to see clearly for more than a fleeting moment.

'It was a while ago, about an hour or something,' said Plunge, as if trying to justify the lack of a Neil Cargill in the corner of the room. 'But I did see him.'

'He got chucked out the Marines, didn't he?' said Jonathan.

'Did he?' said David.

'Yeah, I'm sure I read it in the paper or something. He fought in the first Gulf War – Desert Storm and all that – and then I'm sure I read that he got discharged not long after. Don't know whether it was because he was injured or what, but there was definitely something in the paper about it.'

'Seems weird,' said Nicola, 'thinking that someone our age was out fighting in wars ten years ago. Can't imagine what it must've been like.'

'Just watch the news, we're doing it all over again,' said Gary. David wasn't really interested in talking about politics, the mention of the current conflict flicking a switch in him to off. He wanted to change the subject.

'Right, seeing as how we're here to remember our school days, I can't help feeling that we should be getting into the spirit more. For a start, we are not nearly drunk enough. I suggest some drinking games. You lot grab a booth and I'll get another round in.'

It was past two and the three of them were seriously steaming.

'Check out Mr and Mrs Loverpants there,' said Nicola, pointing at a couple in the adjacent booth, virtually screwing each other on the stained, raggedy seating. 'We were never that bad, were we?'

'What, you mean the two of us?' said David. 'I never got the chance.'

Nicola tried to hit him affectionately on the arm, only she missed and fell slightly against him. She righted herself. 'No, I don't mean the two of us, I mean *us* – our generation. We were never just out-and-out shagging in the middle of Bally's, were we?'

'Maybe *we* weren't,' said Gary, 'but some people were.'

'Really?' said Nicola. 'It's amazing what you don't remember. Like, I don't remember so many of our year being such arseholes.'

'That's about all I remember,' said David. 'Although I was just sitting here thinking they weren't as bad as they used to be.'

'Fuck off,' said Nicola. 'They're twats, the lot of them. Present company excluded.'

'But what about the lot we were in the Lochlands with last night? They're all right, aren't they?'

'Aye, I'm not talking about them either.'

'Who are you talking about, exactly?'

'The arseholes. The twats. Kirsty Boyd and her pals, and all the rest.'

'Now Kirsty,' said Gary, waving a green chartreuse around in front of his face, 'she is an arsehole. And a twat. I'd still shag her, likes.'

'Then you are a sad man, Gary Spink,' said Nicola.

'Nicola, you are absolutely right,' said Gary.

'And what about you?' Nicola said, turning to David. He looked a bit blurry, in keeping with the rest of the room.

'What about me?'

'Would you shag Twinkletoes over there, given the opportunity?'

'No thanks. It would be like having sex with a teacher or an auntie. Not good, in other words.'

'We had one or two teachers I wouldn't have minded shagging,' said Gary. 'And I have a nice auntie, too.'

'You are one sick fuck,' said Nicola. 'Really. Although, our art teacher Mr Thompson was a bit of all right, wouldn't have minded getting him into the art cupboard once upon a time.'

'Gary, which fucking auntie are you talking about?' said David. 'I've met your Aunt Kate, and if it's her you're talking about you really are a sick fuck.'

Gary just smiled. David shook his head then turned to Nicola.

'Mr Thompson!' he said. 'You fancied Mr Thompson? He was so gay. You had no fucking chance.'

'I could've turned him though, eh? Don't you think?' she snuggled up to David's arm and Gary laughed.

'I reckon you could turn anyone,' Gary said and it was David's turn to laugh.

'What, even straight guys?' David said. 'Turn them gay, you mean?'

'Shut up, you cheeky fuck,' said Nicola, letting go of his arm and shuffling clumsily out the booth. 'I've still fucking got it,' she said, doing a drunken shimmy. 'Now, what are you pair of arseholes wanting to drink?'

As Nicola tottered away, both men watched her go.

'She really is something,' said Gary. 'I guess she was worth coming to this reunion for, wasn't she?'

'I reckon so,' said David. 'Although it's been a laugh all round, frankly. Mind you, that could well be down to the fact that I'm steaming drunk and I haven't really done any socializing with anyone except for you and her.'

'So, what now?'

'How do you mean?'

'Between you and her? You going for it?'

'Dunno, just wait and see. We're both old enough to know how the world works. At the moment we're getting on great, so let's just see where we go from here.'

'And what about Arbroath?'

'What about it?'

'Is it going to be another fifteen years before you come back?'

'It'll be another fifty years before I set foot in Bally's again, that's for sure. But I might make it back for the odd game at Gayfield, if you keep me posted. That's if you're going to be here, what with the plans for art college and everything.'

'Yeah, of course.'

Nicola was leaning over the table with a triangle of shot glasses between her hands, careful not to spill anything, when she jumped as if knocked from behind. She quickly dumped the drinks and turned.

She was several inches taller than Mike Clarkson and was looking down on him. He had an evil glint in his eye.

'Did you just pinch my fucking arse?'

'Sorry, love, couldn't resist it,' said Mike, spreading his arms out in a gesture of goodwill, a near empty beer bottle in his right hand. 'You're looking so good these days, Nicky. What are you doing hanging about with a couple of losers like them?'

'Just fuck off, Mike, eh?' David shuffled round the booth to get up but Nicola gently motioned him to stop.

'These two are about the only gentlemen in this shithole,' she said. 'Everyone else in here seems to be a jumped-up little prick with a hardman complex stuck in the fucking 1980s.'

'Shame you think that way, love. I was going to let you come

93

home with me, show you what a real man can do for a woman like you.'

'Does this charm routine work on anyone? Ever?'

'Then again,' said Mike, ignoring her and looking at David, 'I wouldn't want the sloppy seconds of someone like David here, would I? Your bucketfanny is probably fucking rancid, eh, love?'

David made a quick move to get up, but not quick enough and he felt the smash of the beer bottle against the back of his head as he lunged forward, grabbing Mike in a messy rugby tackle. The two of them tumbled to the floor. Like all drunken pub fights, the first few seconds were a ramshackle stalemate as both men clung onto each other, unable to extract limbs from the core of their scrum. But after a few moments Mike managed to wriggle a leg clear and kneed David in the bollocks, and as his grip loosened Mike got above him and smashed a thick forearm across his face. The bottle was gone from his other hand, but he was rabbit punching the back of David's head, until finally he let go completely. Mike stood above him, screaming like a maniac and booting him square in the face when Gary jumped on him from behind. They struggled for a second before Gary also got an elbow in the face, shocking him into half-releasing his grip. Just then, several thick-set bouncers with no necks appeared, seemingly out of nowhere, the crackle of their headsets somehow heard over the throbbing bass from the dancefloor. Almost seamlessly, they separated Gary and Mike and lifted David from the floor, where he was beginning to prop himself up.

'These cunts bothering you?' they said to Mike, and David realized this was only going one way.

'Yeah,' said Mike, wiping his sleeve across his mouth. 'Just jumped me for no reason.'

'That's bullshit and you know it,' said Nicola, glaring at Mike, but even as she spoke Gary and David were being lifted off their feet and marched to the door. She stood for a second looking at Mike, who met her gaze impassively, just a little smile creeping into the corners of his mouth, then she turned on her heels to catch up with the bouncers as they headed through the foyer. Out of the corner of her eye she could sense Kirsty and her cabal soaking up every second of the action. For a moment she thought about turning to shout something at them, but she couldn't think what to say, so instead she fired on, catching up with the bouncers outside the front door as they held Gary and David up against the weather-beaten, puke-splattered pebble-dashed walls.

'We don't fucking like trouble in our club, have you got that?'

'You know as well as I do that Mike started it,' said Gary, before getting a hefty smack across the face.

'We don't give a flying fuck who started it. But we know Mike and we don't know you, so he's staying in and you're out. Now, don't go thinking about hanging about here, maybe catching up with him when he leaves, 'cos we'll be here then as well, and we'll be keeping an eye out for you. And just in case you were feeling really stupid, don't go getting the police involved, because we know them as well, and they don't take too kindly to getting called away from their chips on a Saturday night.'

Gary and David were released and shoved nonchalantly backwards with enough force to make them both stagger and fall over in the patchy grass.

'Now fuck off, the pair of you,' said the bouncer at the front, then, glancing at Nicola, 'and take this slag with you.'

'Fuck you, prick,' said Nicola, but the bouncers were already back inside the front door. The incessant beat of the music died as the door closed, to be replaced by the wash from the sea behind them. They stayed like that for a few moments, David and Gary on their arses, Nicola standing over them, before she sat down next to them on the grass and the three of them started laughing. They couldn't stop themselves, as ripples of laughter passed from one to another, then back again, the volume getting louder as the laughter continued. Eventually they settled down, and were left surrounded by the sound of waves hitting the shore. There was no one else about, except for a lonely drunken figure slumped on a seat over by the crazy-golf course.

'What a fucking arsehole,' said Gary.

'I think that pretty much goes without saying,' said Nicola.

'And those bouncers,' said David. 'They were the genuine article. Real 80s meatheads. I tell you, if anything's going to take me back to my schooldays, it's getting chucked out of this place by a bunch of skinhead bouncers who think they're fucking Sly Stallone and Bobby De Niro. That is priceless. The perfect end to a perfect school reunion, really.'

They got slowly to their feet, swiped at their dusty arses and headed slowly away from Bally's, never looking back. Behind them, the drunk guy at the crazy golf seemed to stir a little as they disappeared round the corner.

The sky was already gaining a watery grey wash around the edges as they said their goodbyes. Standing by the war memorial at the top of the High Common, they could see for miles: Gayfield and the harbour then the cliffs in one direction, Bally's, Elliot Beach and the golf course the other way, and between them miles of slick, grey ocean, filling in the cracks of the world.

Gary was heading west to his folks' house on Monymusk Road, David was angling to walk Kirsty home, past the Keptie Pond and the Lochlands. As he always did at drunken goodbyes, David felt a slight, subconscious twinge of memory, at some base level his mind recalling that night, the last night he'd seen Colin alive. That, combined with the morning dew already forming in the air, made him shiver slightly.

'I guess I'll be seeing you,' said Gary.

'Yeah, keep in touch this time,' said David. 'Have you got a pen? We should swap numbers.'

Nicola raked in her bag noisily, and eventually dug out a pencil and an old receipt. They exchanged numbers with Gary, then there was an awkward silence between them, no one sure what to say next. The evening seemed over, a line drawn under events by this ceremonial exchanging of details, after which nothing more should be said. Gary made awkwardly to hug David, who reciprocated in kind, then he kissed Nicola, and saying final farewells he walked along the path over the railway and headed home.

David and Nicola visibly relaxed as they watched him leave. Being with Nicola was an easy, comfortable sensation, thought David; it felt as if he'd known her for the last fifteen years. He felt a lot more sober than he had even half an hour ago. Whether it was because of the physical exertion or the fresh air or the lack of handbag house pounding in his ears he didn't know, but he felt a lot more together here, walking across the grass with Nicola, their arms entwined the way lovers' arms do. They walked slowly towards St Vigeans Road, neither of them feeling the need to say anything.

Eventually Nicola spoke.

'I'm beginning to think you were right about this whole revisiting your past thing,' she said. 'I thought tonight was going to be a laugh, but it was pretty shocking really. Sorry for dragging you along.'

'I'm not sorry. For a start, if I hadn't come to Arbroath we wouldn't have snogged last night, would we?' He gave her a little nudge, and she smiled a coy smile at him.

'I suppose not.'

'Anyway, I really enjoyed myself tonight, despite getting in a tiny fight and getting chucked out. In fact, that made the whole thing better. And I got to meet up with Gary again, which was pretty cool. I mean, we're not about to start being best mates or anything, but it would genuinely be good to keep in touch with him this time.'

Nicola looked at him.

'You know,' she said, 'it seems we've totally switched our opinions about the past. Isn't that weird?'

'No, we haven't. It just depends on what past you're talking about. That kind of past' – he indicated over his shoulder in the direction of Bally's – 'I can live without.'

'I know what you mean.'

They walked on further, happy in silence for a while, the sky brightening to the east.

Outside Nicola's house they kissed again, both of them more forceful and drunken than last night to begin with, then slowing and relaxing after the first few minutes, soaking up each other's physical presence and drowning in it. Someone wolf-whistled them from the bottom of the street, but they didn't break off, instead just giggled slightly into each other's mouths in a communal sign of togetherness. Eventually they broke apart, and David actually felt dizzy.

'You know, I'm going to go round the abbey tomorrow morning with Amy,' said Nicola. 'Before we head back to Edinburgh. Do you fancy coming?'

'Yeah, that would be good. You can do your tour guide thing on me. Ignorant old history-hating me.'

'I'm part of your history, amn't I?' Nicola said with a nose wiggle. 'And you don't hate me, do you?'

'Hmm, let me think about that,' said David, and they started to kiss again.

7
A Body

The morning sun spread across the mown, stripy lawns, bouncing off the oddly luminescent green moss that clung to the ramshackle stones in the graveyard. Amy ran ahead while Nicola and David sauntered casually up what would once have been the nave of the abbey. In front of them stretched two parallel chains of column stumps, like rows of giant buttons leading to the ruined east end of the nave. A handful of foreign tourists in cagoules drifted around the peaceful, crumbling sandy red walls, touching the warm stone as if hoping to soak up the history of the place by osmosis. Amy disappeared behind a wall and as Nicola raised her hand to shade her eyes she winced involuntarily as the sunlight made her head throb. All those doubles last night hadn't been the best idea, she thought, but they'd done the trick of getting her steaming well enough.

'I take it you don't really want the tour-guide spiel?' she asked David, who passed her a bottle of Irn Bru which she gratefully accepted.

'Yeah, why not? It might distract me from this stupid hangover.'

Nicola took several swigs from the bottle and looked at David. He looked bleary and puffy around the eyes, but apart from that he seemed in much better shape than she felt. He'd been much drunker than her last night, hadn't he?

'Founded in 1178 by King William I, consecrated in 1233, declaration signed in 1320, blah, blah. Fell down gradually in the seventeenth and eighteenth centuries, and everyone started using the stone to build their houses.' She looked again for Amy absentmindedly. 'That enough?'

'I never knew that last bit, that the stone was used to build other houses. I suppose that makes sense. Wouldn't get away with that shit these days, eh?'

They went through a gap in the wall to their right, and found themselves amongst geometric lines mown into the grass, the occasional stretch of stone stubble sticking up here and there. A small sign said 'Cloister Foundations'. They couldn't see Amy anywhere, so they just meandered around the cloister area, soaking up the sun like cormorants at dawn. Just then David's mobile rang.

'So, your mobile sometimes works, then?' said Nicola.

He stuck his tongue out at her as he answered the phone.

'Hello?' he said, then, 'Yes, that's me.'

Nicola's thoughts drifted off as David stood with the mobile to his ear. Her folks' house had been chaotic this morning, Amy carrying on up and down the stairs, the television on loudly, her parents fussing around in the kitchen with Radio Two on (again, way too loud) in the background. Her lazy bastard youngest brother Andrew, the one who still had the nerve to live at home, treating their folks with casual disdain, hadn't come home, preferring to stop over at whichever mate or girlfriend he'd conned into taking care of him. Her folks had obviously been feeding Amy sugar since dawn, judging by how hyper she'd been, and it had been a relief to get to the abbey, to let her off the leash to scoot about the place on her own. It would be a greater relief to get back to Edinburgh and chill out properly, but she was glad to be here with David, and that they'd been through so much this weekend – the booze, the snogging, the fighting – together. It made her feel as if he was a comrade, a partner in crime with regard to the whole thing.

She looked at David now as he put his mobile away. He suddenly looked a lot worse than he had five minutes ago.

'That was Gary's dad,' he said, and seemed to swallow self-consciously. 'Gary's body was found this morning at the bottom of the cliffs. He's in a coma, up at Ninewells in Dundee.'

It took a moment before she understood. Gary? Who they'd said goodbye to eight hours ago? But they'd been nowhere near the cliffs. Nicola's fuzzy head couldn't work out what it meant. She looked at David, who seemed to be about to cry, and she started to feel a knot in her throat.

'I'd better find Amy,' she said, looking around her with a sudden urgency.

They dropped off a reluctant Amy with her grandparents and drove to Dundee as fast as the roadworks let them.

'You must be still drunk,' said Nicola as they headed past golfers silhouetted against a shimmering blue sky. Oilseed rape fields threw pollen high into the air, making their eyes water and their noses run.

'I'm fine,' said David. He was certainly still over the limit, but that didn't exactly bother him now. What the hell did this mean? How the fuck could Gary's body have been found at the cliffs, when the last time they'd seen him was at the other end of town, heading in the opposite direction, and quite clearly making for his bed? He suddenly felt as if he might puke. It was too much like what happened to Colin. The drunken Saturday night, the dawn-lit farewell, the sense of easy-going hangover approaching, and now this. He couldn't fucking stand it. Maybe he was cursed, should get away from Nicola or she'd be next. What else did Colin and Gary have in common, apart from being with him the night they fell from the cliffs? He realized as he thought this that it was stupid, that his current fragile state was making him think illogically, but he couldn't help it. This just didn't make any bloody sense.

Half of him didn't believe the phone call. Gary's dad had sounded too calm, not the voice of a man whose son had fallen from deadly cliffs, and now lay in a coma in hospital, hooked up to all sorts of machines to keep him alive. It couldn't be a joke – who the hell would set up something as sick as this? Maybe it was just a mistake. He wouldn't believe Gary was injured at all until he saw it for himself. Gary's dad had phoned him because they found the scrap of paper in his pocket with David's name on it. He was linked to Gary just as he'd been linked to Colin, as a friend, as a drunken, stupid friend oblivious of this weird fucking shit happening while he slept. He really couldn't handle this any more.

Misjudging a narrowing of the road, he had to swerve to avoid a bus coming towards them. He felt sweat bead up on his forehead. The sun was filling the car with a musty air, and that and the dust kicked up by road diggers and the drifting pollen all made him feel claustrophobic, desperate to get out the car and rest for a moment. He sensed Nicola looking at him after the swerve, but he didn't say anything by way of apology or excuse.

'What do you think it means?' she said.

'I don't know.'

'I don't understand it.'

'Tell me about it,' said David. 'This has happened to me twice. It's like cot death – once is an accident, twice and you're guilty of something.'

'Don't be stupid,' said Nicola. 'You're not guilty of anything.'

'I wonder if the police will see it that way.'

'The police?'

'Sure, they'll investigate, won't they? That's two of my friends found at the bottom of the cliffs in mysterious circumstances. Gary had my number in his pocket, for fuck's sake.'

'Don't be stupid,' said Nicola. 'And anyway, Gary's not dead. He'll be able to tell them what happened when he comes round.'

'If he comes round.'

'He'll come round.'

'He might fucking not.'

They drove on in silence through the painfully bright, dirty day, the hospital drawing nearer.

Gary looked somehow both better and worse than they'd expected. There were no obvious external injuries, but he was hooked up to a ventilator through his nose, and a large, hi-tech contraption which made David think of the Monty Python sketch about the machine that goes 'ping'. For all the lack of evidence of a big fall onto rocks there was still something scary and depressing about Gary's appearance. His body seemed somehow smaller, like it had shrunk in the wash, his straggly hair was like straw and his pale face looked peaceful but lifeless, as if he had already given up.

Gary's parents were sitting at the bedside in the tiny hospital room, in front of a large window so dirty it made the day outside seem wintry and cold. But the room was stiflingly hot and David felt his armpits begin to dampen as soon as he entered, a mix of the humidity and his own nerves. Gary's dad Ian was a small, stocky man, made smaller by a stoop which indicated he had not taken well to all the crap life had dealt him. He stuck his chin out in stoic defiance of the current situation, yet the rest of his demeanour seemed crumpled and resigned, almost as lifeless as Gary. His wife June was distraught. A proud handsome woman with grey hair in a bun, her eyes darted around the room like a frightened animal's, on the watch incessantly for something dangerous and life-threatening.

When David and Nicola entered, June didn't even acknowledge them, but Ian looked up and the sight of his face made David feel queasy.

'What happened?' said Ian.

'Sorry?' said David.

'You were with him last night, weren't you?'

'Yes, but . . .'

'What happened?'

'I don't know.'

'What do you mean, you don't know? You must know. You said you were with him . . .'

'Not at the cliffs,' said Nicola.

Ian seemed to notice her for the first time. 'Who the hell are you?'

'I'm Nicola, Mr Spink, a friend of David's, and Gary's.'

'Were you out last night?'

'We all were,' said Nicola. 'At a class reunion at Bally's. Myself, David and Gary left after there was a fight . . .'

'A fight? Gary was in a fight?'

'Not really,' said David. This all seemed to be going wrong. Just then a sweaty, oversized police officer came into the cramped, steamy room. He was young, younger than David and Nicola certainly, and had a cocky jut to his face.

Ian turned to him. 'These two were with him,' he said to the officer. 'He's David Lindsay. There was a fight. I want to know what the hell happened.'

The policeman angled his head slightly at David, looking for an explanation.

'Look, it's simple, really,' said David. His head was pounding with the heat of the place, and he was soaked with sweat. In this sauna, only Gary seemed dry and calm. 'We were in Bally's, and I got in a bit of a fight with this guy, Gary jumped in, and the two of us got thrown out.'

'What time was this?' said the officer. David expected him to be taking notes, but he just stood there, taking up too much space.

'Dunno,' said Nicola. 'About two. We were all a bit drunk.'

'You were there?' said the officer.

'I left with them.'

'But you weren't fighting?'

'No.'

'Who were you fighting with, Mr Lindsay?'

'A guy called Mike Clarkson.'

The police officer made a face as if this was the least surprising news of his day.

'He didn't get thrown out as well?'

'No, he seemed to know the bouncers.'

'What happened next?'

'Nothing,' said Nicola. 'The three of us walked up the High

Common, then we said goodbye to Gary at the path over the railway. He was heading home, so were we.'

'Where do you live, Miss . . . ?'

'Cruickshank. Nicola Cruickshank. St Vigeans Road.'

'And you?' he said, turning back to David.

'I'm staying at a B&B in Nolt Loan Road. I walked Nicola home, then went back there.'

The police officer raised his eyebrows slightly. 'And neither of you saw Gary again?'

'Not until now,' said David.

'What time did you leave him?'

'I'm guessing around half two, three o'clock?' David looked to Nicola for confirmation, and she nodded.

'And you didn't argue with him about anything?'

'It wasn't like that at all,' said David. 'We didn't argue all night. We're as much in the dark about all this as you are. He wasn't anywhere near the cliffs, and he was heading in the opposite direction. It doesn't make sense.'

Ian became animated. 'It doesn't make bloody sense, all right. But you pair were the last to see him before this.' He nodded towards Gary, sleeping soundly despite the wires coming out of him. 'You must know something else.'

'We honestly don't, Mr Spink,' said Nicola.

The room returned to a kind of stillness, David feeling the heat so much he imagined a tarmac shimmer coming off each of their bodies. June hadn't moved or even acknowledged their presence, and just kept her head down, gazing at her son and then the machines around him as if looking for something.

Ian broke the quiet again. 'What about this Clarkson character?' he asked the officer. 'Shouldn't you be speaking to him?'

'Don't worry, someone will have a word with Mike Clarkson. We know him.'

'You mean he's a troublemaker?'

'We'll speak to him, Mr Spink.' The policeman turned to

Nicola and David. 'I'll need contact information from both of you. We might have to get back in touch for a statement.'

David and Nicola gave him their details. David noticed the badge on his uniform said PC Bell, and wondered if he was any relation to Angela Bell from their year at school. The name popped into his head just like that, although he couldn't picture her, and certainly had no memory of a little brother or anything. He let it pass. Too many memories were coming back to him, and he didn't like it.

The policeman left and Ian turned back to Gary's bedside, putting his hand on his wife's shoulder. She still hadn't stirred since they'd come in. David felt awkward in the room, uncomfortable with the grief that bound Gary and his parents. He started fidgeting with his hands.

'Maybe we should leave,' said Nicola to the Spinks, but there was no reaction.

David realized they had never actually asked how Gary was, how serious his situation was. He couldn't ask now, it seemed obscene to bring it up, so he just stayed quiet. And besides, judging by the faces in the room, Ian's, June's and Gary's, it didn't seem like the answer would be a very encouraging one.

David and Nicola looked at each other, then slipped quietly out the door. There seemed nothing else to do.

They drove in silence back to Arbroath, through the roadworks, past diggers and lorries. David felt ill. He was still hungover and driving made him feel dizzy and disorientated. He imagined gently nudging the steering wheel and guiding the car into oncoming traffic, feeling the impact of metal through his body. He snapped himself out of it. Sleep was what he needed, but he knew he had to drive back to Edinburgh. He also had to get his head round what the fuck had happened with Gary. It couldn't seriously be anything to do with Mike Clarkson, could it? But then if it wasn't, what the hell was the explanation?

Nicola went to get Amy, and David returned to the Fairport

to pick up his things and check out. It was already well after normal check-out time, but Gillian didn't mind, fussing over David as he came in so that it was a relief to finally pay the bill and get out. He sat by the Keptie Pond for a while, watching young families with pushchairs strolling round the park, kids playing football over by the water tower, the stuff of everyday life still going on round about him as if people weren't lying in sweltering hospital rooms in comas. He tried to think about what happened last night, both before and after he and Nicola left Gary, but his mind went round in circles and no clear thoughts distilled themselves out of the thick broth of his hungover brain.

He picked up Nicola and Amy, and soon they were back on the Dundee road, this time heading all the way south to Edinburgh. David remembered his mood on this same road less than forty-eight hours before. His body felt more brittle now, his mind less sturdy. Back then he hadn't seen Gary in fifteen years, now Gary was plugged into a life-support machine. Back then he hadn't spent the end of two nights snogging Nicola, this fantastic-looking woman now sitting next to him.

'Can we listen to the radio?' chirped Amy from the back seat.

'Sure,' said David. He turned the dial. It was Radio One and the charts were on. An innocuous piece of glossy hip-hop slithered through the air, with half the lyrics blanked out. 'That OK?'

'Cool.'

They sat for a while, letting the radio waves fill the car. They passed Perth over the bridge and fired on through another valley of low-lying fields and up a steep, winding slope where the radio reception faltered.

'What happened to your friend?' Amy said.

'What, love?' said Nicola.

'Your friend. The one you went to see in hospital. What happened to him?'

Nicola and David exchanged a look. This wasn't David's territory and he was glad to leave the talking to Nicola. She wasn't exactly keen to explain, but it was part of the job.

'He fell and hurt himself, honey.'

'Where about?'

'You remember the cliffs? We've been there with Granny and Grandpa, and I told you to be careful.'

'He fell off there?'

'Yeah.'

'Wasn't he being careful?'

Nicola looked across at David. 'I suppose not,' she said.

'Were you with him?'

'No, we'd left him and gone home.'

'Was he drunk?'

'What?'

'Was he drunk? Drunk people fall over all the time, and it was Saturday night, and he'd been out with you drinking, so I was just wondering if he fell off the cliffs because he was drunk?'

'We don't know why he fell,' said Nicola. 'Now maybe we should talk about something else.'

'Is he going to die?'

The question hung in the humid air of the car. They couldn't outrun it. It was the question that neither Nicola nor David had yet asked out loud, although they'd both been considering it. David wondered what Nicola would say. It didn't seem like she was going to say anything at all for a while.

'We don't know,' she said eventually. 'He's in a coma.'

'What's a coma?'

'It's like when you're asleep but no one can wake you up.'

Amy considered this for a moment.

'That sounds like being dead.'

'It's different because your body still works,' said Nicola. 'The heart still pumps blood, the lungs still take in air. But he can't wake up, that's all.'

Amy seemed satisfied for now, and didn't ask any more questions. David and Nicola were glad to let the radio fill the silence all the way to Edinburgh.

Going over the Forth Bridge seemed to lift their spirits. The sight of all that open space on either side and the oversized Meccano of the rail bridge seemed to buoy the three of them, and they knew they were nearly home.

It was early evening and trees were beginning to lengthen their shadows as their car crawled round the centre of town heading south. David didn't want to leave them, he couldn't stand the thought of being alone in his own flat tonight, despite the fact he felt exhausted. He had already grown accustomed to having Nicola around in only a few days, and the realization shocked him. He experienced a growing jitteriness at the thought of dropping her and Amy off, and not seeing them for an undetermined length of time.

As if reading his mind, Nicola spoke. 'Do you fancy coming to ours for your tea?'

Before he got a chance to answer, Amy piped up. 'Can we have pizza, Mum?'

'You could live off pizza, couldn't you, munchkin?'

Amy seemed confused by the question. 'Of course. Pizza's great. And I'm not a munchkin.'

'Course not,' said Nicola, and looked across at David driving. She couldn't read the look on his face as he manoeuvred through traffic, but he seemed a touch more relaxed than he'd been earlier on. He caught a glance at her between watching traffic.

'Pizza would be great,' he said with a smile.

The three of them sat numbly watching Sunday night television and eating pizza, Nicola and David with beers in their hands. Amy went to bed around nine, and they sat quietly for a while, not wanting to break the bond of silence. *Midsomer Murders* was on the television, and John Nettles puffed red-faced around a syrupy English village trying to sort out whodunit.

'I can't work any of it out,' said David out of the blue. 'You know? It just doesn't make any sense. The more I think about it, the less I seem to know about what could've happened to Gary.'

'I know what you mean.'

'I suppose it doesn't help that we were all pretty steaming.'

'That's irrelevant and you know it. It might've explained something if Gary had to walk home along the cliffs or something, but Jesus H, he was on the other side of town, and heading the other way. Why would he double back and head to the cliffs?'

'Maybe he was thinking of Colin, and wanted to go see the memorial stone.'

'That doesn't sound too likely.'

'We *were* all steaming. You know what can happen in people's heads at three in the morning after drinking all day. We've all suddenly come to and found ourselves somewhere surprising after a night on the lash. Haven't we?'

Nicola wasn't convinced, although she'd had several such experiences in her younger drinking years. But those were a long, long time ago, and seemed to have happened to a different person entirely, and she couldn't see why someone in their thirties, blind drunk or not, would be wandering around a clifftop in the early hours of the morning, essentially an accident waiting to happen. Because that's what it was, she told herself, an accident. The alternatives were too dreadful to contemplate. That either he had tried to kill himself or that someone was responsible for Gary's fall, someone had pushed him over. The police officer had perked up when he'd heard Mike Clarkson's name, but she didn't think for one second he'd had anything to do with it. He was an arsehole and prone to casual violence, but he didn't hold grudges. Mouthing off and fighting were just part of his average weekend, and she felt sure that he would've forgotten all about her, David and Gary as soon as they'd been thrown out of Bally's. He wouldn't care what happened after that, to do so would be beneath him. So for him to – what? – leave Bally's, secretly follow them up the High Common, follow Gary further, confront him and – then what? Nicola couldn't even conceive what could've happened to get the pair of them up to the cliffs, unless Gary was unconscious *before* he even got to the cliffs. But then that would involve someone driving him there, because you couldn't carry a body that far across town without someone seeing.

Jesus Christ, listen to yourself, she thought. Thinking about how to move bodies around town, how to arrange a fall from the cliffs. This was stupid. It was just a fall, nothing more. And it was just a coincidence that it had been a similar fall to Colin's. Coincidences happen all the time in life, she told herself, there shouldn't be anything surprising in that. She tried to think how she could say this to David. He looked worried. For him the coincidence of it must be terrible. She had hardly known Colin, really, and she didn't know Gary well either, but for David it must be shocking. She couldn't imagine what he must be thinking. And that stuff about him being the common link between the two accidents – that was just stupid. The police wouldn't be thinking along those lines, surely? Even your average small-town copper had more brains than to think David had anything to do with it. And besides, he'd been with her after they'd left Gary.

She wanted to reassure him, let him know that she knew it was just an accident, a stupid coincidence. She looked across at him now, staring at the television screen but clearly churning things over in his mind. She took a swig of beer and spoke.

'Do you want to stay over?'

He didn't say anything, but turned to look at her, and she saw a sadness and some confusion in his eyes. Such cute eyes.

'Sex isn't on the menu,' she said. 'Not tonight. But I could use the company, if you felt like staying.'

His eyes seemed to clear and he took a swig of beer.

'I'd love to stay,' he said, and gave her a kiss.

8

Drawn Back

David woke up in a bed he didn't know, confused as hell for a moment as he lay blinking at the slats of light squeezing through the blinds at the window. He rolled over and there was Nicola, head propped on her elbow, looking at him.

'Morning, sunshine,' she said with a smile.

'Hi, you.'

His heart sang. He tried to think back to last night through the fog of his dreams. They hadn't had sex, they'd just gone to bed after a few beers and held each other, something he'd found surprisingly reassuring. Other memories started trickling back into his mind: the sight of Gary's ashen face in the hospital; the angry questions of Gary's dad; the leering, seething face of Mike at the reunion; the arrogant calm in the eyes of the babyish police officer. They all stared back at him, confusing him and making his head hurt a little. He shook his head and blinked deliberately, then opened his eyes and looked at Nicola again. Her hair was mussed and tousled, falling over her shoulders, bare except for the straps of a black bra top. She was wearing a pair of stripy pyjama bottoms and her eyes were a little sleepy but still full of life. Her smile was beaming as she wiggled her nose and looked around her as if she were thinking, What next?

He was thinking the same thing himself. He wanted to have sex with her now, but what the hell was the form, when you were already in bed together, but you hadn't done anything? He spotted a clock on the table beside the bed. That couldn't be right.

'Is that the time?'

'Half-nine? Yeah, I think so.'

'Shit, I'm already late for work. Why aren't you up? What about Amy?'

'Amy's still on her summer holidays for two more days, and I'm off work looking after her.'

Christ. He toyed briefly with the idea of phoning in sick, but he'd done that once too often on a Monday with a hangover, and considering the state of the company he really couldn't take the piss anymore. He would have to go in.

'I've got to go,' he said with real regret, and to his relief she laughed.

'Fine. Love 'em and leave 'em and all that. Except you didn't, of course . . .'

'Look, shit, sorry, I feel stupid rushing out the door, but I really have to get in to work. Thanks.'

'What for?'

'For everything. For the whole weekend. For asking me to stay last night. For snogging me. For bullying me into going to Arbroath in the first place.'

'Do you really want to thank me for that? Considering?'

'Well, OK, I'll think about that one.' He reached over and kissed her slowly on the lips and she kissed back, arching her neck a little in response. They stayed like that for a few seconds before he pulled away, rolling out of bed and pulling his jeans, T-shirt and trainers on.

'I would say I'll call you, but it's such a cliché,' he said.

'Clichés are good. Cliché away.'

'All right, in that case I'll call you. And I really will call you.'

'Yeah, right.' She put on a fake huff, pouting her bottom lip out. It made David want to jump right back into bed. Instead he just smiled at her, ran his hand through his hair and headed out the door.

Two hours late for work, he staggered sweating and dishevelled into the office, skulked around the kettle making coffee, then parked himself at his desk.

'What the hell were you up to at the weekend?'

It was Spook, looking worse than David felt, poking his head out from behind his monitor.

'How do you mean?'

Spook had a smile on his face, the kind of smile that David didn't like the look of one bit.

'Someone's been phoning all morning, trying to get hold of you.'

'Who?'

'Now, let me get this right,' said Spook, hamming it up as he searched for a note on his desk. 'Ah, yes, a Derek Bell.'

David didn't recognize the name.

'Doesn't ring a bell?' said Spook. 'Pardon the pun. Oh, hang on, you might know him as PC Bell, a constable with Tayside Police. He's phoned a few times, and he left a number to call him back at Arbroath nick.' Spook waved the note over at David, smiling from ear to ear. 'Interesting school reunion, I take it?'

David didn't answer. What the hell did the copper want? He probably just needed a statement about Saturday night, but then why phone three times? David needed to down his coffee before he found out, but just then his phone rang. He picked it up.

'Mr Lindsay? This is PC Bell, we spoke at Ninewells Hospital yesterday.'

'What can I do for you?' David didn't really want to be having this conversation.

'I'm sorry to have to inform you, but Gary Spink died in the early hours of this morning.'

There was a silence, broken only by the buzz and crackle of the phone line. David was looking right at Spook, who was gently gooning at his desk, imitating a copper and grinning widely. David gave him the finger.

'Mr Lindsay?'

'I'm still here.'

'Obviously what we're investigating now is a death rather than a serious injury. We'll definitely need you to make a proper, official statement, since you were the last person we know of to see Mr Spink alive. Yourself and Miss Cruickshank.'

'That's fine,' said David, but his head was spinning. Gary was dead. He had only just met the guy again after fifteen years and now he was dead. Dying in the same way and the same place as Colin all those years ago. Fuck, fuck, fuck.

'Mr Lindsay? We'll need you to make a statement.'

'Sure,' said David, coming to. 'Can we do it over the phone?'

'I'm afraid not. We'd prefer it if you came into the station to make a statement in person.'

'What, in Arbroath?'

'That's right.'

He didn't have any intention of going back to Arbroath. He hadn't had any intention of going back even before all this shit, and he certainly wasn't going now. He told the copper as much.

'I'm afraid I must insist,' said Bell, rather smugly. The tone of his voice said, don't fuck with us, we're the police. There was another long moment's silence, David didn't know what to say.

'If it helps,' said the policeman in a more conciliatory tone, 'Gary's funeral is already set for Friday. At the Western. Perhaps you'll be going?'

David had no such intention, he hadn't had time to think about it, and here was a smug bastard kid copper telling him what to do. He felt dizzy.

'Perhaps if you were up, you could pop in sometime and make a statement,' said Bell. 'I'm working over the weekend, so any time. Just ask for me at the front desk.'

And that was that; it was decided. David seemed to be losing all control over his movements these days, and he disliked the feeling of having all his actions dictated to him. So now what? He was going back to Arbroath to a funeral? To make a police statement about the death of another school friend? Jesus H.

He needed to talk this over. He made another coffee, sat back down and dialled Nicola's mobile.

'That was quick,' she said.

'What?'

'I know you said you'd call me, but that was only about two hours ago. I wasn't expecting a call quite yet. You haven't really perfected the "treat 'em mean, keep 'em keen" approach, have you? Can I expect flowers and champagne back at the house when I get home? Or tickets to Paris in the post?'

'Gary's dead,' he said, regretting the way it came out, but unsure what else to say. Down the phone there was a screeching racket suddenly, making David jump.

'Nicola? What the fuck was that?'

'Monkeys. I'm in the monkey house. At the zoo, with Amy. Hang on a minute, I'll go outside.'

David waited, his mind spinning as he listened to monkey noises receding down the phone.

'Sorry,' he heard Nicola saying. 'I take it I heard correctly? Gary's dead?'

'Yeah.'

'David, I'm really sorry. Christ, what a nightmare. What a fucking nightmare.'

'I know, I know. I just had PC Plod on the phone telling me. He also took the opportunity of coercing me into going back to Arbroath to make an official statement this weekend. I think he'll need something from you as well. Gary's folks have already organized a funeral, for Friday.'

'What about an autopsy?'

'What?'

'An autopsy. Don't you watch *CSI*? Or are they called post-mortems in this country? Either way, presumably there is some doubt over Gary's death or we wouldn't be making statements, so surely they'll do an autopsy.'

David hadn't thought about it.

'I suppose they will,' he said.

Images from forensic television programmes flitted across his mind and he felt queasy. He couldn't equate the glossiness of those American shows with the papery, grey mask of Gary's face as he lay in his hospital bed yesterday, or the thought of his body being opened up. My God, was that only yesterday he'd seen him in hospital? Things were moving fast. They would be cutting him open this week, sewing him back up, then returning him to the earth before the weekend. Jesus.

'I don't know anything about that, all I know is that the funeral is on Friday, and we're supposed to go back to Arbroath to make statements at the police station.'

'We should probably go.'

'To the station, the funeral or both?'

'Both. There's no point getting the police's knickers in a twist over a wee statement about when we saw Gary last. And as for the funeral, we should probably go to pay our respects, don't you think?'

David knew she was right and he was glad that she was telling him what to do. He needed telling what to do, and he needed the company if he was going to head back up there.

'I suppose you're right,' he said.

'I suppose I am too.'

David heard a strange wailing noise in the background, then Nicola muttering 'fuck' under her breath.

'Look, David, I've got to go,' she said. 'I think Amy might have gotten herself into a bit of bother. With a monkey. I'll phone you later on, OK?'

And with that she was gone, the dead tone of the phone ringing in David's ears.

After Nicola had extricated Amy's hair from a rather over-friendly Madagascan lemur, she only had a second to herself before her phone went again. It was that police officer confirming what David had told her, and gently pressuring her into heading back to Arbroath at the weekend. He seemed a little put out that she already knew about Gary's death, but tried to hide it. As she hung up, Nicola thought that if he kept up his snidey manner he was sure to make inspector one day.

She sent a fully-recovered Amy off to find out when the penguin parade was on, and sat down opposite one of the many empty enclosures to think.

It was all getting a little weird. On the one hand, despite herself, Nicola was getting pretty excited about David. Friday and Saturday nights had proven there was definitely something there between them, and the fact that they'd pretty effortlessly picked up each other's lives after a fifteen-year gap was surely an indication that they were in sync with each other somehow. They had – oh, she didn't know how to put it without sounding cheesy – some kind of empathy with each other. Perhaps they didn't have the same attitude towards the past, but they seemed to have a similar view of the present. They had ended both nights buzzing from drink and content in each other's company, and then they had done the same thing, only in more sober and sombre mood, last night too. If anything, the shock of Gary's fall had somehow thrown them together even more. The two of them were now the last people to see him alive, they were a two-person club, and they would always have that inexplicable thread running between their lives.

But then, there was a dead body in the mix. Someone she had been laughing with only two days ago was now dead, and his parents must be distraught. She tried to imagine how she'd feel if anything happened to Amy, but couldn't picture it. No, that wasn't quite right, she could imagine it, she probably thought ten times every day about how desolate, how pointless her life would be without Amy. It was the same for all parents, she assumed, there was something in parenthood that transcended all that other shit about loving till death do you part. The only real love in the world was between parent and child.

She tried to imagine what her parents would be like if anything happened to her, and she couldn't really picture that either. She was the eldest of five kids, so she'd always been like an extra parent to the rest, looking after her little brothers and sisters, helping out around the house, grown up before her time, really, which was why, she always suspected, she had taken to mother-hood so easily.

She realized with surprise that she wasn't really as shocked as she should be about Gary. He wasn't her friend, she hadn't known him, really, so his death hadn't had that much impact on her. Secretly, she admitted to herself, she was a little bit excited about it. It was a terrible thing to admit, and she felt genuinely awful for Gary's parents, but the mystery of his death also offered a horrible vicarious thrill, as if she'd been watching a film or reading a book. It was bizarre, how he'd ended up at the cliffs on that night. She'd been reading Nancy Drew books for Amy recently – when she herself was little she'd loved the ham-fisted adventures Nancy would blunder in on, always sorting things out by the end, with or without those two Hardy Boys twats who would sometimes turn up and ruin things. She felt guilty and vaguely absurd thinking these things, but also strangely keyed up. Kirsty had snidely said the other night that Nicola had led an adventurous life, trekking round the world and coming back with a baby, but the reality of her round-the-world jaunt had been mundane. You never learnt anything, racing through other people's cultures and countries, sampling the pre-prepared tourist trinkets, or hanging out with the other globally migrant workers in the same way that Australians now seemed to congregate in Edinburgh as some kind of coming-of-age ritual. It wasn't the grand adventure she'd hoped for, her trip, and the only good thing to have come out of it, really, was Amy, and while she didn't regret a minute of her life with her daughter, changing nappies and cleaning up puke for years wasn't exactly James fucking Bond. Now she worked a steady job, looked after her daughter, didn't get out much and liked the odd large glass of wine – hardly the stuff of high-powered professionals, let alone something as glamorous as undercover agents or millionaire arms dealers. She loved her life, she *did* love it, every aspect of it, but it really wasn't exciting.

And yet, what was a mysterious dead body if not exciting? The trouble was, Gary's death could well be a mystery that was unsolvable. After all, they had never come to any conclusion about Colin's death fifteen years ago. That was the terrible uncertainty of life – that sometimes you just never get to find out what really happened. It was nothing like a Nancy Drew story, was it? In both Gary's and Colin's cases, there were three possibilities. Either they'd fallen by accident, jumped on purpose, or been murdered. If it was an accident, then the trail ended there. If it was suicide, did anyone ever know the real cause? Even those that leave notes – not very many, she remembered from a forensic show on telly – leave big gaping holes in the hearts of those they love, don't they? Big, unanswered questions, as well as anger and shame. But what were the chances? She didn't know anything about statistics or probability, but she remembered something recently from the news about cot deaths – in fact hadn't David mentioned it? – that once was a tragedy, twice was murder. Did that apply to other similar deaths? Maybe that was stupid, but it lodged in her brain as an idea, it seemed to logically make sense that the same thing happening to two people in the same place, two people who had the same backgrounds and who had known each other, well, that couldn't be coincidence. Which left murder.

But that was ridiculous as well. For a kick-off, who the hell would be murdering people? And at Arbroath cliffs, of all places? That sort of shit just doesn't happen in a place like Arbroath. But then again, there were stories on the news every day about deaths, murders, terrible things happening in small towns all over Scotland, all over Britain, everywhere in the world, so why the hell shouldn't it happen in Arbroath, just because it was the place where she grew up?

She felt confused, her head cloudy with the swirling possibilities of it all. That she might never know what happened to either Colin or Gary nagged at her a little, gnawed away at her sensibilities, raised as she was on easily-compartmentalized and solvable problems, murder mysteries that were over in an hour or two on television.

She wanted to talk to David about all this, but she wasn't sure how to bring it up. They were both going to be heading back to Arbroath, she realized; maybe they would do it together this time, and maybe she could discuss some of it then. Their relationship was getting off to a strange start. So far they'd been to a museum, a school reunion, Arbroath Abbey and a hospital together, and their next dates were at a cemetery and a police station. It wasn't normal, but it was interesting, she gave it that.

She saw Amy coming round the corner with a glum look on her face.

'They don't do the penguin parade today,' she said. 'They only do it on special occasions now.'

Nicola looked around her. This zoo was going to the dogs, she thought. When she was little she'd been brought here for a special treat, all the way from Arbroath, and they'd had elephants back then. Admittedly they were squeezed into a tiny enclosure and looked like fat businessmen bursting out of grey suits, so it was maybe better that they weren't here any more. They'd also had bears which, unbelievably, some kids had fed orange juice. Recently the zoo had got rid of their giraffes as well, and most of the big cats. Now the penguin parade was being scaled down. What was the point? It had become a steep hill with some monkeys and lizards. Maybe it was for the best, she didn't really approve of zoos anyway. Still, she regretted that Amy wouldn't be having the kind of eye-widening experience that she'd had when she came here for the first time. She wondered for a minute whether other aspects of life were being similarly scaled down, all the risk being taken out of life in an ever more litigious world, but then she thought that was just her grumpy, thirty-something side getting the better of her. Fuck that, there was still plenty of excitement in life. Not least what had happened to Gary Spink.

She took Amy's hand and headed slowly up the hill in search of an animal enclosure that might also contain some excitement.

All day the phone never stopped ringing, driving David nuts as he tried to avoid working. So when it rang just before five, as David was putting his computer to sleep and throwing things into a drawer, he considered for a moment not answering it. But then he thought it might be Nicola, and picked up.

'David Lindsay?'

Oh shit. It was Mr Bowman. David's mind pictured the old soak across the table from him and Gary in Tutties, and fast-forwarded through the conversation that was about to happen. He knew how this was going to go, and he didn't like it, but he couldn't see how it could be avoided.

'Yes,' he said with a heavy sigh.

'It's Jack here, David. Mr Bowman. I'm just calling because I heard the terrible news about Gary. Shocking, absolutely shocking. I can't really believe that we were sitting chatting on Saturday, and now he's dead.'

'Tell me about it,' said David, already wanting this conversation to end.

'How on earth did it happen?'

'How the hell should I know?' David felt like he was back at school for a moment, being accused by the teacher of something someone else had done. He felt his cheeks flush involuntarily.

'I'm sorry, what a ridiculous thing to ask you. I do apologize. I'm just a little shocked, you understand.'

You're fucking shocked, thought David, but he kept his mouth shut.

'What do you want, Mr Bowman?'

'I'm sorry?'

'I said, what do you want? Why did you phone me?' It sounded unnecessarily harsh, David realized, but he knew exactly why Mr Bowman had phoned, and he wanted to get through it as quickly as possible.

'Ah, well,' said Mr Bowman. 'And please call me Jack. Of course you remember Gary agreeing to come to the school this week, to talk to some of our older pupils about the dangers of . . . well, this is incredibly awkward, I suppose, considering . . . but anyway. He was going to talk about tombstoning, you recall, and now . . . But considering what has happened, I think it's probably more important than ever that someone comes to the school to have a chat with some of the kids about the cliffs and the dangers.'

'And you thought of me.'

'I know it must seem terribly heartless, considering Gary's death, to bring it up just now. But don't you see? Things could really get out of hand now. Word will get out about this straight away, and we could have two dead martyrs for these tombstoning idiots to worship. We both know Gary would never have been doing anything so stupid, but teenagers are very impressionable, and they don't often take much notice of the truth unless it's shoved down their throats, unless they're faced with it in person. Which is where you come in, if you'd be willing. I think it would be fantastic if you would take Gary's place, and come and talk to some of the pupils.'

David had already decided he would have to say yes before Jack had even started to ask. He absolutely did not want to be standing in front of some belligerent schoolkids, spraffing shit about not jumping off cliffs, in the vain hope that none of them would break their stupid fucking necks in the future. He absolutely did not want to be put in that position, but for some strange reason – some masochistic instinct, some kind of penitence for the deaths of his two friends, for which he was utterly blameless but felt guilty about nonetheless – he knew he had to do it. It was his own pathetic little exhibition of martyrdom, except only he would know about it.

'That's fine,' he said. 'I'd be happy to do it. I'm going to be back in Arbroath on Friday for Gary's funeral. I could do it then, in the morning sometime. How about eleven?'

Jack obviously couldn't believe what he was hearing, and there was silence down the phone for a second's beat.

'That would be fantastic, David, really it would,' he said. 'I'll make the arrangements at this end. If you just ask for me at the school reception when you arrive. I'll take you out for lunch afterwards, if you like. It's the least I can do. If that doesn't clash with the funeral.'

'That should be fine,' said David. He felt exhausted.

'Well, I'll let you get on with things,' said Jack. He sounded delighted with how his day had gone. David wished he felt the same way. 'I'll see you on Friday, then.'

'See you then.'

David had the receiver halfway down when he heard the teacher again.

'Oh, I take it you met up with Neil on Saturday?'

'What?'

'Neil Cargill. We discussed him briefly, you remember? I wondered if he was going to the reunion at Bally's.'

'Yeah, well, he didn't show up, as expected.'

'Really? Only I saw him when I left Tutties.'

'What?'

'I saw him, just a short while after you left Tutties. I finished my drink and headed off, and I literally walked past him outside the pub. I have a good memory for faces and names, you see, and of course we'd just been discussing him, so he was at the forefront of my mind. Anyway, it was only after we'd passed each other that I remembered who he was, so I shouted after him, but he didn't turn round. It was definitely him, though. I assumed he was in the area because he was heading along to Bally's for the reunion.'

'You're sure it was him?'

'I might be getting on a bit but the old grey matter still works, just about. My family is blessed with cancer and heart disease but not senility, so the memory remains intact, for now. It was definitely Neil.'

'Well, he wasn't at the reunion,' said David, but then thought back to what someone had said in Bally's, who was it again? One of Gary's mates had claimed to have seen him in the place. His memory was hazy, soaked in the booze of the night.

'I suppose some people just don't go in for that sort of thing,' said Jack. 'Anyway, I'll let you get on. I'll speak to you on Friday.'

David put the phone down and sat for a moment. It was only Monday but already this week had gone to shit. He had a talk to give at a school, a funeral to attend and a police statement to file before the week was out. Great. Better get home and get a drink inside me fast, he thought as he slung his jacket on and headed out the door.

The week dragged grudgingly towards Friday, and as it did something started to creep into David's mind. That name that seemed to keep popping up at odd moments in Arbroath finally lodged itself in his subconscious, then slowly floated up to the surface of his thoughts – Neil Cargill. He gradually started thinking more and more about Neil, mentally picking at the scab of his childhood memories of the two of them – the four of them including Colin and Gary – and how their lives had been together back in the 80s. It seemed like an entirely different universe, the 1980s. People were still worried about nuclear bombs and the cold war, for fuck's sake, so it really *was* a different universe. Not that any of the four of them had been worried about that sort of thing. Most of the time all they worried about was which girl they were going to try and get off with, or where they'd get enough money to get drunk at the weekend. That was life in a small town, David thought: they were like goldfish swimming in their own tiny bowl, minuscule attention spans and flapping mouths agog, while outside the bowl a whole world was getting on with wars, love, death, famine, politics, all the stupidly important shit that teenagers everywhere resolutely ignored, never mind those in a dead-end former fishing town flung half way up the east coast. In eighteen years of childhood, David could

125

remember visiting Edinburgh and Glasgow on only a few occasions for a gig or football match. It wasn't that these places were impossible to get to – both were a couple of hours on the train or bus. The nearest city, half an hour down the coast road, was Dundee, seen as something of a seething metropolis by the vast majority of Arbroath residents. The fact that it was seen as a culture-free joke of a city by the rest of Scotland spoke volumes for how far adrift Arbroath and the people in it were from the larger scheme of things in Scotland, and beyond into Europe and the rest of world.

David almost couldn't believe he was the same human being now as that teenage boy who went drunkenly skinny-dipping at Elliot Beach, made petrol bombs on the High Common and unearthed other kids' porn stashes from the railway embankment. It seemed impossibly distant. Not that he was exactly worldly-wise now; he hadn't been trekking around the globe like Nicola had. They said that travel broadens the mind – well, he had only had to travel the length of Fife to Edinburgh to get plenty of broadening. Having said that, the people he met at uni were invariably like him, small-town kids with wide eyes, pretending they weren't impressed to be walking around the cobbled Old Town where a thousand years of mischief had taken place. He had gravitated towards people of his own kind, people with the same outlook on life, the same down-to-earth demeanour, as if there was an invisible pull between them all, as if they were all destined for the same kind of life, despite coming from all corners of the country.

These people were different from his schoolfriends. They had got out, like him, from the oppressive emptiness of their small-town origins, they had escaped the mundanity, the mind-numbing boredom of drinking on street corners, vandalizing toilets and bus shelters. His schoolfriends hadn't. But his uni friends, like him, still carried a little of that with them, they still bridled at cosmopolitan Edinburgh and the university establishment with its swankier (almost always English) students, lecturers and professors. They showed disdain for authority, they lacked respect for, well, for just about everything, including each other and themselves. They had been brought up in a culture of disrespect, and that was something they would take with them to the grave.

Take to the grave. The thought brought him back to Colin, Gary and Neil. Two of them dead, and now the third name kept popping up. It was so clear now that David wasn't the only link between Colin, Gary and the cliffs. There was also Neil. Neil, who had joined the Marines, fought in the Gulf War, then quit, only to go into the police, quit that too, and who was now, apparently, living as a hermit somewhere up the coast.

He had to find out more about Neil, about what had happened to him in the fifteen years since they'd last seen each other. When, exactly, had they last seen each other? He tried to think back, but his memories weren't date-stamped and he struggled to piece it all together. They had been together the night Colin died, and then they hadn't seen each other for a few days, but then there was the funeral – but wait, Neil wasn't at that, was he? And David had left town a couple of days later. So the last time he had seen Neil was when he watched his and Colin's backs as they walked unsteadily up the High Street in the early hours of that Sunday morning, the same morning a dog walker would come across Colin's broken body at the bottom of the cliffs a few dawn-filtered hours later.

He googled the name. What else would anyone do these days? he thought. How the hell did anyone find out about anything before the internet? Now, and surely more so in the future, no one ever had to remember anything ever again, now that the source of all possible knowledge, most of it wildly inaccurate, was only a mouse click away. What would happen to future generations' minds, if they never had to retain a single fact?

He got millions of hits for 'Neil Cargill', so he combined it with all the obvious things: 'Royal Marines', 'Arbroath', 'Tayside Police'. After five minutes he had nothing. Who in the world didn't have an internet presence? A bit more rooting around and he eventually unearthed a tiny news story from a Dundee newspaper, dated 22 July 1992, a general round-up of army news from the Condor base which ended with a mention of a 'Private N. Cargill' who was apparently discharged on medical grounds from 45 Commando. Was that Neil? The dates seemed to match up with having left after the Gulf War. A further five minutes in front of the screen and he had the name of the sergeant major for the regiment and his number at the Condor base. Looking at the sergeant major's profile, he noted that he had been in charge of the regiment back when Neil had been discharged. He decided to give him a call.

It was all surprisingly easy. Pretending to be a journalist researching the Royal Marines in the northeast (he was deliberately vague), he got through to Sergeant Major Wilkins' office straight away. Wilkins wasn't available, but his secretary made an appointment for him to interview Wilkins on Sunday afternoon. Sunday, thought David – didn't these people have weekends? Apparently not. He put the phone down, buzzing from his little deception. This must be what it feels like to be a spy, he thought. It wasn't exactly James Bond, but it was pretty exciting all the same. He tried to picture the forthcoming meeting and how he would play it, face to face with a military man, trying to brazenly lie about why he was there. But why was he there? He wanted to find out more about Neil Cargill, that's why, and there hadn't been anything else on the internet. How did private detectives track people down? How could he find out where he lived, and what he'd been doing for the past ten years? Wasn't there a central website for Arbroath-based gossip? Apparently not, which he thought was strange, because there had been plenty of fucking gossip around when he was a kid – it seemed at times as if the town ran on the stuff. It fuelled the conversations in shops, on streets, in offices and pubs. And now he couldn't find out more than one small fact about the life of Neil Cargill? Strange.

He felt thrilled and a little apprehensive at the idea of the subterfuge involved in his meeting this weekend. He wanted to tell someone all about it. He thought of Nicola and picked up the phone.

'You're a daftie.'

Nicola had a point. After David had left the office and headed home, the excitement of his little undercover mission had waned quickly. By the time he'd got home he wasn't sure at all about why he'd set up the meeting with this Wilkins character, or what he was hoping to achieve with it. A couple of hours later, sitting in the Abbey with Nicola, he had lost sight of any real purpose to the whole thing.

'You're probably right,' he said. 'Maybe I won't bother going. I gave his secretary false contact details anyway, so I can just not bother if I don't fancy it.'

'What are you hoping to find out?' said Nicola.

'Good question.'

David looked around him. Most of the pubs in the Southside were predominantly full of either students or locals, with hardly any mixing of the two. That wasn't the case with the Abbey, in which both sets of punters coexisted in an uneasy balance, the mutual dislike between the groups usually never boiling over into anything more than the odd muttered comment. The large mahogany circular bar and ornate plate-glass windows were reminiscent of days long gone, when pubs took a certain pride in their appearance, and didn't get needless facelifts every two years to try and pull in a few more punters. Across the room, at one of the window seats, an elderly decorator, judging by his paint-spattered overalls, was slumped asleep in his chair. A handful of giggling student girls waving Aftershocks in the air were taking it in turns to drape themselves over him, while their friends took quick snaps with their camera phones. The old man woke up finally, to shrieks of laughter, looking utterly bemused like a little boy lost in a supermarket. He frowned at the girls and got up to get a fresh pint.

David turned back to Nicola, and was immediately lifted by the look on her face, a wry, squint smile and an arched eyebrow. It was amazing what the look on a particular woman's face could do to a man's insides, he thought.

'I suppose I want to find out about Neil, find out what the hell he's been up to for the last decade and a half,' he said. 'I don't know why, except that there used to be four of us in a gang – a stupid little gang, admittedly, but a gang nonetheless – and now the other two in that gang are dead. I can't really explain it, but there seems to be a bond, something pulling me towards him. I need to find him, speak to him about all this.'

'You think he's involved?' said Nicola.

The suggestion shocked David, but secretly not as much as it might've. Deep down he had been thinking the same thing, although he hadn't voiced it out loud. To hear Nicola say it now it sounded obscene, monstrous – to suggest that there was somehow a connection between Neil and the deaths of Colin and Gary – but if he was being honest with himself, David had had the same thought himself.

'I don't know,' he said. 'I don't really know what to think. It's all a bit of a mystery.'

'It's a real Nancy Drew job, for sure.'

Nancy Drew, thought David – wasn't that the girly version of those Hardy Boys books he'd read as a kid? Kind of murder mystery adventure things? Pretty dumb, he vaguely recalled.

'I preferred the Hardy Boys myself.'

'You would, being a boy.'

'And what's wrong with being a boy? I suppose you think it would be better if I was into girly pink Nancy Drew shit, aye?'

'Nah, I like my men to be all men. Like lumberjacks. Ever sung a song about chopping down trees, David?'

He laughed at the reference. It was easy to talk to Nicola. They made the same references, laughed at the same stupid jokes and drank the same cheap lager. He really wanted to sleep with her. But he also didn't want to blow it. And anyway, this whole

Gary thing – or Colin thing or Neil thing, whatever you wanted to call it, an Arbroath cliffs thing? – was kind of putting a dampener on that kind of action. Having said that, as his eyes drifted involuntarily to the small, firm breasts under Nicola's tight T-shirt, the thought of sleeping with her brought about a stiffening in his cock, so maybe it wasn't putting a dampener on anything after all.

'I have to go soon,' said Nicola, smiling as if reading his dirty thoughts. 'Amy's only staying over at a friend's for a wee while. I've got to get her home and to bed, or she'll be a right pain in the arse come morning. Speaking of which, are you still OK with giving us a lift up the road? We can get the train or bus, it's not a problem.'

'Don't be stupid,' said David. 'It'll be my pleasure.'

'Yeah, a talk at our old school, followed by a funeral, a trip to the police station and now an undercover interview with a man trained to kill with his bare hands. It'll be a hoot, I'm sure.'

David downed what was left of his lager.

'Gets me out the house, doesn't it?'

9

Tombstoners

'*Altiora petamus*' roughly translates as 'Let us aim for higher things'. David read the school motto as he drove in through the front gate, an unassuming entrance nestled in a residential area which led to the sprawling complex of crouching, modern, dusty red buildings scattered across Lochlands Hill that was Keptie High School. He swung right into the staff car park and got out.

It was a muggy kind of day, a high-level haze diffusing the heat of the sun and spreading a sticky closeness, a claustrophobic blanket over the land. The buildings in front of him were much as he remembered them, slightly garish and clumsily-built rough brick rectangles radiating out from a central hub which housed the hall and cafeteria.

It was only eleven o'clock and already he'd dropped Nicola and Amy off at Nicola's parents' and checked into the Fairport. Gillian with a hard 'G' seemed unsurprised to see him, as if strange men naturally kept returning into her life unannounced.

He stood for a moment at his car door and soaked up the sight of the school. He had only spent three years in this place because it was built halfway through his secondary education. The original high school had been down the road, round the back of the Keptie Pond, but when that gloomy Victorian hulk of buildings started shedding masonry on pupils' heads and sprouting leaks from lead plumbing, it was time to move. David had once been playing with a large storage heater in the old school's overspill huts, knocked up quickly post-war, when he discovered some asbestos fibres stinging his hands. Another time Gary had badly sprained an ankle when a set of stairs gave way under him. This was before anyone knew about lawsuits so neither of them had profited from the school's crumbling haplessness.

They moved to the current school at the beginning of fourth year, just in time for the serious business of exams. As a younger kid David had often mucked about in this part of town, running through the long grass playing Japs and Commandos with mates. He could remember when this was all fields, and the thought made him laugh, but also made him feel old for a moment.

As he stood looking at the school a Fiesta skidded round the corner, a blast of hardcore hip-hop causing its suspension to bounce and windows to throb. Two teenage boys covered in Burberry and Nike swooshes sat posing with the windows down, the engine on high revs. After a couple of minutes two girls about thirteen years old in tiny pleated black microskirts and white blouses came hurrying out the school, giggling and egging each other on. They ducked past the staff-room window and into the back of the Fiesta, which screeched off in a show of burning rubber. The weekend starts here, thought David.

He headed towards the official entrance to the school – a door which no pupils were ever allowed to use – at the front of the admin wing, which seemed a damn sight nicer than he remembered the rest of the school being. He thought again about the school motto – 'Let us aim for higher things' – and about how he was here to talk about people doing exactly the opposite, plummeting to deadly depths. It was a black thought but it made him chuckle nonetheless.

He checked in at reception and was quickly met by Mr Bowman, who ushered him along a corridor and up some stairs into the library. Every second of the walk was disorientating, memories of his schooldays rushing back. Over there at the bottom of the stairs was where he was once battered by one of the extended Clarkson clan, essentially for being brainy. Round the back of the cafeteria was where Elaine Mackenzie had agreed to go out with him – a date which ended in disaster when he didn't have enough money to stand her a bag of chips. Further over in the corner was where he and Neil had raided the tuck shop, making off with pockets stuffed full of Wham bars and Rhubarb and Custards, while over at the other side of the hall was where he had whispered a joke about Davros behind the girl from the year below them in the motorized wheelchair. A few of the memories were good, a lot of them bad, most of them embarrassing beyond words, especially the ones which revealed in spotlight what little shits he and his mates had been for large swathes of the time they spent as teenagers. There was no doubt about it, being back here, haunted by the ghosts of a feral childhood, made him feel mostly ashamed.

The library was packed with PCs taking up every available desk space, while a few perfunctory peeling bookshelves hid in one corner of the room. A gang of about twenty boys lounged about on cheap plastic chairs in that overcooked nonchalance that teenage boys have. Their postures were attempting to say that they couldn't give a fuck about anything, but it was an unconvincing message – the boys who really couldn't give a fuck were already long gone from school. These boys were sixth-years – their lanky height and almost adult faces making David feel suddenly old as hell – so they had chosen to be here, for whatever reason. They weren't exactly welcoming when David and Mr Bowman came into the room. David wondered why there were no girls in the group, and if the boys had been forewarned about this little impromptu meeting Mr Bowman had laid on. He didn't have long to wonder, because Mr Bowman fired straight into introducing him. Before he realized it he was standing up in front of them. It was only then – with the sticky sunlight treacling in through the large bank of fusty windows and his armpits getting itchy from the heat – that he thought maybe he should've prepared something for this. All week his head had been swimming with thoughts of Gary's death, thoughts of Nicola and her goddamn smile as she lay in bed across from him, thoughts of Neil and Colin walking away from him up the High Street and out of his life seemingly forever. He hadn't thought about this at all. He hadn't considered what this morning might actually entail; in truth he had assumed he was maybe just going to be here to answer the odd question or something.

But now here he was, expected to say something meaningful, something about tombstoning, and about two people he'd known who died at the cliffs but who had nothing to do with tombstoning, if that even really existed anyway. Was Mr Bowman perhaps over-exaggerating the extent of what was going on amongst Arbroath's kids? How did he know that these particular kids had anything to do with it? Was it only a one-off thing that had been reported in the paper? He'd said there was graffiti all around the town, glorifying Colin's death, apparently at his memorial stone as well, but David had been there last weekend and there had been no sign of anything like that.

He felt his scalp get hot, and the backs of his knees were moist with sweat. His mouth was dry, the dusty air in the library catching at the back of his throat. He felt like he'd been standing in front of the kids for an age, so he decided just to talk and see what happened.

'Thanks. Erm, I'm not exactly sure why Mr Bowman asked me here today. What I mean is, I know why he asked me, but I'm not sure that I'm the right person to be doing this. He seems to be worried that, well . . . OK, let me start with the basics. I was friends with Colin Anderson.' Was it his imagination, or did some of the boys sit up a little straighter in their seats? Their half-arsed masks of disinterest fell slightly, and David realized that they hadn't been told what this was about after all. He was somehow encouraged by that idea and fired on. 'I was with Colin the night he died. Not at the cliffs, well, I was there earlier with him, but I wasn't there when he fell. Anyway, Mr Bowman tells me that some kids in town have this weird idea that Colin was involved in something that the papers are now calling tombstoning. They seem to have this idea that he's some kind of underground legend, or an extreme sports hero or something equally stupid. I'm sure you all know what I mean.' He could see that they did, and he noticed that every one of them was paying attention now. 'Anyway, I just wanted to tell you that nothing could be further from the truth. Colin did not jump from the cliffs that night. He would never have done anything that stupid. He fell. Why the hell would someone like Colin Anderson jump off a cliff, even if it was for a thrill? He was about to start pre-season training as a professional footballer; he had everything going for him. This tombstoning, or whatever you want to call it, is just a ridiculous idea based on absolutely nothing at all. Anyone who does it isn't hard or clever or whatever, they're just stupid. There's thrill-seeking and then there's just plain stupidity, and that's what tombstoning is.'

He stopped for a moment, wondering what else to say. One of the kids piped up quietly from near the front.

'How do you know?'

'I'm sorry?'

The kid had the collar of his shirt up and a spiky, streaked haircut that David remembered being in fashion about 1985. Christ, was that shit back in again?

'I said,' the boy said, leaning forward and growing in confidence, 'how do you know?'

'How do I know what?'

'That Colin didn't jump? If you weren't there, how do you know he didn't jump off the cliffs for kicks?'

'Because he wouldn't have, that's why.' David realized the inadequacy of the answer, and thought that he sounded like a teacher as he said it. 'It's just not the kind of thing Colin would've done. What would be the point?'

'Maybe it *was* for a thrill,' said the kid, his long limbs arranged around his seat like a pile of snakes. 'Maybe he just thought it would be a buzz.'

'There's no buzz in jumping off a cliff and killing yourself.'

'How do you know?'

The rest of the boys were shuffling around in their seats, trying to hide smiles from their faces.

'How do you know if you've never tried?'

'Have you tried?' David tried to stare the boy down, but got nowhere.

'That's not the point,' said the boy, remaining cool. 'The point is that you don't know what you're talking about. You don't know what it's like to jump off a cliff into the sea, and you don't know what happened to Colin Anderson. Or Gary Spink.'

News had obviously spread fast around town. There was no reason why it wouldn't, David supposed, no reason why Gary's death wouldn't be the talk of every pub, club, office, shop and home, as it must've been for the last five days. But he wasn't about to let this little shit tell him off in front of his mates, especially when the wee bastard knew nothing.

'Gary didn't jump either.'

The boy smiled at David.

'Again, how do you know?'

'I just know. I was with Gary on Saturday night, we sat and got fucking pissed together all afternoon, then all night, and when I left him he was on the High Common, heading in the opposite direction from the cliffs.' He could hear his voice rising in pitch and volume, and he felt a trickle of sweat start to run down his forehead. 'So you tell me why the fuck he would turn round, walk all the way across town and then throw himself off the cliffs. For kicks? Suicide? You don't know anything about Gary, or Colin, you jumped-up little prick.' He could see Mr Bowman getting out his seat from the corner of his eye but kept on regardless. 'You don't know a fucking thing about me or my life, or about either of them. So don't go claiming they're martyrs or heroes, because they're not. All the pair of them are is wasted potential, guys who could've amounted to much more. You don't know how the hell they came to be found at the bottom of the cliffs, so don't fucking tell me you do.'

The boy with the streaked hair was nonplussed. He held David's gaze and gradually got out of his seat.

'The problem is,' he said, hissing through his teeth, 'you don't know how they came to be at the bottom of the fucking cliffs either, do you? What kind of mate were you to the pair of them? You don't know anything about them. You haven't even lived in this town for the last fifteen years. You can't come here and tell us what happened to Colin back then, or Gary at the weekend, because the simple fact is you don't know, and you never will.'

David knew he was right. The little shit was right, that was the worst thing. This visit had been a huge mistake. Birdshit hair was absolutely right, who the fuck was he to come and tell them that Colin and now Gary weren't tombstoners, or whatever? Really he knew nothing about it. Maybe they both committed suicide. Maybe they were both murdered. Maybe he had mis-judged their banter that night all those years ago and Colin really had gone back and jumped off as a dare to himself, or just to get a buzz. Maybe David had secretly feared that was the truth all along and felt guilty about it. Maybe the two deaths weren't connected at all. Who was to say that one wasn't an accident and the other a suicide? Gary had seemed fine when they met at the weekend, but after fifteen years, was one day enough to form any kind of valid judgement?

The truth was, David didn't know. He didn't know what the hell had happened to either of them, all he had to go on was his gut instinct, but what the fuck use was that? It was nothing, it was superstition, it was a feeling, it was nothing concrete, nothing as certain as two dead bodies lying in a heap at the bottom of a cliff face, fifteen years apart.

He slumped back into his seat with the realization and put his head in his hands. He felt exhausted and no longer even had the energy to lift his head up. The boy with his collar up sat down with a satisfied grunt and folded his arms, and a heavy silence rushed in and drowned the room. Mr Bowman started ushering the boys out of the door, then came back to sit opposite him. After a while David looked up.

'I'm sorry,' he said.

'Don't worry about it,' said Mr Bowman. 'I suppose I should've known it was a stupid idea. But I really thought it might be worth a try. It's not easy talking to these little shits, they're so sure about the world all the time, they never listen to common sense. Especially young Derek Clarkson back there, your little pal.'

So he was a Clarkson as well, thought David; they bred like fucking rabbits in this town. He wondered if the lad was related to Mike Clarkson, if he'd heard about the fight last weekend.

'The trouble is, he was right, wasn't he? I don't know what the fuck happened. To either of them.'

Mr Bowman looked at him for a long time with something resembling pity. Eventually he glanced up at the clock on the wall.

'Sun's just past the yardarm,' he said getting up. 'I could use a stiff drink. Want to join me?'

Right at that moment, David couldn't think of anything he'd like more.

The Lochlands was surprisingly busy for midday, but it was a Friday, thought David, so some folk were clearly getting a head start on the weekend. The handful of punters at the bar looked as if they'd never left the place since David saw them parked on the same barstools a week ago. They grabbed the last free table next to the gents and Mr Bowman got the round in, ordering up a couple of token pies at the same time.

David couldn't help feeling bad about what had just happened at the school, not least because that Clarkson kid had highlighted exactly what had been gnawing away at him. The past seemed to be intertwining with the present the more he came back to this fucking place, and he felt like he was getting dragged down by an undercurrent of memory, a rip tide of lives half-formed, people half-forgotten and places that he hadn't thought of in a long, long time.

He'd let Mr Bowman down. He didn't really owe the old bastard a thing, but he had turned up with the genuine intention of trying to help out and he had hardly gotten started when he'd given up, let himself be talked down by a fucking teenager with a haircut that wouldn't've looked out of place on *Top of the Pops* twenty years ago. Little wank, thought David, although it was hardly Derek Clarkson's fault that Bowman's half-arsed idea had been misguided in the first place.

He thought again about what Clarkson had said. He really didn't know what had happened to Colin and Gary but he *did* have a glimmer in the fog, a lead that might shed some light on the matter – Neil. He hadn't thought of him while he was losing it in front of the school kids, but now, sitting with Jack Bowman in the pub, it came back to him.

'I wanted to ask you about Neil,' he said, taking a deep swig of lager.

'It's funny you should mention him, because after I spoke to you on Monday I did a little asking around, in the staff room and such like. I thought it was curious that I'd seen him, and yet he never turned up at your reunion. I was just being nosy, I suppose, but after what you said in Tutties, I got to thinking that it is rather strange for someone to have lived in this area for so long, and yet for no one to really know anything about him.'

David had drunk half his pint already. He really needed to slow down, but it was nervy drinking, nervy with what had just happened, and what Jack was telling him now.

'And?'

'Well, you know that he served in the Royal Marines, don't you?'

'Sure, he was in the first Gulf War, then he was dismissed on medical grounds.'

'Ah, well, that was the official line, I gather.'

'And you know differently?'

'Remember that this all comes from the staff room, so it has to be taken with a whole mountain of salt, but one of the other teachers had heard that there was a lot more to it than that.'

'How do you mean?'

'A number of the lads came back unwell, suffering from both

physical and mental problems. I believe they refer to it as Gulf War Syndrome.'

'I thought that was never proven.'

'It's still open to debate in the courts.'

'And you're telling me that Neil had Gulf War Syndrome?'

'One of the teachers' cousins was a nurse at Ninewells, and a number of squaddies came in with complaints.'

'Wait a minute, wouldn't they have gone to a military doctor with this?'

'I understand they didn't trust someone on the military payroll to look into it properly.'

'OK, so he had Gulf War Syndrome,' said David. 'That's still medical grounds, so that's presumably why he was given his discharge, yeah?'

'I'm sorry, I seem to have misled you,' said Jack, finishing his pint and looking at David. David got the hint and quickly got the pints in, irritated at Jack for stringing this out.

'As I was saying,' continued Jack as David sat back down, 'he claimed to be suffering from Gulf War Syndrome, but that wasn't why he was discharged.'

'Well why the hell was he discharged?'

'It seems there was a fight, at the Condor base, between two commandos. One of them ended up in a coma. The other was Neil.'

'And you know this how?'

'The nurse again. Apparently it was a matter of life and death, and they had to go to Ninewells for the sake of the other squaddie, to give him a chance of survival. The guys that brought him in told our friendly nurse off the record what had happened.'

'Which was?'

'Neil beat him half to death over next to nothing. It started as an argument over something trivial, I don't know what, but escalated until half a dozen military police had to drag Neil off the other fellow.'

'And what happened to this other guy? Was he OK?'

'Afraid not. He didn't die, but he never fully recovered. Brain damage. When his condition didn't improve, they moved him to Sunnyside after a few weeks.'

David felt his stomach drop and tighten, like he'd been punched himself. Neil had half-killed someone, a fellow marine. Beat the shit out of him so badly he'd ended up in the local mental home. He took a few seconds to digest the whole thing.

'Surely this would've been in the news,' he said. 'Weren't the police involved?'

'The police were given the brush-off, apparently,' said Jack, obviously revelling in his role of gossip spreader. 'The military police took over the whole situation. And you know what the army's like for sweeping stuff under the carpet. They just covered their tracks, acted like nothing had happened. Gave Neil a medical discharge to get him off their hands and avoid any scandal. I mean, they couldn't have him stay at Condor after what had happened, the other squaddies would've killed him.'

'But didn't this other guy have any family? Didn't they kick up a stink?'

'According to our nurse, there was no immediate family. There were a couple of cousins, but it's not always easy to get anyone to listen to you, especially when you're up against the muscle of the army. They probably figured there was no way they could get this fully investigated, so they gave up trying. Remember, all this could be absolute rubbish, you know what small-town rumours are like. It's always easier to think the worst of people, and bad news spreads fastest of all. I haven't heard of anyone corroborating this story, and it *was* over ten years ago.'

'So, you think Neil became a recluse after what happened?' Something didn't quite click in David's mind. There was something missing here. 'Wait a minute, someone told me that Neil joined the police after the Marines. How the fuck could that happen, if he had this cloud hanging over him?'

'Maybe no one knew at the time,' said Jack, his second pint finished already.

'Come on, everyone seems to know everything about everyone else in this place. And anyway, wouldn't he need a reference from the Marines when he applied to the police?'

'I assume so,' said Jack. 'But then again, if it got Neil out of the Marines' hair, maybe they thought it would be a good idea if he joined the police.'

'And Tayside Police wouldn't have a vetting procedure in place to stop violent ex-marines with Gulf War Syndrome from joining their rank and file?'

'How many dodgy coppers do you know?' said Jack.

It was a fair point. In a place like this it seemed to be a prerequisite for joining the force that you had to be at least partially fucked up. He remembered his own teenage years, trying to avoid hassle from jumped-up little Hitler cops down the West Port on Friday and Saturday nights, getting lifted and cautioned for nothing much, just because they didn't like the look of your face or they knew your mate's older brother and didn't like him. The outrageous behaviour of Dirty Harry Reid had been legendary amongst them all – happily arresting kids, keeping them in the cells overnight, beating them when he thought he could get away with it. The nickname Dirty Harry had started as a joke, but he had grown into it, grown to live up to it, grown to love it. His daughter Sophie was the year above David at school, and she had copped a lot of flak for being related to Dirty Harry, but in the end most people gave her the benefit of the doubt, since she clearly despised her own father more than anyone else in the whole town, the scars on her wrists were testament to that.

David didn't know what to make of everything Jack had told him. He knew how things got exaggerated in a place like this, how rumours and gossip spread, but even so, there was something about Jack's information that somehow seemed to ring true to him. Neil had always had a quick temper as a kid so he could just about imagine how, after a few years of training as a soldier followed by the stress of actually seeing combat, he might have the capacity to do something like beat a man half to death. But even if he did do what Jack had told him, that didn't really have any bearing on what had happened at the cliffs, did it? All this would make his trip to Condor on Sunday more interesting, and he was glad that Jack had been nosy enough to ask around. He decided not to tell Jack about his meeting with the sergeant major. He didn't really know how to explain it, anyway.

Jack was playing with his empty pint glass. David checked his watch. There was still time for another couple of cheeky wee pints before the funeral, so he got up and got the round in. At the bar, two of the pupils from the debacle at the school earlier came in and ordered pints. When they spotted Jack at the table, a knowing look passed between them. They wouldn't grass on him if he didn't grass on them. Jack was clearly in no position of moral authority here, half-past twelve on a school day and already ganting on his third pint. The fact that the boys were still in school uniform didn't seem to bother the barman. They saw David and smiled sarcastically at him. David wanted to smash their smug little faces in. They reminded him so much of himself at that age he felt sick. He paid for his pints and returned to the table, his mind returning to thoughts of Neil, smashing another man's head in until he was barely alive. It was an image he could see all too clearly in his imagination, and it sent a shiver through his body as he gulped at his lager.

10

The Funeral

In her sombre black trouser suit, Nicola stood self-consciously amongst a handful of Gary's relatives at a funeral plot stuck so far up the back of the cemetery it might as well have been in the tattie field over the fence. She was being scowled at by Gary's father, who obviously remembered her from the hospital. His wife had the glassy-eyed look of the terminally inconsolable. Mourners were taking it in turns to comfort her with platitudes and gentle arm movements, but her silent, raging grief was awesome to behold. She was like a landmine waiting to explode under someone's feet, and Nicola stayed well away, lurking at the back, almost hidden amongst the hedges.

Where the hell was David? she thought. He was supposed to be here already, and they were about to start. She'd assumed there would be other people from their year at school here, but she couldn't see anybody. As far as she could tell there were only a few relatives, presumably aunts and uncles, a couple of cousins and a shellshocked grandmother. There was Gary's sister, Susan, the brainy one from a couple of years below her. She looked like a media executive or something, in a designer outfit and shades, and Nicola couldn't help thinking that she didn't look suitably grief-stricken. That was unfair, there was no reason why people couldn't look good at a funeral; it just seemed somehow obscene to be so obviously doing well at life when your brother's body was being lowered into the ground.

The minister was coughing politely to stop the murmur of the sparse crowd when David appeared panting at her side. He stank of stale lager and his face was a sheen of sweat. His suit was a little dishevelled and his black tie was squint. Nicola was reminded of that joke about what you call a Glaswegian in a suit – the accused. David clearly wasn't the kind of person used to dressing this way, but he looked sort of haplessly cute despite the fact.

'Sorry,' he whispered, a little too loudly. 'Have I missed anything?'

With no other sound but the twittering of starlings, David's voice seemed to carry itself off into the atmosphere, and a couple of nearby mourners turned to tut at him. He looked apologetically at them then lowered his voice to a proper whisper.

'I couldn't find the plot. There was no one at the front gate to ask.'

'Maybe if you hadn't been to the pub you might've been here on time,' said Nicola. She was surprised at the tone in her own voice, but she was annoyed that he'd left her here alone and conspicuous while he was lagering himself, and she wanted him to know it.

'Sorry, sorry,' said David, sounding genuinely apologetic. 'But I was in the Lochlands with Jack Bowman, he had some interesting things to tell me about Neil.'

Nicola was intrigued, but this shit could wait. They were here to show some respect, so that's what they would do.

'Tell me later.'

David took in the scene around him. The sun had beaten through the haze and was blazing through the gaps in the trees. They weren't too far from Colin's grave, and David was immediately reminded of that funeral. He'd only been a kid then, confused and disorientated by the weird ceremony of it all, and it had seemed to drift past without him actually interacting with it. Today's turn-out was tiny in comparison to Colin's. The pathways had been crammed for Colin's funeral, a fact which maybe added to his confusion on the day. Apart from that, the two ceremonies seemed remarkably similar, thought David, the banal numbness of the minister's intonation, the pointless platitudes in the air, the inappropriately warm weather. Back then he had admired Nicola by the graveside from a distance, his teenage lack of confidence preventing him telling her how he felt. Now here she was, standing at his side, half-heartedly tutting under her breath at his late appearance. He remembered seeing that row of marines' graves near here, the neatness and uniformity of the gravestones as if the bodies under the ground were still on parade. He wondered if any of Neil's colleagues from the Gulf War were there.

Gary's eulogy was short and vague enough that it could've been about virtually anyone. Was this all a life amounted to, thought David – a handful of relations showing face, a couple of people you'd been out on the lash with the night you died, and some meaningless generalizations about life and death? Five minutes of platitudes and a handful of dirt thrown onto a coffin? It wasn't much to shout about. He wondered who might come to his funeral. Daresay it wouldn't be much better than this, he thought. A few more mates, maybe, but ultimately it would be a day of formulaic misery, acted-out woe. He hated whenever celebrities were asked about their funerals, and they always claimed that they wanted them to be celebrations of their lives rather than miserable displays of grief. Fuck that. When he died he wanted women wailing in the aisles, men beating their chests in grief, hair being torn out and teeth being gnashed in unbearable torture. Fat chance. More likely it would be a few tepid sausage rolls at a wake and a raised pint in a pub somewhere.

He shook his head to try and clear it of thoughts of himself, and as he did so he caught a slight movement at the corner of his vision. He turned to see someone disappearing behind a large monkey puzzle tree, then a shadow passed behind some adjacent bushes. He'd only caught the face for a second but was sure he recognized it – it was fucking Neil! He hesitated for a second. He turned quickly back to look at Nicola, but she was still watching the ceremony in front of them, the minister's flatlining voice casting a veil over events around the graveside. Then all of a sudden he was off, jogging towards the tree, accelerating into a proper run and instantly wheezing with the effort of it. The sounds of his movements reverberated around the small gathering, so much so that the minister stopped his solemn intonation to look up and see what the cause was. Along with most of Gary's relatives, he was just in time to see David slip on the greasy grass in his proper black shoes and skid sideways onto his arse with a hefty bump that Nicola, watching slightly agog, couldn't help thinking would leave one hell of a bruise on his bum cheek in the morning. David quickly scrambled upright again and was round the tree moments later. The minister and the congregation returned to the matter in hand, Nicola silently shaking her head.

David caught a glimpse of movement up ahead, as if someone had just turned the next corner and was heading along the path perpendicular to the one he was on. He could hear the crunch of gravel underfoot. It was definitely Neil, he thought, as he made for the corner up ahead. What the hell was he doing here? This really meant something, that Neil really *was* connected somehow to whatever the hell was going on here. His mind was reeling through the possibilities as he felt his legs start to ache with the effort of running. Don't criminals always return to the scene of the crime? He'd learnt that from *Columbo* or some other shit 70s show. But then this wasn't the crime scene, if there even was a crime scene, this was a funeral. But maybe Neil's guilt had driven him here, if he'd had something to do with Gary's death, or maybe . . .

He turned the corner and ran straight into a stocky kid in his late teens, carrying a rake and wearing overalls. A wheelbarrow full of cut grass sat on the verge behind him. The collision knocked the wind out of David for a moment, but not the guy he'd run into.

'Whoah! What the fuck?'

David stood bent over with his hands on his knees, glancing round the side of the kid to see if there was someone further in the distance. He puffed as his chest heaved. Gradually his breathing regulated a little.

'Was there someone else round here?' he asked.

'What?'

'Someone else. I thought I saw someone else come this way.'

'No one's been past me the last five minutes, mate,' said the boy. 'You all right? You look fucked. I would apologize, but *you* ran into *me*.'

'Have you been here all the time?'

'I just came from the same direction you did, mate. Round by that big tree there.' The kid pointed to the monkey puzzle tree. He had seen this gardener, that was all, and the few pints in his system and his imagination had made it add up to much more. Fuck, what an idiot, he thought. He was letting this whole Neil thing mess with his head. He didn't have any proof that Neil had anything to do with this, or even if Neil was still living in this area, or even still alive for fuck's sake, so why the hell was he running around a cemetery like a demented idiot?

'Sorry, mate,' he said to the gardener. 'I thought you were someone else.'

'And trying to knock them over, aye?' said the kid. 'Running into folk is no way to behave in a graveyard, you know.'

'Yeah, you're right, of course.' He was taking a telling-off from a teenager earning minimum wage. He deserved it.

He sauntered back to the funeral, but as he rounded the tree the small crowd was already dispersing. He had loosened his tie after bumping into the gardener, and he had a large, sticky grass stain on his trousers. His brow was glistening with sweat and he realized he looked a bit of a state.

Nicola clocked him and almost laughed. She didn't know why he'd run off, but he looked so sheepish and gormless standing there in the shade of the tree that she couldn't help smiling. He trudged over towards her but before she had a chance to speak she noticed his eyes moving away from hers to somewhere immediately behind her. She turned to see Gary's sister standing there.

'I'm Susan.'

'Nicola. I'm so sorry about Gary.'

'Thank you. It doesn't seem real,' Susan said, although the sound of her voice didn't indicate that she was failing to comprehend the situation, thought Nicola. Perhaps she was being harsh again, but Susan seemed far too composed for someone who'd just lost a brother. David introduced himself to Susan. Nicola noticed that the sun had burned all the haze away from the day and it was another scorcher, at least by Scottish standards. This must be the best summer in years, she found herself thinking for no reason. She felt hot, and the faint smell of beer from David made her wish she had a pint of lager in her hand right now. She wondered briefly what she would've been doing today if this whole stupid school reunion had never happened, if she'd never met David, if Gary had never fallen, if things had gone on the way they had for the last few years. Susan and David were talking and she drifted back to the conversation.

'*Please* come to the house for a drink,' Susan was saying. 'Mum and Dad have organized a wake, but I don't think there will be another person there under fifty, and I don't think I could stand it alone.'

'Sure,' said David, looking at Nicola for confirmation only after he'd agreed already. She didn't mind; she could do with a nice cold beer. And what else would she be doing today otherwise? Her folks had Amy, so for the second weekend in a row she was free to do whatever she wanted. Hopefully, this weekend wouldn't end up with someone dying, she thought to herself with a thin smile. As they left the cemetery, the sun beat on their backs relentlessly but Nicola still somehow felt a little cold.

Gary's parents' house was a grey and joyless post-war, pebble-dashed semi in a street of identical houses. The walls were thin and the windows small. It was the kind of street that had suburbia written all over it, except Arbroath wasn't big enough to have suburbs. David had been here plenty of times as a kid but it had never struck him as being this dowdy and depressing. David remembered Susan as being sweet and likeable at school, but the years had changed her. She talked non-stop about her jetsetting career with a self-confidence spilling over into arrogance. Clearly she considered small-town life far beneath her now. Then again, didn't David think exactly the same thing? Susan didn't even seem that bothered about her brother's death, although David gave her the benefit of the doubt. She might be putting on a brave face, suffering from shock or maybe it just hadn't sunk in yet.

At the house Susan stuck to Nicola and David like glue. The conversation between the three of them avoided all mention of Gary. David wondered if she even knew that he and Nicola had been with Gary the night he'd died. Maybe she knew and she was deliberately avoiding the topic.

They sat out in the small back garden. Nicola tickled Jody, the Spink family dog, while Susan talked about her job in Prague, shamelessly namedropping Hollywood actors she'd met filming on location there. David couldn't care less, but he felt a little sorry for her, filling the air with chatter so that she didn't have to think. It was as if by talking she'd be able to keep the death at bay, stop it from entering into the real world.

He wanted to talk to Nicola privately. Over the next couple of hours they tried a few times to excuse themselves from the wake, but each time Susan wouldn't hear of it. There were glowers from her father, no doubt wondering what his only remaining child was doing talking to the last two people to see his son alive, but Susan blanked him. So David and Nicola were persuaded to stay put, fresh drinks pressed into their hands as they sat watching the sun beginning its slow descent behind next door's identical slate roof.

Eventually, despite the free beer, David could no longer toler-ate Susan's painfully incessant chatter. He looked over at Nicola and the look on her face told him she felt exactly the same. He finished his beer and got up to go to the bathroom, making a gesture to Nicola with the angle of his head. Once inside, he hung about in the front hall, and sure enough, a few minutes later there was Nicola, actually tiptoeing along with a finger to her lips.

'How did you get away?' he whispered, a laugh in his voice. She waved him away, pointing at the door, and the two of them tumbled outside, giggling like a pair of five-year-olds, before breaking into a jog until they were round the corner and free.

'I feel terrible, bolting like that,' said Nicola.

'Yeah, but I couldn't stand any more of it.'

'It must be awful for Susan, for all of them.'

David thought about it for a moment. It had brought it home to him how monumental a thing it must be to have someone in your family die on you. Before they'd gone to the Spinks' house he'd been thinking selfishly about Gary's death, about how it impacted on him alone.

Nicola took his arm in hers and planted a deliberately wet kiss on the side of his face.

'Right, enough of this misery,' she said. 'It's a beautiful summer Friday evening and I've got a free pass from babysitting for the night. What the hell are we going to do now?'

David looked her in the eyes and besides keeping on drinking, which was a given, he could only think of one thing he wanted to do with Nicola Cruickshank tonight.

Nicola sat listening to David recounting everything Jack had told him. It was intriguing, she gave him that, but she wasn't sure what it all meant. Was it really front-page news that someone trained to kill people with his bare hands had almost done exactly that? And did it have anything to do with Gary or Colin? She couldn't see how, although she was prepared to admit that Neil's violence (if any of this third-hand stuff was to be believed) was cause for at least a little bit of suspicion.

She passed the red wine to David and watched as he swigged it out the bottle. To their right was an empty Gayfield, the corrugated iron roofs of the stands bouncing angled evening rays of sunlight back up into a darkening cherry-pink sky. To their left was the Signal Tower Museum, a cluster of pristine whitewashed regency buildings which now housed a twee exhibition about what life had been like in this place in the past. Nicola wondered if museums of the future would house remnants of today's impossibly shallow lifestyle, and if there was anything about living in Arbroath today that made it distinct from living in any other small town in Scotland, or anywhere else for that matter. In front of them was the sea, an unusually calm expanse which seemed bluer than she'd seen it before and hazier off into the distance, as if it were trying to do an impression of the Mediterranean. One toe in the freezing waves at the shore would blow that impression out the water.

David had stopped talking and seemed to be looking for some kind of response. He looked at her with eyes that matched the hazy blue of the sea she'd just been staring at, and a small, pursing smile on his lips. Right at that moment she really wanted to kiss him. She wondered how much of an influence she was having on him, if any, and in turn she wondered how much of an influence he was having on her. In the last fortnight she'd been drunk more often than in the previous six months. On balance, at this precise moment, she figured that was overall a good thing, but it couldn't continue. She wasn't going to be one of those mums that need a quick G&T for breakfast, then a sherry mid-morning.

He was still looking at her, so she took the wine bottle from him, leaned over and kissed him, deeply, forcefully moving her tongue around in his mouth and sensing his surprise. She broke off after a while and took a swig of wine, giving him a moment to recover.

'So what are you going to do about Neil?' she said.

'I'm not sure. What can I do?'

'Mention it to the police tomorrow, that would be a start.'

'But he was in the police.'

'So?'

'You'd trust the police of this place to properly look into the fact that one of their ex-colleagues might have something to do with a couple of deaths, both of which look like accidents or suicide?'

'You never know. He probably wasn't in the police for long. To them, maybe he's just another punter now.'

'Anyway, we've probably got it all wrong. That story about Neil is just gossip, and it's probably got absolutely nothing to do with anything.'

David didn't sound convinced.

'You're probably right,' said Nicola anyway. She thought about it for a moment longer. 'What about your meeting at Condor?'

'What about it?'

'Are you going to bring it up?'

'I think I have to, don't I? He won't tell me anything, but I have to ask about it.'

'And then what?'

'I don't know. Depends on what happens at the police station and the Marine base.'

'Oh yeah,' said Nicola, 'I nearly forgot to ask – what was with your disappearing act at the funeral?'

David explained sheepishly and Nicola laughed, shaking her head in disbelief. After a moment she looked at him, slouching like a teenager on the bench they were parked on. He was smiling widely at her.

'What are you smiling at?'

'I was just thinking, despite everything that's going on, I'm having a great time being here with you.'

'You smooth bastard,' she said, laughing, and he joined in. 'But I know what you mean. It's strange, isn't it? We've just been to a funeral, but I feel pretty good.'

'That's just the booze talking.'

'It doesn't hurt,' she said, taking another swig and passing the bottle back to him. 'But the company helps plenty too.'

She nudged him, he nudged her back and they started kissing again. They kissed for a long time, getting deeper and deeper into it, until David had one hand under Nicola's blouse, gently stroking her breasts, the other down the back of her trousers, feeling her arse, while she rubbed the crotch of his suit with her hand. She climbed over to sit astride him on the bench, thrusting herself up against him, kissing him deeper and deeper, as he moved both hands round to cradle her bum and push her down against him.

'I really want to fuck you,' he whispered in between kissing her neck and her ear.

'That's lucky, cause I really want to fuck you too,' she said.

'What are we going to do about it?' he said, and she could hear his voice getting a little frantic, a good kind of frantic, she thought. She could feel his cock bursting to get out of his trousers.

'Why don't we fuck?' she said.

'I mean, where?'

'What's wrong with here?'

He pulled back slightly to look at her face, and she saw in his eyes that he knew she wasn't joking. She looked around quickly, and there wasn't a soul in sight.

'Why not?' she said.

'I haven't got a condom.'

'I have.'

She took his hand, led him from the bench to the grass a few yards away and they lay down.

'Let's see what you've got, then,' she said and he laughed, undoing his trousers and pulling them down so that his cock sprung out suddenly. She faked a start. 'Christ, nearly had my eye out there,' she said, smiling.

'Are you going to sit there laughing at my cock all day?' he said, laughing but beginning to look nervously around him. 'Or were you planning to do something with it?' She took a condom from her bag, ripped it open and slowly rolled it down his cock. He arched his back a little and closed his eyes. She slipped her trousers and pants off, climbed on top of him and felt him slide easily and deeply into her. They stayed motionless for a few moments, looking into each other's eyes, then she started to move up and down on him, slowly at first, then into a steady rhythm. After only a few minutes she could feel him tensing his body, getting ready to come, so she ground down harder and faster and then, as she felt his body spasm beneath her, she surprised herself by coming as well, waves of it sweeping over her so that her legs went weak and she had to move her hands from his chest to the grass either side of him to support her weight. She instantly started laughing, a slow, quiet laugh in time with her breathing.

'What the fuck are you laughing at?' he said between heavy breaths from beneath her.

'I'm fucking happy, you idiot,' she said, and collapsed on top of him.

11

Cruising

Arbroath police station was a boxy new building that sat, exposed and ugly, next to a roundabout in the centre of town, towered over by a spindly radio receiver mast. It was Saturday lunchtime and the streets contained a steady trickle of shoppers plus the occasional tourist trying to find the abbey up the hill. The sun poked through high, flossy summer clouds, but there wasn't a breath of wind and plenty of bare Scottish flesh was on show amongst the locals traipsing up and down the street. Nicola and David crossed the road, headed in the front door and were met by the typical gloom that dowdy buildings contain on hot summer days. A miserable-looking spotty copper behind the front desk took their details and got on the phone as they sat looking at a corkboard covered with cheesy, slogan-heavy anti-crime posters. David examined the plastic plants next to him absent-mindedly. He was thinking about last night, and trying unsuccessfully to keep a large smile from spreading across his face. She had seduced him (well, that's how he liked to see it) at Inchcape Park, after which they had pulled on their clothes, laughing to each other, and gone for a long walk around the western part of town, avoiding the pubs and clubs, drunken brawls, puking teens and all the rest. Instead they headed to the West Links arm in arm, the sea panting quietly nearby, the pair of them joking and laughing and kissing as if they were teenagers, just discovering what all this love and sex stuff was all about. On the way back they'd fucked again, this time standing up against a wall at the back of the West Common, then again back at Fairport House after tiptoeing in the front door and up the stairs. Three times in one night, thought David with a grin. It had been a long time since he'd had sex three times in one night, but that seemed to be the effect Nicola was having on him. He wondered what she made of the whole thing. She hadn't seemed awkward or regretful or anything like that when they'd met up today. They'd spent the short walk to the station laughing and joking again, referring coyly and flirtatiously to last night and being naturally relaxed in each other's company. It was only when they caught sight of the station and remembered what they were here for that the laughing and joking stopped. Now, waiting in the pallid light of the station's reception, he longed to leave, to drag Nicola with him out into the sunshine and the fresh air. Just then PC Bell appeared and took him through to an adjacent room with a high window throwing the dusty promise of a sunny day across one wall.

It was straightforward enough, and within five minutes Bell had his statement in the can. The policeman was being surprisingly polite, thought David, considering what a snide arsehole he'd been on the phone earlier in the week. That is, until David brought up Neil. At the mention of the name Bell immediately narrowed his eyes to look at David more closely.

'Who?'

'Neil Cargill,' said David. 'I was wondering if you'd heard of him.'

'It's a common enough name around this town, there's bound to be a few of them kicking around.'

'This one is my age, and I think he was in the police at one point.'

'I think I know who you mean. Why do you mention him?'

'I don't really know. I was wondering what you knew about him.'

'Why?'

'Well, I was mates with him at school, so was Gary. And Colin Anderson, who I'm sure you know died at the cliffs back in 1988.'

Bell's impassive face was trying not to give anything away, but David could tell he wasn't hearing anything new here.

'Why bring him up now? Do you think he might have something to do with Gary's death?'

'Well, not really, I don't suppose . . .' David didn't really know what to say next. *Did* he think Neil had something to do with it? Faced with the question out in the open like this, he began to realize that's exactly what he had been thinking. But he also realized that he had no basis for that accusation, none at all.

'I was just wondering if you could tell me anything about him. I wouldn't mind tracking him down, for old times' sake.'

Bell eyed David suspiciously. It was clear he didn't believe David wanted to find Neil for a pint and a chat about the good old days.

'I don't know anything about him.'

'But he was in the police, wasn't he? He did work here?'

Bell looked uncomfortable being on the receiving end of questions.

'He left not long after I joined.'

'So you knew him?'

'Not really.'

'What was he like?'

'I thought he was *your* mate at school,' said Bell, back on the offensive.

'He was, but I was wondering what he seemed like by the time he worked here. He was in the Marines before he joined the police.'

'I heard.'

I'll bet, thought David.

'And he apparently had a bit of trouble there.'

'No shit,' said Bell.

'So I was wondering what he was like when he was in the police.'

'And I told you, I didn't know him.'

'But you must have . . .'

'Look, Mr Lindsay,' said Bell, 'I think we're done here, don't you? I have your statement about Mr Spink's death. Unless there's anything else you want to add officially?' He waited a second. 'Thought not. If you want to track down Neil Cargill I suggest you do it elsewhere and on your own time.'

David sat in reception waiting for Nicola to finish her stint with Bell, wondering how much the copper really knew about Neil. He had to make contact with the one person who knew himself, Gary and Colin on equal terms from all those years ago, if only to talk through what a stupid fucking thing these deaths were, if only to find out what had been happening in Neil's parallel universe for the last fifteen years. If only to put his mind at rest.

When Nicola emerged from the interview room, he looked at her smiling face and all thoughts of Neil, Gary and Colin left his mind completely.

'Can we, Mum, *please*?'

They were standing at the edge of the harbour with ice cream dripping from cones down their hands, like something out of an old-time seaside comedy film. The harbour wasn't exactly picture postcard, despite the presence of a handful of almost quaint pink and yellow houses, a fish smokehouse puffing a thin trail of brownness into the shimmering air and a smattering of tied-up sailing boats clanking in the dock. Larger rusting hulks of fishing boats were scattered around the harbour, and the smell of diesel, rotting fish and woodsmoke made for a pungent aroma hanging over the oily water down below. Blue sparks wheeled into the sunlit air as a filthy man with homemade tattoos and a blowtorch tried to keep his boat in one piece. The boat in front of them didn't look in much better nick. A small fishing vessel converted to take passengers, it rocked gently in the water, its ferric hull and peeling white paint appearing and disappearing below the water with the gentle bobbing motion. The boat was offering sightseeing tours up and down the nearby coast for a few quid. The guy in charge was like a Captain Birds Eye gone to seed, his beard was yellowy grey and unkempt, the uniform was greasy and faded and his gut was trying to burst some buttons at the front. Nicola had difficulty thinking of him as a captain, with the responsibility and seafaring knowledge that went along with such a title, although his leathery face had certainly seen enough time on the sea, a lifetime of fishing ingrained in the heavy lines under his eyes. For all that, he did have kind eyes and an endearing gummy smile, and she warmed to him. He was using his charms to gently work on them, claiming he only had three more spaces on the boat to fill. She looked at David, who smiled a little hesitantly and shrugged.

'Why not?' he said, and the three of them, David, Nicola and Amy, stepped on board.

The thin phutter of the engine as it made its way out the harbour beefed up to a proper chug as they turned right (Was that port or starboard? thought Nicola, she could never remember) and headed out to sea. Nicola was immediately embarrassed by the sight, directly in front of them, of the Signal Tower Museum and, beyond it, Inchcape Park only a couple of hundred yards away. From here on the water, illuminated by beaming sunshine, it looked amazingly exposed to the elements, as well as prying eyes, and she couldn't believe it was the place where she and David had sex last night. She sneaked a look at David who was doing a bad job of suppressing a giggle and she felt herself chuckle too.

'What are you laughing at?' said Amy, a vision in coordinated bottle-green T-shirt, trousers and trainers today.

'Nothing, love,' said Nicola.

'Tell me.'

Just then their captain's voice boomed through the small PA on board the boat, much to Nicola's relief.

'Up ahead is the Signal Tower Museum, and beyond it is Inchcape Park. The park doesn't see much action through the year, just the occasional military display, circus big top or travelling show in the summer. As you can see there's nothing to see there at the moment. The Signal Tower was originally built in

1813 as the shore station and family living quarters of the famous Bell Rock lighthouse, which lies eleven miles out to sea, built on a dangerous semi-sunken reef. The Bell Rock lighthouse was a tremendous feat of engineering, built by Robert Stevenson, founder of a dynasty of lighthouse engineers and grandfather to writer Robert Louis Stevenson . . .'

Nicola tuned out. She knew all this stuff more or less off by heart from her time working at the abbey. Although the Signal Tower wasn't run by Historic Scotland, all staff at their sites were encouraged to bone up on local history, so she knew the ins and outs of the Bell Rock lighthouse, the Stevensons and all the rest of it.

She stared at the park bench where they'd been last night. Although drunk, she'd been very much in control, there'd been enough pissing about and it was time to get it on. The sex had taken the tension out the air, the strange tension of not having done something they both clearly wanted to do. The rest of the night had been like a bit of a weird dream, walking and talking and kissing and shagging in places she'd been a hundred times before but seemed to be seeing fresh. Then again, maybe she was just drunker than she thought. But she didn't regret a minute of it. And the way David had been today, didn't that indicate that he didn't regret it either? He seemed to be one of the good guys, and Christ knows there aren't too many of them around, she thought.

By this time they were past the breakwater and had turned left (Port? No, starboard? Fuck it, she thought) and were heading past the tiny, squatting fishermen's cottages in the oldest part of the harbour called the Fit o' the Toon. Thick walls, tiny windows and narrow streets were all designed to keep the fearsome sea weather at bay, and despite a bright coat of paint the cottages looked like they had always expected, and received, a hard time from the sea.

They were gathering speed now and heading east, out past Victoria Park to the start of the cliffs. Nicola had never seen the cliffs from this angle, and it was disorientating seeing a place you were familiar with from thirty years of visits, but from the completely opposite direction. If anything they looked more sinister than she had ever imagined them, more imposing, dominant and immovable. There were dark nooks and crannies everywhere, birds nesting improbably on tiny ledges, small partially-submerged rocks. It looked a long, long way down from the top, much further than it ever seemed from up on the grassy ledge. Even with the sun beating down and the water relatively calm, there was something ominous and unsettling about the place, or maybe she was just projecting the deaths of Gary and Colin on to her feelings about what was, after all, just a simple slab of sandstone rock.

The captain cut the engine not long after they reached the cliffs and started a commentary about the geology of the area and the birdlife you were likely to find. A few of their fellow passengers whipped out binoculars. There were nine passengers apart from themselves, and as Nicola looked at them she realized that most of them were birdwatchers – there was just something about the way they dressed that gave it away, the geeky waterproofs, the shorts and hiking socks and boots, the insulated jackets with pockets everywhere. The captain was talking now about cormorants and shags; terns, oystercatchers and curlews; kittiwakes, razorbills and, if we were lucky, maybe the odd puffin. There seemed a slight flurry of excitement at the mention of the bird world's comedy character.

With the geology and wildlife taken care of, the captain quickly got on to what was clearly his favourite topic, the shady history of the cliffs. Every headland, bay, cave, den, rock and overhang had a name and a story to go with it. Here was Whiting Ness, then St Ninian's Well, Steeple Rock, the Horse Shoe, the Elephant's Foot, then, rather unimaginatively, thought Nicola, the Stalactite Cave.

'. . . and the headland overlooking the Stalactite Cave is known locally as Monk and Maiden's Leap,' the captain said.

At the mention of the word 'leap', David's ears pricked up. It was somewhere around here that Colin's body had been found. From this angle he couldn't tell exactly where. There was no sign of the small memorial stone, but then they surely couldn't see it from down here anyway. He didn't know where Gary's body had been found. Was it in the same place as Colin's? He couldn't believe he hadn't asked the copper, he'd just assumed it was the same place.

'It's thought that the name relates to a local lass called Mary Scott who was commemorated in a poem by Arbroath poet David Balfour in the early eighteenth century. The story goes that when Mary's mother died she was comforted by an abbot. Unfortunately he comforted her a little too closely, if you know what I mean, and she fell pregnant. The abbot arranged for her to be thrown from this point of the cliffs, then became insane with the guilt and jumped from the same spot. It's said that both of them were buried near here, a wild rose blossoming on Mary's grave while a stunted, gnarly thornbush sprouted from the abbot's.'

Probably a lot of old bollocks, thought David, but the idea that people had been chucking themselves off the cliffs for centuries gave him a strange sensation. How far back did the idea of suicide go? Did cavemen do it? What about the Bronze or Iron Ages? When did people start feeling so bad that they couldn't go on? He imagined a time line stretching back into the far past and it made him feel tiny and insignificant. Then again, he thought, maybe it was this precarious bobbing up and down in a tiny boat on a colossal sea next to an uncaring cliff face that had something to do with that feeling.

The boat's engine started up again, and they were heading east along the cliffs. More quaint old names came booming through the PA: Needle's E'e, Pebbly Den, Mermaid's Kirk, then a small bay with steep sides and several stacks called Mariners' Grave.

'This was the site of a terrible shipwreck in 1800,' said the captain, hamming it up. 'But not all the seamen were lost, thanks to the initiative of some locals, who lowered a basket from the clifftop to pull up the sailors who were still alive. The incident was widely reported at the time, and Sir Walter Scott used it in his famous book set in Arbroath, *The Antiquary*, as did R. M. Ballantyne in his Bell Rock story called *The Lighthouse*.'

Walter Scott wrote a book about Arbroath? thought David. Really? Why had he never heard of it? Then again, he wasn't much of a reader. The Antiquary was the name of a boozer round the corner from his work. Small world.

As they progressed north-east up the coast there were more and more sea caves, so many that a lot of them didn't seem to have names. The captain assured them they had all been heavily used for smuggling in the past. Many of them had apocryphal tales linked to them, no doubt invented by the smugglers to keep superstitious locals away. There was Smuggler's Cave (a bit obvious, that one, thought David), Lady's Cave, Dark Cave, Mason's Cave (which at one time had a door and was used by the local lodge for meetings), Forbidden Cave (which contained the ghost of a lone piper, allegedly) and a host of others. There were blowholes, ruined castles and forts, secret dens, a stack called the Deil's Heid and a place called Gaylet Pot, David missing the explanation of its name, or even what it actually was, but catching the fact that Robert Burns had supposedly once visited it. Why on earth? he thought. They puttered up past Hermit's Cave, where a lone elderly man used to live not that long ago, apparently, surviving on fish and cockles from nearby. David thought it was fantastic, somehow, that within living memory people had actually been able and willing to live in a cave and survive on what the sea brought them. As if the whole of the modern world had passed them by: the development of towns and cities, the improvements in transport and infrastructure, the concepts of leisure and entertainment – all of it happening to other people somewhere else, while you sat hunkered down in your cave next to your fire, waiting to see what tomorrow would bring in the way of flotsam, jetsam and food. It was scarcely believable, but somehow comforting in a strange kind of way. How had he lived an entire childhood in Arbroath and never heard any of this? But then again, when he was a kid he'd rather have had his teeth pulled than listen to some boring old fuck prattle on about caves.

They tootled past another bay and headland with a handful of old cottages arranged on it. According to the captain these were formerly coastguard houses, but now in disrepair. A couple of steep paths led down the cliffs from the cottages to a secluded beach. Round the headland and they were confronted with the harbour of Auchmithie, little more than a ramshackle stone wall covered with seaweed and algae and crumbling into the sea, with a huddle of small boats lurking behind it. A couple of rusty old cars and vans were parked along the seafront, old timers working on upturned boats hauled out onto dry land. Behind them a thin road snaked up between cliffs to the village of Auch- mithie, little more than a cottage-lined street running along the headland and petering out in an overgrown field. David had been to the village a few times before as a kid, but could remem- ber next to nothing about the place, except there was a tearoom, a pub and that was it. They had been press-ganged into doing a sponsored walk once at school, and had walked the few miles out to Auchmithie and back, but they hadn't used the cliff path – presumably because the kids couldn't be trusted not to fall in the sea – instead tramping along the inland road from town. Pretty ironic, thought David, considering what had then happened to Colin.

'And here we have the fishing village of Auchmithie,' the captain was saying. 'Although Arbroath is thought of as the home of the smokie, in fact the world-famous delicacy originated here in Auchmithie. Sometime in the early nineteenth century the fisherfolk migrated to the larger harbour of Arbroath, bringing their secret for smoking the haddock with them. Amongst the families who flitted were all the famous smokie names, the same ones that continue to produce smokies to this day, such as Swankie, Spink and Cargill.'

David spotted Nicola looking at her. She had been keeping Amy entertained for most of the trip, pointing out seabirds and weird shapes and colours in the rocks, but now, at the mention of both Spink and Cargill, she was looking at David with raised eyebrows. He didn't know exactly what the expression meant. Arbroath was crawling with Swankies, Spinks and Cargills, there had been hundreds of them at school, so it was hardly surprising that these names would come up now, he supposed. He thought of Neil again, and how someone had said that perhaps he lived out in Auchmithie. It seemed too remote, too far from civilization, almost, for anyone to bother living here, yet there was clearly activity both at the harbour and up in the village. Maybe some people liked the seclusion, the peace and quiet that living in a dead-end village gave them. Maybe there were more hermits in the world than David had thought. Maybe Neil was one of those hermits, driven to live here by whatever it was that he was running away from. Destroying a fellow marine's life, for example. Or maybe more than that.

He looked up at the village again, ridiculously hoping to get sight of a stocky figure with Neil's rolling gait striding clearly along the clifftop. He knew it was stupid, but he felt that any minute Neil was going to come walking into view and clear up everything, every lingering doubt in his head.

'Auchmithie also featured in Walter Scott's tale *The Antiquary* as the fishing village of Musselcraig, where the Mucklebackits lived,' said the captain. The fucking *Antiquary* again, thought David. I'll need to get a hold of a copy, see what it's all about. But then he'd started one of Scott's books at school – was *Ivanhoe* by Scott? – and he'd got about five pages in and given up. He wondered idly if anyone had ever made a film of *The Antiquary*, maybe he could watch that instead.

Their boat was already turning to head back south-east down the coast. This was apparently as far as their captain was willing to take them for a fiver. On the return journey the captain's voiceover concentrated on the wildlife of the area, mostly the different seabirds on offer, although he did tantalize everyone on board by claiming that seals, porpoises, dolphins and even very occasionally minke whales could be spotted up and down the coast. Needless to say, they spotted none of those, but David managed to borrow an old pair of binoculars from the captain and spent the rest of the journey picking out guillemots, shags and kittiwakes and pointing them out to Amy, who was surprisingly excited by it all, although he still kept one eye on the sea in case Moby Dick or his pals showed up. At one point Amy spotted two puffins scudding across the sea surface, their tiny wings a blur and their chubby bodies struggling to get any height. She squealed as they crash-landed further along the coast, and David and Nicola smiled at one another. The sun was still on their backs and David looked at Nicola, picturing her naked astride him in the park, and couldn't help thinking he was the luckiest bastard in the world.

'I'm hungry,' said Amy, turning to her mother and spotting David's stray hand which had come to rest on Nicola's waist. He removed it, not quickly enough but Amy ignored it and asked: 'David, do you want to come to Granny and Grandpa's for tea?'

David looked at Nicola who just smiled and shrugged.

'I'd love to,' he said, as Arbroath appeared from behind the headland at the start of the cliffs, looking from this distance at once beautiful and serene in the soft late afternoon sunlight.

12

The Search

'There's more of everything, so don't be afraid to get stuck in.'

A massive, steaming plate of steak pie, roast potatoes and veg was plonked down in front of David and he smiled.

'Thanks, Mrs Cruickshank.'

'Oh, for goodness sake, call me Bel, everyone does.'

Isobel Cruickshank was a handsome, petite woman in her mid-fifties with an air of amused and friendly authority about her. Her long brown hair had flecks of grey through it and was tied up in an untidy knot at the back of her head with a pencil sticking through it. She looked considerably younger than she was, as if bringing up five kids had been the easiest thing in the world. She was at least six inches shorter than Nicola, but that aside there were striking similarities – the wide mouth, the slight frame, the animated nose all clearly linked Bel to her eldest daughter. David watched as she headed back towards the kitchen and considered the notion that looking at a girl's mum tells you what she'll be like when she's older. He liked what he saw, and he smiled again.

Nicola's dad appeared from the kitchen drying his hands on a towel. He was a stocky man with thick forearms and greying hair swept back from his forehead. He wasn't much taller than Bel, so Nicola's height was just one of those strange genetic quirks, David supposed, but he wasn't lacking in authority either. A lifetime of engineering lent him a keen analytical mind, something he applied as much to people and conversations as to the aircraft parts he dealt with at work, or the motorbike he was currently trying to reassemble in the back garden.

'Know anything about bikes?' he asked David.

'Afraid not,' said David.

He had met Alex Cruickshank a few times as a kid, and always been slightly intimidated by him, but so far today he'd seemed a perfectly likeable character. Admittedly he had been stuck out the back tinkering with gaskets and spark plugs with oily hands since David arrived, but still, he didn't seem nearly as ominous a man as David remembered. He wondered what Alex would make of the fact he had screwed his daughter less than twenty-four hours before, in a public park no less. But then Alex had five kids, three of them girls, and umpteen grandchildren, so he supposed you got over that sort of thing eventually.

Alex sat at the head of the table. Nicola was opposite David, with Amy next to her, and Bel bustled back through and sat at the opposite end from Alex. The table was one of the extendable types, and had clearly seen plenty of usage over the years – gouges here, scuffs there, scratches covering the faded varnished wood – but it was at its most compact these days, all of the kids having left home except the youngest, Andy, still sponging free board and rent from his parents at the age of twenty-three. Andy had already skipped out to meet mates and go out on the piss, something David was glad of because he knew Nicola and Andy didn't get on. So it was just the five of them for a cosy family dinner. It made David think about his own parents, no doubt sitting sipping the local *vin de pays* in the garden of their converted barn. As an only child, he'd never had the noisy security of big family meals, familiar chaos ringing in his ears, it had just been him and his rather bohemian parents who, outnumbering him two adults to one child, had pretty much treated him as a grown-up through most of his childhood, boring adult conversations and all.

'So you were back for the funeral,' Alex was saying. 'Terrible business, really.'

'Alex, I'm sure David doesn't want to talk about that,' said Bel, although she was looking at Amy as she said it. It must be good, having grandparents looking out for you, thought David. He had never known any of his own grandparents, something which led to inevitable self-pity, although thinking about it now, for the first time he thought about how it must've been for his parents, having their own folks die at an early age. He felt slightly ashamed he had never considered it before, but then he rarely considered his parents at all these days, something they'd made easy by living in another country.

'It's all right, Mum, Amy knows about what happened to Gary,' said Nicola.

'He fell off the cliffs when he was drunk,' said Amy, matter of fact.

'Were you good friends with him?' said Alex, looking at David.

'Not really. We were mates at school, but I hadn't seen him in years until last weekend.'

'Awful business,' said Bel, seemingly resigned to the topic. 'His parents must be distraught. How were they at the funeral?'

'As you might expect,' said Nicola. 'In shock, I think.'

Nicola's dad seemed to be considering something as he chewed a lump of steak.

'David, you were friends with the Anderson boy at school as well, weren't you?'

'Yeah.'

'Another shocking business,' said Bel. 'Such a waste. Such a terrible waste.'

'It always is,' said Alex, taking a swig of Guinness from a can. 'Remember when that Cargill boy killed himself in his car, Bel? It was the same for his parents.'

David realized straight away that this was Neil's older brother, Craig, who had died when he and Neil had been about ten. The name Cargill just kept cropping up.

'Did you know the Cargills, then?' asked David.

'We did a little, back then,' said Bel. 'Of course they're both dead now.'

'Are we talking about the same people, here?' asked Nicola, a little wide-eyed. She'd clearly never heard this chat from her parents before. 'The parents of Neil who was in our year at school?'

'And his older brother Craig, who crashed his car – yes, that's them,' said Alex, looking to Bel for agreement.

'Connie and Jim,' she said. 'Jim died years ago, now, maybe ten years ago? Lung cancer I think it was that got him. Connie died a few months later, from a massive stroke.'

'Jesus,' said David under his breath.

'Bit of a cursed family,' said Alex, wiping his plate with a slice of bread. 'I feel sorry for Neil, being the only one left.'

'I never knew you knew the Cargills,' said Nicola.

'Everyone knows everyone around here, dear,' said Bel. 'Anyway, we didn't really know them too well by the time Craig died. We knew them from when we were all at school together. Jim was quite a hard man, with a temper. I felt sorry for Connie sometimes. I don't really think she knew what it was going to be like, with him and the two boys in the house. I met her occasionally in the street, but she never really said much.'

'Well, people change, Bel,' said Alex, 'and circumstances change. None of us really know what it's like in anyone else's home.'

'It must've been terrible when Craig died, though,' said Bel. 'Just like it must've been awful for the Spinks, and for the Andersons back when Colin had his accident.'

There was so much death around, thought David. He had never really considered how the deaths of the young affected everyone in a community like this, in the spider's web of lives intertwined genetically and geographically and spread across the generations. He hadn't ever given much thought to how Colin's parents, or his two younger sisters, must've felt when Colin was found dead. He had been so young and selfish at the time, and his tunnel vision shamed him now. He wondered what Colin's sisters were doing. He struggled even to remember their names – one was called Jude, was it? Or Judith? And the other was

Emma or Emily – definitely Emma. He had carried Colin's death around for years, but for them it must've been – must still be, presumably – a thousand times worse. They would only just have been in their teens, if that, when he died. How did the uncertainty of his death affect them? How did the death affect them, full stop? He hoped they'd found a way to work through it all.

Was *he* over it? What did that even mean? The event had irrevocably changed his life, but then every other event in his life had also affected him in some minute way. He felt dizzy as he imagined the infinite twists and turns his life took every microsecond of every minute of every day, how all other possibilities vanished, all other alternate universes collapsed into the one existing one, all potential futures simply fizzled out of being once every infinitesimal decision was made, moment by excruciating moment. It terrified him, both the myriad of possibilities his life could take at any moment, and the way those possibilities were only that, just possibilities, and then they were gone, phut, quicker than the blink of an eye.

He thought about what Nicola had said about the past making us what we are. He had disagreed with her back then, insisting in his obstinate naivety that you made yourself up every morning brand new, you could reinvent yourself with every second of every day. And in a sense maybe that was right, you could be an entirely different person from moment to moment, with each event that occurred changing the concept and reality of the you that existed from then on, but it *was* all built on the bedrock of past experience, it was all down to what had gone before, it was all based on the person you were the moment before that, and the moment before that, right back to when you were conceived, and beyond, into the past of your parents, their parents and your ancestors further back beyond that, right back to the creatures crawling out the primeval swamp and breathing the air around them. The past *did* make you who you were, and not just your own past, but the history of the world, the way people had struggled to survive for centuries, all so that he could be sitting here right now, sticking a forkful of steak pie into his mouth and thinking about the endless terrifying possibilities of life. He felt idiotic for ever suggesting to Nicola – this wonderful girl sitting across the table from him – that human beings were clean slates, that reinvention was easy, that the past didn't matter to the present. It was a revelation, and he felt the weight of the generations suddenly pressing down on his shoulders. All those millions of eyes from the past watching him from the ether, waiting to see what he was going to do next. He didn't know what he was going to do next. But whatever it was it would change him, it would change the world, it would change the future. He felt sick at the thought.

The conversation was going on around him, and Alex had just finished saying something. Nicola was staring at him as if he should be listening, as if he'd just missed something important.

'Sorry, what?'

'I said he used to do the lobster pots,' said Alex. 'Gerry, that I know from the snooker club, said that he just turned up one day with a boat and a few pots and started fishing for lobsters. It's a pretty tight-knit community out there, and they didn't take too kindly to having an outsider pitch up and start fishing the same water as the rest of them. They tried to speak to him about it, but he just brushed them off. After that he pretty much kept himself to himself. Fished his own little corner and never spoke to the rest of them. Gerry reckoned it didn't impact on the rest of their catches much so they just let him get on with it.'

'I'm sorry, who are we talking about?'

'Your friend, Neil Cargill. We were talking about how hard it must've been for him to lose his parents, after what had happened to his brother and all, and I was telling Nicola that he just turned up one day in Auchmithie, started fishing for lobsters.'

'Is he still there, do you know?' David couldn't prevent his voice rising a little in pitch.

'That's the thing. One morning he just didn't turn up at the harbour. He stopped the fishing as suddenly as he started it, according to Gerry, and they never saw him again. They didn't think too much about it, and they weren't sorry to see him go, since all he'd done was take a few of their lobsters and never said anything to anybody.'

'When was this?'

'Oh, must be a couple of years ago, now,' said Alex. 'Would that be right, Bel? All that business was before Gerry's daughter's wedding, so it would be almost two years ago, I think.'

David thought about the past. He wondered how the past had affected Neil, how the events of his life had played out, and how that had shaped him. What was he like now? Where was he now? Still alone in the world? Parents dead, brother long dead. He'd left the army, left the police and left the fishing. What was he doing now? David thought about those collapsing possible universes. Surely that meant there were infinite possible future universes ahead of him? That every decision he made from now on could take his life any direction he wanted? There were infinite futures for him, for him and Nicola, for him and the rest of the world. But actually it didn't feel like that. He felt like he was getting drawn into something that he wasn't sure he wanted to be drawn into, a future that somehow was going to involve Neil. Although theoretically he was free to choose whichever path he wanted, the past bore down on him with magnificent graceful pressure, guiding his hand, pushing him towards the one person left alive who could try to make some kind of sense out of all the death and hurt around him.

The conversation had moved on. He looked at Nicola, who was laughing and joking with Amy. She was serenely beautiful, he thought, and his heart swelled with admiration, with lust, and with the beginnings of love for her. He wanted a future with her, with her and Amy. He felt as if he knew that for the first time now, but he couldn't see how it was possible until he sorted out the past. He had to untangle everything, the knotted threads that linked the death of Colin with the death of Gary, the past with the present.

He had to find Neil Cargill.

The Condor base was an unprepossessing green expanse set back from the Forfar road, surrounded by a ten-foot fence topped with barbed wire and razor wire. David drove right up to the front gate and, without having to show any ID, was ushered through by a teenager in camouflage gear pointing a rifle at the ground. The road wound past an airfield, an artificial ski slope and an assault course before coming to a complex of dozens of small brick buildings, their corrugated metal roofs glinting in the sunlight.

David had been here once before when he was a kid, about ten or eleven. Every now and then the Marines had an open day, when locals were encouraged to go along and presumably see the human face of the killing machine that was the 45 Commando Unit. He'd had a go on the assault course, and needed a leg up over the climbing wall from one of the marines watching over proceedings. There had been ice cream and games to play, as well as a tank they were allowed to clamber over and pretend to drive. The incongruity of it all had passed him by as an eleven-year-old. A year later kids in his class had dads who were fighting in the Falklands War on the other side of the world, but he never equated them with the friendly guy helping him over the wall.

Before he'd left the Fairport David had found a couple of local maps on a bookshelf in the residents' lounge through the back. He looked for Condor on both and while the buildings and airfield were outlined, there were no names anywhere for what they might be. Was this down to security? To prevent terrorists from blowing the place up? If so it wasn't much use, and the same went for the razor wire and fence surrounding the place, if you could just drive right up to the headquarters of the place with a bomb in your car. He momentarily felt a bit unnerved by the fact he was on military soil under false pretences, but since he'd come this far he might as well get on with it. He got out the car and went into the building he'd been directed to at the front gate.

Two minutes later he was sitting opposite Sergeant Major Wilkins, a clean-cut man with a Home Counties accent, muscles bursting out of a casual camouflage uniform and a turquoise beret perched at a clinically precise angle on his head. The only previous experience of sergeant majors David had was watching the guy with the 'tache who shouted at everyone about being a bunch of pooftas in *It Ain't Half Hot Mum* when he was a kid. This man in front of him seemed an altogether more real and balanced prospect. He was poised and composed, polite but firm, and almost immediately David knew he wasn't going to get anything out of him.

He started by asking general questions about the Marines and the 45 Commando. It turned out they were back on base after having spent time in Iraq, and before that, Afghanistan. David tried to equate this with the pictures of both conflicts he'd seen on the television, but here, with the sun beaming in through the blinds of a neat and tidy office, and a view of typically nondescript green rolling Scottish fields out the window, it seemed impossibly far away.

Wilkins was clearly media trained, thought David. He answered questions efficiently and pleasantly, but without giving anything much away. David asked about the relationship between the marines and the local community, and got the expected platitudes in response. It turned out that the 45 had been awarded the Freedom of Angus a couple of years ago, a symbolic gesture from the local council, but one which meant that any member of the unit was technically entitled to march 'bayonets fixed, drums beating and flags flying' anywhere in the county. David laughed as he thought of the running battles between the casuals and the marines that used to go on down the West Port when he was a teenager. A gang of casuals, in a spectacular display of

177

idiocy that only mindless thugs could muster, would jump a marine and batter him one night, only to have the whole unit descend on the centre of town the following night, picking fights with anyone who looked even vaguely like they might know a casual. The fact that these men were trained to kill with their bare hands seemed to pass the casuals by, or maybe that was the whole point. Either way, David learnt quickly to keep his head down and keep out of trouble. Around that time Arbroath had featured in a centre-spread story in a national tabloid under the headline 'Arbroath: A Town in Conflict'. A framed copy of the article had found its way behind the bar in the Malacca, the casuals' favourite haunt which sat right across the road from the Waverley, where the marines used to hang out. He imagined the faces of casuals sitting drinking their bottles of Grolsch in the Malacca, if dozens of marines had come marching out the Waverley towards them, 'bayonets fixed, drums beating and flags flying'. He wondered what had happened to the casuals. It was a frightening phenomenon of Thatcher's Britain in the 80s. The guys he knew that ran with the Arbroath Soccer Society had been well educated, well turned out, aspiring young men who just happened to turn into animalistic thugs every Saturday, using a football match as a thinly-veiled excuse. They used to phone rival gangs – either one of the local crews from Montrose or Forfar, or bigger gangs like the Aberdeen Soccer Casuals or Hibs' Capital City Service – for orchestrated fights in town centres. It was ritualistic, violent madness. It seemed to have died out, from what David could tell, although maybe it had just moved else-where, moved underground, changed from being organized into sporadic pockets of random violence. After all, it was the same attitude which now pervaded Lothian Road in Edinburgh, and the main drinking streets of towns and cities all over Scotland, on Friday and Saturday nights.

David drifted back to the conversation. Wilkins was still talk-ing, emphasizing the unit's close links with the local community, all that dull jazz, and David started thinking about last night. As if by telepathy, both he and Nicola had been slightly cooler towards each other than the previous night of blustery, passionate sex, as if two successive nights of that sort of thing was somehow not quite where they were at yet. It didn't mean they weren't somewhere, although they didn't talk about it, and David could feel that Nicola hadn't regretted anything they'd done together; she was just taking it easy, needed an early night, something which also suited him, despite the hardening in his trousers when they'd kissed goodnight at the Cruickshanks' front door.

As he walked round the inky teardrop of the Keptie Pond towards the Fairport, David had been unable to get the thought of tracking Neil down out of his head. How do you get hold of a private detective? How do private detectives actually do their job? Isn't there something he could do himself to find the guy? Was Neil still in Auchmithie? There weren't that many houses there, say a few dozen – what if he just went door-to-door, see if anyone knew him?

Here, sitting in Wilkins' office, he was getting nowhere. He wasn't going to be told anything useful by the mouthpiece of an organization only too used to warding off bad publicity. There had been more than one case, when David was growing up, of a marine losing the plot and killing himself, or worse, taking his wife and kids with him. The stress of actual combat on men with a tendency towards violent killing had some pretty terrible consequences, but it seemed to be a price the military were prepared to pay. Just don't expect them to shout about it. And anyway, he had realized last night that it no longer really mattered to him what this sergeant major told him. Even if he told him the details of Neil's discharge from the unit, it wouldn't make any difference. Either way he knew now that he definitely had to find him, to talk to him about everything, to try to make sense of it all.

But he'd come this far with the whole undercover bullshit, so he asked anyway.

'What about instances of trouble with individual marines? Either with other soldiers or local people.'

'I'm not sure what you mean.'

'There have been incidences of marines fighting with locals, or fighting with each other while on base, haven't there?'

Wilkins gave him a look which said he knew all along that this was why David was here, and that he wasn't going to get anything.

'Very occasionally,' he said with a small sigh. 'But we deal with any kind of insubordination swiftly and through the proper channels.'

'Is that what happened with Private Cargill in 1992?' David thought he might as well go for it, just to see Wilkins' reaction.

'I'm afraid I'm not at liberty to talk about individual cases,' said Wilkins with a smile. 'And besides, that seems like a very long time ago, so I wouldn't even have that sort of thing to hand, even if I wanted to tell you about it.'

'But you were Sergeant Major of the 45 back then?'

'I was.'

'So you might remember.'

'I might.'

'But you won't talk about it.'

'I won't.'

And that was pretty much that. David asked a few more questions to try and disguise the fact that he obviously wasn't really a journalist. He didn't know if Wilkins had him pegged, but he thought he might. He didn't much care. He now just wanted to be away from here, away from this pristine, unreal office, with its dagger-and-globe coat of arms on the wall, its framed pictures of men in uniforms standing on parade or hunkering down in a foreign land on some training exercise. He wanted to be away from the smug authority of the sergeant major, the easy assuredness, and the face which knew that he could kill this little shit sitting opposite him given half a chance and different circumstances. So in the best form of undercover tabloid journalists everywhere, he made his excuses and left. Sergeant Major Wilkins saw him to the door with a toothy smile, and David felt like punching him in the face. Instead he shook hands and headed out the door, away from the base and back towards town, where Nicola and Amy were waiting to be picked up and taken back to Edinburgh. As he drove past the kid at the gate with the gun he tried to imagine Neil handling a similar weapon. He found he could picture it all too easily.

The drive back to Edinburgh seemed to take forever. The sun slowly baked them in the rusty can of David's car, and roadworks on the Forth Bridge left them stationary for an hour amidst angry drivers, shimmering tarmac and clammy exhaust fumes. Amy seemed sullen in the back, quietly sighing in between picking up and putting down a book about witches, wizards and trolls. David told Nicola that the visit to Condor had been a waste of time, and she didn't pursue it.

When he dropped Nicola and Amy off, David wanted to go inside with them, but he could clearly see that some mother-and-daughter time was needed, that things were maybe moving too fast between him and Nicola for Amy's liking, so he reluctantly left them to it.

Nicola was grateful that David had got the message. Whether Amy was cranky about David, or about being taken up to Arbroath all the time, or about all the talk recently of death and funerals, or just about having to go to school tomorrow, she didn't know, but she felt as if she had been neglecting her daughter over the last couple of weeks, as if this whole thing with David had taken over. She silently chastised herself for it. When they got in the house, Amy seemed to cheer up, especially when they ordered out for pizza, got the ice cream out and put the *Shrek* DVD on. Snuggled up on the sofa, Nicola tried to put all thoughts of David out of her head for the evening, leaving behind the grown-up world of sex, flirting, death, police stations, funerals and all the rest, at least for a few hours. She didn't want David to think that she thought shagging him at the weekend was a mistake, so she didn't want to totally cool off on him, but she sensed somehow that he got it, that he realized she had to spend some time with Amy, her number-one priority, that she had to take at least a breather from him, from whatever was going on between them, for both her own sake and for Amy's. This relationship (she was using that word to refer to herself and David now, that was a step in itself) was going somewhere, but she sensed it was still fragile, and they were going to have to take it easy if they didn't want to spoil it, damage it, break it early on, before it had barely got going.

She thought about Gary's funeral. The look on Gary's parents' faces as they stood by the graveside. This was real life, and it hurt. She didn't know the details of David's visit to Condor, but he'd said it was useless. Maybe that was for the best. She sensed that David was being drawn towards Neil somehow, but what good would that do?

David was greeted at work on Monday morning with an official written reprimand for poor timekeeping. One more warning and he was out the door. It was bullshit, really, an excuse to fire him. He wasn't the most punctual, but then neither was anyone else, and if they were being strict they would have to fire every bastard in the whole of Still Waters, something they would probably be doing soon enough anyway.

He spent the day on the internet trying to work out how to find Neil. It turned out there was a huge online industry based around trying to find people, most of which involved credit card details and a fee. He tried the free ones first, directory inquiries and the like, but there were no Cargills listed for Auchmithie. He tried for Arbroath and got 150 replies but none with the N initial. He eventually bit the bullet and signed up for a service which claimed to trawl through electoral rolls, birth, death, marriage and divorce certificates, title deeds, land registers, bad debtor lists and so on. By the end of the day, for his thirty-five quid he had a long email detailing just about everything he already knew about Neil Cargill, and precious little else. Born in Arbroath in 1969, went to school, joined the Marines in 1988, left in 1992, joined the police force the same year, left in 1994, parents died the same year, not long after that he sold the family home and then . . . nothing. He just disappeared. He wasn't on any of the lists they'd searched: not registered to vote, or to pay tax or receive benefits, or with any banks or credit card companies, he didn't seem to own any property, or run a business, or even exist. Except Nicola's dad said he had turned up in Auchmithie only a couple of years ago. So much for the paper trail.

David thought about complaining to the internet company who had essentially just fleeced him, but then he started wondering about how easy it might be to simply hide yourself away, to disappear from society if you wanted to. Presumably he had been trained in the Marines how to survive on his own, how to use the land resourcefully to stay alive. He wondered if there were many people doing that in Scotland – it seemed unlikely, more like the kind of thing you'd hear about people doing in the States. But then there was plenty of room in this country, plenty of space to disappear into if you wanted, there was that whole big dumb middle of the country with nothing in it but hills and forests if you seriously wanted to be on your own. And he had no way of knowing if Neil had even stayed in the country. He was a trained fighting machine – maybe he was abroad somewhere, earning money as a mercenary? David was letting his imagination get away with him, but it was possible, wasn't it? Or then again, maybe he had changed his name and identity, and he *was* still living in Scotland. But wouldn't that show up on this internet search he'd just paid for? Not if he hadn't done it officially, if he was living under an assumed name somewhere, keeping himself out of mischief, and nobody was asking questions.

By the end of the day, he was no further forward. As he struggled across town through the festival traffic (would this fucking festival never end, he thought) he realized that there was only one thing he could do. Neil had last been spotted in

Auchmithie two years ago, so he would go there and ask. It was simple. Maybe if he asked the right question to the right person, he might get a lead. Sitting baking on a sweaty bus stuck in traffic on South Bridge, he resolved to go back up north at the weekend, see what he could uncover.

During the week, the good weather finally broke. Thunder and lightning rolled across Edinburgh, pellets of rain punching free from bellies of clouds and down onto the city, leaving behind squally showers and the fresh smell of wet concrete. David phoned Nicola to tell her what he had planned and, more importantly, just to hear her voice again. He had spent the last few days obsessing about Neil, but every time he thought of Nicola he perked up a little, and would feel a slight pang of regret that he wasn't with her at that moment. He wanted to concentrate on her, on making sure this relationship (that's what he was calling it now, he realized) worked, but he kept getting sidetracked with this search for Neil.

'You're beginning to get the hang of the "treat 'em mean" thing, I see,' said Nicola.

'What?'

'We finally get round to shagging on Saturday, and it takes you until Wednesday to phone?'

'Jesus, Nicola, I'm sorry but I've . . .'

'I'm joking, you idiot. Wind up. What happened to your sense of humour?'

'I've been a bit preoccupied the last few days.'

'Let me guess – Neil Cargill?'

'Wow, telepathy, I'll need to add that to the list of your many gifts.'

'You're compiling a list of my many gifts?'

'Not really.'

'But if you were, what would be on it?'

'You know, the usual – wit, beauty, charm, intelligence, ability to fuck outdoors at the drop of a hat.'

'Yes, that is one of my best attributes. I notice wit came before beauty in that list. Funnier than I am pretty, aye?'

'Well, you're pretty funny.'

'Boom, boom.'

'Anyway, sorry for not calling sooner. I really enjoyed last weekend, despite there being a funeral involved.'

'Yeah, I know what you mean. I had a great time too. Let's do it again sometime. Although maybe without the funeral part. Or maybe that's what got us randy. Maybe we should go and hang out at cemeteries every weekend, get ourselves going. I'm talking shit, amn't I?'

'Yup. Kinky shit. The best kind of shit, so don't let me stop you.'

'I've stopped already.'

'Shame. Anyway, guess what I'm doing this weekend?'

'Let me see, taking me out for a romantic dinner for two in a top Edinburgh restaurant? I've always fancied the Atrium. They apparently do a magnificent squid starter.'

'It sounds great, but no, not this weekend. Maybe next. Another guess?'

'Well, if you're not keeping me in the manner to which I am not accustomed, would it have something to do with tracking down Neil, perhaps?'

'Bingo. I'm going to Auchmithie.'

'Do you have an address for him?'

'No. I'm just going to ask around.'

'That doesn't sound like much of an idea.'

'It's all I've got. I've spent all week on the internet trying to find out about him.'

'Ah, the fount of all knowledge. What did people do before the internet?'

'Good question. Anyway, I got nowhere. It seems he stopped existing around ten years ago.'

'And yet he was seen two years ago in Auchmithie.'

'Exactly. Wanna come along?'

'I don't think so. Much as I would like to tramp around strangers' doors in a tiny, close-knit community asking about a man last seen in the area two years previously, I have a daughter to look after, remember? Even though Amy likes her granny and grandpa, she's been in a huff about continually getting dragged up to Arbroath. So I think sticking around in Edinburgh for the weekend might be best.'

'I thought she might be in a huff with me – you know, the new man in her mum's life and all that.'

'There might be some of that involved as well, to be honest, but don't let that worry you.'

'But I do.'

'Well don't, it's to be expected.'

'I really like her, you know.'

'I know.'

'And I really like you as well.'

'I know.'

'And I'm serious about us.'

There was a moment's pause.

'That's good to hear, David, because so am I.'

'That is also good to hear.'

There was another pause.

'Good,' said Nicola. 'Now that we've got the awkward serious relationship stuff out the way, how about we joke some more about your daft idea of going to Auchmithie?'

'It's not daft.'

'You think?'

'I think.'

'OK.'

'What does OK mean?'

'Is this the start of our first argument?'

'I don't think so.'

'Shame, I always like the first argument in a relationship, there's something so fresh about it that other, later arguments never quite capture.'

'Maybe we'll never have any arguments.'

'Now that *is* a daft idea. Anyway, you have fun in Auchmithie. When are you going?'

'Friday after work. I'll stay in the Fairport, but I'll probably go straight to Auchmithie in the early evening, see what I can find out, and then go back on Saturday.'

'Will you phone me when you get to the Fairport?'

'Sure. You worried about me?'

'Nah, I just want that saucy housewife landlady to know that you've got a woman waiting for you elsewhere. She's definitely after you, you know.'

'It's so nice that you care.'

'Yeah, well, just phone, OK? I am genuinely interested in what you find out, you know.'

'I know.'

'Not that you'll find out anything.'

'Thanks for the vote of confidence.'

'You're welcome.'

'I miss you,' said David. 'Sorry if that seems a bit weird to say, since we've only just re-met and stuff, but it's true so I thought I might as well come out and say it.'

There was a pause, the line crackling slightly.

'I miss you too, doofus.'

There was another silence down the phone.

'We really have got the awkwardness of the awkward serious relationship stuff nailed, haven't we?' said David.

'Damn straight.'

13
Auchmithie

It was seven o'clock as David turned off the Arbroath back road for the last couple of miles to Auchmithie. High, grey clouds raced across the evening sky and a flustered wind made the trees along the roadside whisper secrets as David rounded a bend in the road and was suddenly in the village.

He hadn't been here in God knows how long, but nothing much seemed to have changed. A line of low sandstone cottages with small windows crouched along the single street which ended abruptly at a cliff top. A couple of more recent houses had been built at the cliff end, presumably because the older ones had been battered to death by the elements. He looked south, the colossal slate expanse of sea taking up most of his vision, with the small pebble beach of Auchmithie Bay and the harbour two hundred feet below him, both dominated by the adjacent headland, the lumbering, lonely Castle Rock, worn away almost to the point of being detached from the mainland altogether. In the bay, slabs of spotted pale brown rock jutted out of the sea like broken bits of oatcake. Beyond that were three or four derelict old cottages perched precariously atop the next headland, looking as if they might crumble into the waves at any minute.

He turned the car and headed back through the village as small spots of rain started appearing on the windscreen. Didn't there used to be a hotel with a bar here somewhere? He had planned to start asking around in there, as he didn't fancy going door-to-door, but the hotel seemed to have disappeared, at least there was no sign of it now. As he drove back down the tiny street he noticed the lane – a rough, grass track really – which came off the road and headed steeply down the ravine next to the headland, winding its way down to the stony beach and harbour hundreds of feet below. From here he could only just make out a couple of small fishing boats draped in ragged tarpaulin and hauled up above the high-water mark next to two tiny lock-up sheds and a line of lobster and crab pots.

Opposite this lane was the one building in the village which wasn't a house, the But 'n' Ben. If there was no hotel and no bar in Auchmithie any more, this was going to have to be where David started asking around. He parked the car and went inside. The But 'n' Ben maybe called itself a licensed restaurant, but really it was just two twee cottages knocked through, with a scattering of tables, chairs and some frilly patterned curtains framing the windows. The low-ceilinged space was full of random seafaring junk, and the walls were lined with local artwork, all seascapes and all for sale. The pine furniture was pure country kitchen and as David looked around he noticed that he was the youngest person in the place by a good thirty years. The room was packed with old folk, either posher sorts from elsewhere in Angus sporting Berghaus fleeces and enjoying a quaint evening out, or more seasoned, spirited locals getting fired into the drinks menu as much as the old-school granny cooking on offer. The air was thick with the smell of smoked fish and noisy with the chatter of three dozen patrons at varying stages of deafness. A doddery old man in filthy blue overalls with grey hair sprouting from his ears was standing at what passed for the bar, really just a till on a bench with a couple of whisky optics mounted behind. He was chatting to the old dear behind the till who was dressed in regulation restaurant uniform of white blouse and black skirt, making her smile and laugh so that the wrinkles on her forehead bunched up together in a way that reminded David of curtains being drawn open to let sunlight in. She spotted David in the doorway and cut short her conversation with the salty dog.

'Can I help, dear?' She gave him the once-over. Clearly thirty-somethings in T-shirts, jeans and trainers were a novelty in the But 'n' Ben. 'I'm afraid I don't have any tables free at the minute.'

'That's OK, I'm actually trying to find someone. I wondered if you knew of a Neil Cargill living around here?'

'There have been plenty of Cargills pass through over the years, dear,' said the woman. 'But I'm fairly sure there isn't a Neil Cargill in the village at the moment.'

'If Edith doesn't know him, then he's not from Auchmithie, that's for sure,' said the old man at the bar. 'She makes it her business to know everything about everyone, don't you, Edith?'

'Och, away and boil yer heid, you,' said Edith with a laugh, before turning back to David. 'He's making me out to be a terrible gossip, so he is.'

'Are you saying that you're not?'

'That's exactly what I'm saying, Fergus. I'm just interested in people, that's all. There's nothing wrong with that, is there?'

'So, neither of you have heard of a Neil Cargill, then?' said David. 'He's about my age, stocky with a square jaw, and I think he used to fish for lobsters here a few years ago.'

'Jesus!' said Fergus. 'That guy? Is that who you're looking for? He was a right strange one, so he was.'

'Oh, I remember him,' said Edith. 'He was a Cargill then, was he? He was never from the village, though. And he kept to himself – never spoke to anyone around here, not even to say hello in the street. A right unsociable sod. To be honest, we were glad when he stopped turning up.'

'When was that?'

'Oh, a good couple of years now,' said Fergus. 'We were glad to see the back of him. There was no law against him fishing these waters, you understand, but there's an agreement amongst the villagers that this little patch is just ours to fish. He turned up one day and started laying down his pots. We tried to reason with him, but he just ignored us. There was nothing we could do, really. So when he stopped showing up, we never asked any questions, we just got on with it.'

'If he didn't live in the village, do you know where he stayed?'

'For a while, I think, he stayed in one of the coastguard cottages, over on Meg's Craig,' said Edith.

'Where's that, exactly?'

'I'll show you,' said Fergus.

The old-timer headed out the door, motioning for David to follow. For a moment, he thought the old guy was actually going to take him there, but as soon as they were outside he stopped and pointed. Across the ravine and a row of muddy brown fields, David could just make out the short line of houses, almost floating at the edge of the land, balanced precariously over the sea's edge.

'How do I get there?' he asked. The old man was already walking inside, as the rain started to thicken a little, becoming a solid drizzle, and David followed.

'Oh, he'll not be there any more,' said Fergus, settling back down at the bar. 'Those cottages have been abandoned and boarded up for two years now.'

'That's right, dear,' said Edith, who hadn't moved to serve anyone in the place. 'The Thompsons – they're the farmers who own all that land from Meg's Craig down to Tanglehall and inland to Windyhills – they were using the buildings for storage for a while. Not sure what they were keeping in there, right enough, but then apparently one of the roofs fell in, and they didn't think it was safe any more, so they've just been boarded up and left.'

'And that's where this Neil Cargill stayed, before all that?'

'I think so,' said Edith. 'But he never spoke to anyone, so I'm not entirely sure.'

'But how do you get there? Just out of interest. Do you have to go across the fields?'

'No, son,' said Fergus. 'There's a farm track leads out there.

Don't know what state it'll be in these days, but it should still be useable. You'll have gone past the start of the track just before you came into the village. But there's nothing out there, not now. If that's where your man Cargill was staying, then he'll be long gone years ago.'

'Thanks anyway,' said David, ignoring the curious looks he was getting from both of them. 'You've been a big help.'

He headed outside, where the wind had picked up and the rain was settling in for the evening, it seemed. The sky had turned into a solid, low bank of grey above his head. He looked over at the cottages on the next headland, about a mile or two away, but you couldn't get there directly. From here it looked like a remote and abandoned place, thought David, just the kind of place Neil might've liked the seclusion of. What the hell, he thought, as he got in the car, started the engine and headed back out the village.

The farm track was easy to miss, hidden by some overgrown bushes along the roadside, and once David reversed back a little to drive down it, he noticed a rusted old sign warning it was a private road and no unauthorized vehicles were allowed. Past the bushes and the sign the track opened out a little, but it was full of potholes and rocks, with large clumpy tufts of grass and weeds sprouting up the middle. Maybe in a four-wheel drive or a tractor this was easy going, but not in his wee town car, creaking and clunking as he trundled slowly over stones and divots, rocking the car from side to side. The rain was coming down heavily now, and the rhythmic wheeze of his windscreen wipers made his car sound asthmatic.

At five miles an hour, it took him longer than expected to reach the cottages. Once there, he wondered why he'd bothered. There were three houses, terraced together. The one nearest the sea was only really half a house; the roof had collapsed in on it, and the sea-facing wall was little more than a pile of sandy red rubble. The other two houses were in relatively good nick, their roofs a little saggy but still intact, and their windows boarded over with plywood. The paintwork had peeled and damp areas were spread over the exposed walls.

David switched off the engine and the car's heartbeat stopped, leaving just the sound of the rain and wind outside gently rocking him in the driver's seat. He got out and started to walk around the cottages. He could see through the rubbled wall that the tumbledown house had nothing in it – bare internal walls now exposed to the elements, a fireplace full of masonry debris and an old bird's nest. He walked round its far wall, and was amazed at how close to the cliffs this side of the terrace now was. He wondered when the houses had been built, and how much the erosive battering from the sea had dragged the buildings towards the precipice they now stood on. The rain was even heavier now, and from here he could barely make out Auchmithie back across the ravine. Between them was Castle Rock, and from here he could see how it got its name: it looked like a giant sandcastle that a kid might have made on a beach, its edges beginning to crumble and decay. He looked down at the sheer drop from the headland he was on, and felt dizzy for a moment as he imagined himself as a raindrop, plummeting down into the frothy, yellowy foam that ebbed and flowed, occasionally crashing into the rocks below as wave after wave gradually beat the land into submission. He looked in the opposite direction from Auchmithie and thought he could just about make out another bay, cutting its crescent shape into the land beyond Meg's Craig. This was completely hidden from Auchmithie, and he didn't remember seeing it from the sea when they'd been on the boat trip, but he must've done because it was completely exposed to the sea. He tried to remember that trip, in the summer heat, laughing and joking with Nicola and Amy, and it seemed like a different country to the one he was now inhabiting, miserable and isolated, with the rain beating down on it and the wind making the high grass and weeds around his feet jerk this way and that in protest.

He rounded the tumbledown house and examined the backs of the other two cottages. The windows and small back doors round this side were also boarded up. As he looked closer, though, through the rain, he saw that the corner of one of the boards on a window was loose, slightly peeled away from the window frame at the bottom. He went over to it, having to tramp through a tangle of nettles, weeds and dandelions to get there. He tugged at the corner, and the whole board came away quite easily in his hands. Behind it there was no glass left in the window frame, and beyond that only the gloomy darkness of the house's interior. He thought he smelled something, a smell which reminded him of the But 'n' Ben, a smoky sensation, but with the underlying scent of something unmistakably from the sea behind it. He peered into the house. As his eyes got accustomed to the dark, he started to make out shapes inside – a doorway here, an empty fireplace there. Then he spotted something in the corner furthest away from the window. As he gazed at it, David's eyes widened. It looked like a bed with a sleeping bag on it, and there was a large holdall lying on the floor next to it. Further along the same wall seemed to be a small, portable gas stove. Jesus H! Someone was living here!

He thought he heard something through the whoosh of the wind and the sound of rain hammering the ground around him. He turned to look behind him but before he'd even got halfway he felt an unbelievable and shocking pain shooting from the back of his head, down his neck and shoulders and tunnelling down into his spine. Sudden sparkles of light filled his vision as he reeled forwards, smacked his head off the gritty, crumbling wall of the house and passed out into unconsciousness, a dark emptiness filling his mind completely.

The first sensation he felt was pain, unfocussed but brutal pain, ebbing and flowing through his body, coming in wave after wave, making him feel nauseous and dizzy. He drifted like that for a while, surges of overwhelming sickness and aches pulsing through him so that he could do nothing at all except have his mind battered about like a piece of flotsam caught in a tidal rush.

After a while he started to drift in and out of consciousness, the pain becoming more focussed, more localized. His head. His head throbbed agonizingly, and it felt as if his pulse would burst his eardrums. His back ached too, lower down and to the side; more than just muscular, it felt like some organ or other was collapsing. And his wrists, his wrists felt as if they were slit.

He suddenly jerked awake with the thought. His body spasmed, causing each of his now distinct pains to increase, and as he tensed his arms he realized that his hands were tied behind him with some kind of wire. That explained the wrist pain. His head continued to pound so that it was the only thing he could hear. He opened his eyes but all he could see were little explosions of light bursting out of darkness like sub-atomic reactions creating particles out of nothing. He was hit by another wave of nausea and felt himself drifting back into the hole of unconsciousness. He tried to fight it, but the hammering of his head became too much and he passed out.

He dreamt he was standing on the ocean floor with Colin, Gary and Neil. Somehow it was the bar of Tutties Neuk, except underwater. They could see a torrential storm happening way above them on the sea's surface, but down here they were safe from harm, quietly supping their pints and chatting about the football as crabs scuttled past and fish meandered in between them. The puggy flashed invitingly next to them. It felt good. He wondered why more people didn't live underwater when it felt this reassuring. All pubs should be like this, he thought. The storm raged overhead, and they kept drinking their pints and laughing. They stayed like that in comfort for a long time.

Suddenly he felt wet. Had the storm managed to penetrate their haven after all? Another splash, this time more real, more cold, across his face and chest, and his lungs froze momentarily in shock. A third drenching and he was awake. His head was pounding with pain again, somewhere at the back of his skull and on his forehead, the pain seeming to pass back and forth between the two via the backs of his eyes and through his brain.

He opened his eyes again. This time there were no flashes, but he couldn't focus on the grey around him. Gradually he started to differentiate the sound of the sea shushing against the shore from the rhythmic throbbing of his head. He distinctly heard a gull cry somewhere nearby. The swimming grey in front of him started to separate into shapes. There was the disused fireplace, the one he'd seen earlier when he looked in from outside the house. That meant that over there must be – there they were – the bed and the portable stove. The holdall was gone. The board was removed from the window he'd looked in through, and the empty window frame was casting a tepid, soupy light into the room. Outside the rain was still falling, but he could just make out patches of lighter sky overhead.

'Thank fuck.'

It had been fifteen years, but he recognized Neil's voice straight away. It was coming from behind him. He tried to turn but the pain in his head threatened to overwhelm him, so he jerked forward uncomfortably. He realized now he was sitting on a chair, or more accurately, he was tied to a chair by his wrists and ankles.

'Neil? What the fuck is this?' He tried to indicate his wrists and ankles, but could hardly move, and just shunted the chair a little sideways.

'Do you always sleep that long when you get knocked out? I've been bored out of my fucking mind waiting for you to come round. If I'd known, I wouldn't have hit you so hard. But then you did bang your head off the wall on the way down. Apologies for the water to wake you up, by the way, but I got tired waiting.'

'Why are you doing this, Neil? Untie me, for fuck's sake.'

'Sorry, no can do.'

'I came here to find you.'

'No shit.'

'What's that supposed to mean?'

'It means I knew you would come and find me eventually. I've been waiting. I'm surprised you weren't here sooner.'

'Well, you seemed to have disappeared off the face of the earth.'

'Good. That's the way I like it.'

'But I found you. And so will others. In fact, there will be people coming here looking for me soon, if I don't report back tonight. They knew where I was going, and they knew to come and look for me if I didn't check back with them.'

David heard laughter behind him, a full-throated laugh with a chesty rattle to it, and Neil walked round to face him.

David didn't know what he'd been expecting, but the figure in front of him wasn't much different to the boy he'd last seen that Saturday night all those years ago. He wasn't as heavy-set as he used to be, but his muscles were more clearly defined under the plain green T-shirt he was wearing. His forehead had more lines across it and his eyes were darker and sadder than they ever were before. His close-cropped dark hair had flecks of grey through it, as did the week or so of stubble on his jutting chin. His face still fell naturally into a frown, even, as now, when he was laughing. He had the look of a man who knew a hundred different ways to kill someone, but he also looked as if that knowledge weighed heavy on him. His forearms were covered in tattoos, and he wore a chunky watch, combat trousers and heavy black boots.

'Is that the best you can do?' he said, sitting down on the bed next to David on the chair. 'For a start, it's already tomorrow, you fucking idiot. You slept so long after I smacked you that it's now' – he made a show of looking at his watch – 'eight forty-five hours. Saturday morning. And for another thing, I know full well that you haven't told anyone you were coming here to look for me. Who would you tell? The police? I don't think so. What would you tell them, exactly? So don't give me that bullshit about people coming to find you, it's not going to happen. Oh, and don't bother looking for your mobile, I took it out your pocket and chucked it over the cliff.'

'Look, Neil, just untie me. There's no need for this. I just came here to find you and talk.'

'I think it's painfully apparent that we're past that, don't you?'

David tried to concentrate. He looked at Neil, who was staring back at him from no more than a yard away, smiling thinly and playing with a large torch, spinning it in his hands. The pain in his head was making David's vision blur; he was finding it hard to think. All this had come at him so quickly. One minute he was ambling around the countryside in a largely theoretical search for an old friend, the next he was trussed up in a disused cottage at the mercy of . . . well, what was Neil now? A psychotic ex-marine? A killer?

'I know what you did,' said David. Neil stopped tossing the torch into the air, instead bringing it down sharply on the side of David's face. The pain made David scream out, and his eyes and nose started to run. He felt the metallic taste of blood in his mouth and spat a stringy maroon gob onto the bare floor.

'You don't know fuck all about me,' said Neil, 'so don't start saying you fucking do.' He got up and started walking easily around the room.

'I know you killed Colin.'

Neil stopped. For a moment David thought he was going to get the torch in the face again, but Neil seemed to be considering him closely.

'That just shows you know fuck all,' he said. 'Which is the whole problem, now, isn't it? Everyone knows Colin fell. Tragic accident, blah, blah, blah. But I always knew you and Gary thought differently. I always knew, the way you ran away to uni and the way Gary looked at me when I saw him in Arbroath, I knew that you thought I'd killed him. That would've been easier for sensitive little you, wouldn't it? A nice, neat answer. Colin, the shining fucking light of our stupid shithole of a town, shoved over a cliff by the fucking illiterate monkey Neil, the cunt no one ever had fucking time for, the grunt only good for sending into fucking war. Eh? Isn't that right? Nice and simple – good guy versus bad guy, that's how you'd like it to have been, isn't it? Well, you fucking prick, that is not how it was, sorry to tell you, sorry to burst your little fucking bubble, but Colin fell off that fucking cliff, despite what everyone thought, and if I could've fucking stopped him, if I could've fucking grabbed him, I would've. But I didn't, did I? And he died, just like people die all the fucking time, sometimes much worse fucking deaths than Colin's, let me tell you. I've seen plenty of worse deaths, bodies blown to fucking bits by tank fire and worse even, so don't bleat away about a wee laddie who probably would've amounted to fuck all who fell off a stupid fucking cliff.'

'You were there,' said David quietly. 'You said if you could've grabbed him – that means you were there when Colin died.'

'Congratulations, brainiac, well worked out. Of course I was fucking there, how the fuck else would I know how he died?'

'But that's not what you told me, or the police.'

'My god, you're fucking slow. Catch up. Of course I fucking didn't. You think I wanted to have them place me at the scene of the crime?'

'I thought you said he fell.'

'He did.'

'Then there wasn't a crime.'

'Fuck off. Figure of speech. If I were you I wouldn't be so fucking smart. Mr Torch here might pay your face another visit.'

'If you lied about that, how do I know you're not lying now? How do I know you didn't kill Colin?'

'Well, you'll just have to take my word for it, won't you, sunshine?'

'What were you doing back up there anyway?'

'What do you fucking think? We were drunk, we were arsing around. We dared each other. We had a pretend fight, then he fell.'

'It sounds like you're still trying to convince yourself. That you feel guilty.'

David felt the torch before he even saw it, this time striking him on the temple, sending searing needles of pain through his brain.

'Fuck off with your amateur psychology bullshit,' said Neil, sitting back down and leaning into David's face, which was dripping blood. 'I know all about psychiatrists and their fucking little word games, I had it all in the fucking Marines, then again in the fucking police. Let me make this as plain as I fucking can: I. Did. Not. Kill. Colin.'

'I don't believe you.'

'Which is why I have to kill you.'

It took a few moments to sink in through the pain spread across David's body and head. He realized now this was painfully real. He could die. He *would* die if he didn't start thinking of a way out.

'Like you killed Gary,' he said.

Neil let out a snort.

'Finally, we're getting somewhere,' he said. 'Yes, David, like I killed Gary.'

'So you admit that?'

'You catch on fast, don't you?'

David felt suddenly sick. He pictured Gary a fortnight ago, sitting in the pub talking sheepishly about going to art college.

'For fuck's sake, why?'

'Why do you think? Because he knew.'

'Knew what?'

'He knew I was there when Colin died. He thought I killed him. He was going around telling people I killed Colin. I couldn't let that go on.'

'What the fuck are you talking about? He never said anything like that to anyone.'

'That's nice, covering for him, but I know he told you. Why else did the two of you spend the whole day of the reunion together?'

'How do you know that?'

'How do you think? I followed you. I saw him meet you in Tutties. I saw the pair of you at the football. I saw you getting thrown out of Bally's. I spent the whole day watching the pair of you. I've known for a long time that he knew, I could tell. I've been watching him for months. Waiting for him to slip up. And then you turned up – out the fucking blue – just like that, and who did you meet? Gary. Very convenient. It was then that I knew for sure. I knew he knew, and I knew that he told you, and that I'd have to take care of it.'

'You are insane, you know that? I don't know what the fuck has happened to you over the last fifteen years, but you are a fucking headcase, you do realize that? One minute you're telling me that you didn't kill Colin, that it was an accident, the next that you killed Gary because he knew you killed Colin.'

Another slam of pain, this time concentrating on his jaw, which rattled and jarred with the force of the torch against it. David felt nauseous, and spat more blood and slavers on the floor.

'If you fucking *listened* you would've heard me say that Gary knew I was there, not that I killed Colin.'

'But he didn't even know that,' said David, wincing as his jaw moved. 'At least, he never said anything to me.'

'Yeah, right. You expect me to believe that?'

'I'm telling you he didn't. Even if he did, and even if he thought you killed Colin and he was telling everyone under the fucking sun about it, that's no reason to kill the fucking guy. It's just someone's opinion, that's no grounds for killing them. Unless you did do it.'

'Careful,' said Neil, coming towards him, thumping the torch against his thigh.

'What the fuck has happened to you?' said David.

'What happened? What fucking happened? That would be easy, wouldn't it? That would fit into your stupid fucking psychology profile, I suppose. "Oh, Neil was a nice kid at school, then he joined the Marines and fought in the Gulf War and got fucked up with Gulf War Syndrome and saw some terrible things and it turned him into a monster." Is that what you think?'

'Well, you were never an insane killer when I knew you before.'

'I'm not insane. If anything I'm more sane than ever.'

'But you killed Gary, that's not the act of a sane man.'

'You think everyone who kills someone is insane? That's the stupidest thing I ever heard. There would be no murderers in prison then, would there? They'd all be in the fucking funny farm. No, David, I'm a killer, in that I have killed, but I am perfectly sane.'

'You don't sound it to me.'

Neil sighed and leaned in towards David's face.

'I'm fucking sick of this. I wish I'd never woken you up.' With that he brought the torch down again, this time heavily thudding into the back of David's skull, wrenching his neck and head forward. David felt dizzy, and the flashes of light appeared before his eyes again, then his body slumped in the chair.

Nicola checked her mobile again – still nothing. She swerved slightly as a lorry approached her on the Arbroath back road and threw the phone back onto the passenger seat. David hadn't called. She'd waited and waited last night for a call from him, then tried his mobile number a few times but got nothing – did that bloody thing never work? She'd left a couple of messages, hoping she sounded nonchalant, telling him to get in touch. He had probably just forgotten or something, or was in the pub in Arbroath, so she had decided to leave it until the morning. But she'd been unable to sleep properly, so at eight a.m. she tried the Fairport, only to discover that he'd never checked in. She tried the mobile a few more times then made a decision. Within the hour Amy had been packed off to a mate's house for the day, and she was on the train to Arbroath. There, she'd borrowed her folks' beaten-up old Volvo estate, the car she was currently negotiating along the road to Auchmithie, to try and find out what the hell had happened to him. Maybe this was stupid, she thought, but she had a bad feeling. She wasn't usually one for intuition and all that crap, but this didn't feel good, and she felt that she had to try and do something.

It was lunchtime when she parked the car and headed into the But 'n' Ben. It was the only place in the village that wasn't a house, so she thought it would've been the obvious place David would've gone.

Inside, the place was swarming with pensioners, the air heavy with the reek of smokies. A lot of the old men turned to take in her slim frame in the doorway as she stood waiting for one of the waitresses to come over. A teenager with rolling hips and an ample bosom waddled over to see her. She explained she was looking for David, but the girl said she hadn't been working last night.

'Maybe Edith saw him, she was on yesterday. She's in the kitchen. Just a minute.'

Nicola was getting curious stares from everyone in the place, and she stood returning the looks until everyone was sheepishly heads down, back to examining the plates in front of them. Nicola saw an old dear with a crinkly face emerge from the kitchen.

'I'm looking for someone, David Lindsay, might've been around here yesterday asking about someone?' She started to describe him but before she could finish, the old woman interrupted.

'Aye, he was here, right enough,' she said. 'Looking for a Cargill.'

'That's him,' said Nicola. 'Any idea where he went?'

'No idea where he'll be now, dear, sorry. The fellow he was looking for used to live over at the coastguard cottages on Meg's Craig, and he seemed awful interested in that. But I don't know whether he went over there, or where he'll be now.'

'How do you know this Cargill doesn't live there any more?'

'No one lives there any more, they've been abandoned for years.'

Nicola asked for directions, and the old woman took her to the doorway and pointed back the way she came, explaining the track that led back out to the adjacent headland. Nicola thanked her, and the old woman walked slowly back inside, shaking her head slightly as she went.

Nicola looked south towards the cottages. The sky was low and dampness hung in the air as banks of cloud drifted past, seemingly almost at head height, rolling in over each other from the sea. She could only just make out the tiny row of houses, which seemed to be defying gravity by hanging off the end of the cliff. She wondered if David had gone there. Surely he had, since that would've been his only lead. But after that, where had he gone?

She got in the car, turned it, and headed back through the village towards the track to the cottages.

David gradually swam back to consciousness, the pain sharpening in his head, his face, his wrists. It took him a moment to remember where he was, and when he did his heart dropped like a stone into his stomach. He felt sick suddenly and gagged a little, spitting onto the floor at his feet.

'Lucky I'm not house-proud, you're making a right fucking mess of my floor.'

'This is insane, Neil, just let me go.'

'Is that you starting with the insane thing again? Careful now, you've only just come to, I wouldn't want to knock you out again. Actually, I probably would, but never mind.'

David tried to think. How could he get out of this? How the fuck could he escape? Neil had presumably been trained in all this sort of stuff when he was in the Marines, and what had David been doing all that time? Sitting on his arse in front of a computer or a television, unfit and lazy. He had no chance of physically matching Neil, and precious little hope of escape. He would have to talk to him, try and talk him round, talk him out of this madness.

'Where have you been living, Neil?'

'What?'

'Have you been living here for the last two years? When I tried to track you down, you just seemed to have disappeared about two years ago. I was wondering where you'd been.'

'Oh, you know, here and there. Around. A man with my skills can be in demand these days, especially where there's conflict.'

'A mercenary?'

'One man's mercenary is another man's freedom fighter.'

'That's terrorist.'

'What?'

'One man's terrorist is another man's freedom fighter.'

'Whatever. Anyway, I spent some time in Azerbaijan, since you ask, and a while in Chechnya.'

'Nice.'

'Not as bad as you'd think, some of it. Amazing scenery, when you got a chance to look at it between the snipers and the bombs. Nicer than here, anyway.'

'So why did you come back?'

'Good question. I've been wondering that myself, recently.'

'And you've been staying here?'

'What's with the questions? What the fuck does it matter to you where I've been?'

'I'm just trying to understand.'

'Understand? Don't make me fucking laugh. You're trying to stay alive is what you're doing. I learned all this kidnap situation psychology in the Marines as well, you know. Opening up a dialogue with your captor. Letting them know you're human. Bet you're surprised that old Neil could learn stuff, aren't you? The fucking runt of the litter, the fucking grunt of the ADS, the butt of all your and Colin's fucking jokes, eh?'

'You were never that, Neil.'

'Wasn't I? A wee bit of the selective memory going on there, my man. You were always so fucking superior, with your fucking Highers and your middle-class parents pissing off to France. You and Colin both. When you weren't having a pop at Gary, you were taking the piss out of me.'

'Is that what all this is about? Getting back at us for schoolboy shit?'

'This isn't *about* anything except survival. Don't you get it? I'm trained to survive. Recently I've seen things that have compromised the chances of that survival, so I'm dealing with them.'

'You're fucking mental.'

Neil had been walking up and down in relaxed fashion in front of David, but now he stopped and glared at his captive. David didn't like the look on his face.

'If I hear you say one more time that I'm insane, I swear, I'll fucking kill you right here.'

He was leaning forward and his face was close to David's now, close enough for David to smell a mixture of sweat and something else – alcohol? – coming off his body. There was silence for a while, as Neil turned away and started arranging things in a holdall in the corner of the room. Eventually David spoke again.

'Did you have Gulf War Syndrome?'

'What?'

'You mentioned Gulf War Syndrome. Did you have it?'

'I've still got it, it never leaves you.'

'But I thought it didn't officially exist.'

'Lots of things don't officially exist, doesn't mean they're not real. I don't officially exist, as you discovered trying to find me. But I'm here, aren't I, and I've got GWS.'

'What are the symptoms?'

'What's it to you?'

'I'm just interested.'

'Jesus, you must think I'm an idiot.' Neil continued packing things away for a few moments before stopping again. 'Headaches, insomnia, skin rashes, memory loss, stomach ulcers, you name it, I've got it. Fucking army and their secret weapons.'

'Is that what caused it?'

'What else?'

'Stress?'

'Are you saying I'm mental again?'

'No, no,' said David quickly. 'I was just . . .' He tailed off, not knowing what to say next. This wasn't going too well. He still couldn't believe what Neil had told him. Despite what he said, David thought he must've killed Colin, otherwise why go so nuts about Gary?

'How did you kill Gary?'

'You're fucking pushing it.'

'I mean, logistically. We were away over the other end of town. How did you get him to the cliffs?'

'My powers of persuasion.'

'Meaning?'

'Meaning I stole a car, beat him over the head, chucked him in the back, drove up there and pushed him off.'

'Just like that?'

'Just like that. It's easy to push a body over a cliff. Want me to demonstrate how it's done?'

'Look, Neil, I realize you've had a hard time of it in the past . . .'

'Don't fucking patronize me, you little piece of shit. This is just like fucking school all over again. You never, ever thought I was a real human being, did you? I was just a fucking amusement to you, like everyone else was. You never fucking cared about anyone else in your life, so don't start taking the fucking moral high ground with me. I don't care about people either, but at least I'm honest about it. And don't talk about a hard fucking past – you don't know anything about life. My folks are dead, my brother died all those years ago, and I've seen some terrible fucking things in the world, but that doesn't make me a fuck-up.'

'You are a fuck-up.'

'I'm not, you little prick. And even if I was, there doesn't have to be a reason, does there? You just don't get it, do you? It's all cause and effect with you. There has to be a reason for everything. Well, wake the fuck up to the real world, there's a whole world of pointless pain and suffering out there, with no reason for any of it.'

'I don't need a reason, I'm just trying to understand.'

'There's nothing to understand, that's the fucking point . . .'

Just then they heard the stutter and grumble of an old car engine coming from outside. Neil snapped alert. He pulled a pair of socks out of the holdall, stuffed them in David's mouth and secured them with masking tape around his head. David gagged and had to choke back spit and bile. The engine noise stopped, and they heard the clunk of a car door opening and closing above the spatter of raindrops outside. Neil went to the open window frame and glanced out sideways. He seemed to relax and become annoyed at the same time.

'Jesus H,' he whispered. 'You *did* tell someone you were coming here, didn't you? Nicola Cruickshank, eh? Better go and deal with her. Back in a minute.'

David tried for all he was worth to make a screaming noise, but all that would come out of his blocked throat was a pathetic whimper. He started to jerk around in the chair, trying to make a sound with the chair legs against the stone floor. But Neil appeared at the edge of his vision and he felt yet another almighty whack on the side of the head, making him feel sick and dizzy all over again.

'Jesus Christ,' said Neil, 'you are truly fucking pathetic.'

It was the last thing David heard before he passed out again.

Nicola got out the car in the rain and headed towards the cottages. There was nothing here. No sign of David, or any other life for that matter. She took in the collapsed house nearest the sea, then rounded the back of the cottages. She thought, briefly, that she heard something, a windy, whining sound, but with the blustery rain in her ears she quickly dismissed it. As she neared the next cottage she spotted that one of the window frames was unboarded. She headed towards the opening, but just before she got there she spotted a glimpse of metallic colour to her left, down in the ravine just past Meg's Craig. She changed direction and headed towards the ravine. As she neared the edge, she could see, hidden amongst the dense foliage, a car. It was angled downwards and to the side so that she could see the car's exposed underbelly, about a hundred yards away, caught up in some ancient, wiry tree branches and thick bushy undergrowth. She moved round to the side and more of the car began to be revealed. It was David's car, and judging by the angle, it had been pushed or driven off the cliff, only it hadn't made it past the first bursts of greenery. Her pulse boomed in her ears as she reached for her mobile. She was about to venture further down the steep incline to see if anyone was still inside when suddenly her head exploded with pain, crippling debilitating pain which swept instantly through her body. She felt a strong, thick arm cradle her, preventing her from falling forwards, and then she was gone, descended into blackness.

14

All at Sea

Her head hurt like hell and at first it felt like she'd pissed herself, but as she gradually became more aware of the dampness in her pants and jeans she realized it was cold, not warm. She opened her eyes and tried to focus, and saw that she was sitting in a puddle of water on a rough concrete floor. Her back and arms were awkward and painful, and as she tried to move she became aware she was somehow tied to a radiator against the wall, the sharpness of a metal edge jutting into her back, the empty pipework clanking as she struggled. She looked around the room, trying to get her bearings.

'Welcome to the party.'

She heard the voice before she could locate the owner, but then he came into view on her left and she recognized straight away the boy from school who had gone off to be a marine. He looked older, of course, and somehow more composed than the angry little coiled spring she'd vaguely known at school. So this is how it was going to be, she thought. She heard a muffled, throaty noise coming from the other direction and turned to see David, trussed to a chair, straining so that it looked as if the veins in his neck were going to burst.

'For fuck's sake,' said Neil and strode over to David, tearing the masking tape from his face and pulling the socks out his mouth. 'Are you going to shut up with that pathetic whining or what?'

'Let her go,' said David.

'Yeah, right.'

'You've got a problem with me – that's fine, but Nicola's got nothing to do with it, you can let her go.'

'She's here, isn't she? That means she's got everything to do with it.'

'He's got a point,' said Nicola, finding her voice.

David looked at her as if she was growing an extra head.

'Whose side are you on? I'm trying to get you out of this.'

'I'm just saying,' said Nicola. 'He's not stupid, are you, Neil? He can't let me go, now that I know about him and this place. Talk sense, David.'

'Yeah, talk sense, David,' chimed Neil.

'Jesus H,' said David.

'But seeing as how I'm here now and a bit of a captive audience, any chance I can get an explanation about why exactly I've been knocked unconscious and tied to a radiator?'

'I've already done all this with laughing boy over here,' said Neil, nodding towards David. 'He can fill you in if he likes.'

Nicola looked at David, who rolled his eyes. There was silence for a minute before David said, 'Are you serious?'

'Well, I'm not going anywhere,' said Nicola.

David looked at Neil who swept his hand towards him, as if giving him the floor. David shook his head.

'Well, Neil says that he was there when Colin died, on the cliff-top, and claims that it was an accident.'

'There's no fucking "claims" about it.'

'He joined the Marines, got Gulf War Syndrome, saw terrible things, quit, joined the police, quit, his folks died, he went abroad to fight as a mercenary, came back, started getting paranoid about people thinking he killed Colin, started following Gary, and killed him by shoving him off the cliffs a fortnight ago. Now he's going to do the same to us.'

'He sounds mental.'

'Don't call him that. He doesn't like it when you call him that.'

'Oh, a sensitive type of killer, is he?'

'I am fucking here, you know, you pair of smart-arse cunts. Very nice banter, considering the situation you're in.'

'We're just making the best of things,' said Nicola. 'You do know, of course, that folk will come and find us. You don't think I trekked out here without informing the authorities about our suspicions.'

'Nice try, but laughing boy already tried that one,' said Neil. 'And all that happened was that his girlfriend turned up. It's hardly the fucking SAS. What next, is your daughter gonna show up and try to overpower me?'

At the mention of her daughter Nicola's heart sank. She had been deliberately upbeat since she'd come round, trying to persuade herself that the situation they were in wasn't real, wasn't dangerous, wasn't fucking deadly. But the mention of Amy brought it all home. This wasn't a laughing matter, not by a country mile. It was deadly serious and she was going to have to keep her wits about her and hope for some kind of a way out. She looked at David more closely. His face was quite badly battered – his left eye had just about closed and his mouth seemed misshapen and swollen – and there was blood on the back of his head which had trickled onto his T-shirt. He had obviously had more than just the single smack to the head that she'd so far experienced. She looked now at Neil, trying to gauge the man. He didn't seem edgy, manic or mad; he looked quietly confident, as if he were about to go in for a job interview and he knew fine well he was the best qualified candidate. She looked back at David again, whose hangdog face seemed bereft of ideas.

'You look like shit,' she said, but with a kind edge to her voice.

'He does, doesn't he?' said Neil. 'He needs to look after himself.'

'I was talking to David.'

'I'm OK,' said David, in a voice that sounded far from it.

She turned to Neil.

'This makes you feel like the big man, I take it?'

Neil pretended cartoonishly as if he was considering what she said. 'Yeah, pretty much.'

'I assume you realize that all this violence and paranoia come about because of an inferiority complex brought about by your parents' lack of encouragement when you were younger.'

'Ah, I see we have another student of popular psychology. Did you ever consider that I just like being violent? It's what I'm trained to do, after all, and there's a certain amount of professional pride in doing what you've been taught to do well.'

'Jesus Christ,' said David. 'Professional pride? Don't make me fucking laugh. That's not what this is about. This is about you being a fucking madman.'

Nicola watched as Neil strode over towards David and belted him full force with a large, solid torch across the back of the head. A small splurt of blood flew from the injury and David slumped unconscious in the chair. Neil turned to Nicola, shaking his head and checking the torch for damage.

'I have warned him repeatedly about calling me mad,' he said, sitting down on the bed next to the chair and David's slumped body. 'The question now is, what the fuck am I going to do with the pair of you?'

'I suppose you've already considered letting us go, and decided that's not an option.'

'You suppose correct.'

Nicola didn't know what to say next. All the snappy banter in the world wasn't going to talk the pair of them out of this hole, that was obvious. She thought about her family. She hadn't told her parents why she'd turned up in Arbroath, or why she wanted to borrow the car, because it seemed like such a silly escapade, that she was just worrying over nothing, and she didn't want them to think she was daft. Mistake. She thought of Amy, how she'd hurriedly packed her off at a friend's house earlier this morning, just a quick kiss goodbye at the door and not even turning back to watch her go in. She felt her pulse quicken in her throat, almost choking her, as she briefly considered that might be the last time she'd ever see her daughter, that her daughter's last memory of her mum would be getting shunted off to a pal's and left while she headed north. After a moment she managed to control her emotions. That sort of shit wasn't going to get her out of this. She had to stay strong, keep her wits about her. Looking at Neil now he seemed cleverer than she remembered him, more aware, more slyly intelligent and knowledgeable. He was also built like a brick shithouse and clearly knew how to handle himself. She couldn't think of a way out. She would just bide her time, wait and see if an opening arose.

'Well, I'm going to have to move you while I think about what to do,' said Neil, as much to himself as to Nicola.

'Why?'

'Don't get me wrong, love, I don't think for a minute the police are haring it up here to arrest me. But you pair both found me in this place, and I guess others will in time. It just isn't safe to use it any more.'

'And where are you going to take us? To your secret underground lair?'

Neil looked at her closely, a thin smile spreading across his face.

'Close, but no cigar,' he said. 'I do have a place that I use for contingencies, though.'

'What, more of a hideaway than an abandoned cottage about to fall into the sea?'

'Much more. Trouble is, I can't carry the pair of you to the boat at once, and I can't be arsed with you trying to run off.'

The boat? thought Nicola. Where the fuck were they going? Neil had gotten up off the bed and was slowly walking towards her.

'Wait a minute, Neil. I don't know what you're thinking, but you don't have to do anything rash, you can trust me not to try to escape.'

'We both know that's not true,' said Neil, playing with the torch in his hand. He looked as if he had made a decision. 'I'll carry you to the boat one at a time, laughing boy first. But I'm afraid that means I'm going to have to knock you out.'

'Now, hang on, Neil, there's no need for that, I promise I won't be any trouble.' She was squirming against the radiator at her back, the metal clanking out rhythmically in time.

'Sorry, love,' said Neil as he raised the torch and swung it down hard over the back of her head, sending shards of burning pain through her body.

She dreamt that she was a horse and Amy was riding on her back, digging sharp heels into her sides. She came to with a start, the room solidifying around her. She hadn't moved; she was still tied to the radiator in the cottage. She had no idea how long she'd been unconscious. She was alone. The only sound was the squawk of gulls. She struggled a little, causing more clanking from the radiator, which was digging right into the small of her back. Surely the clanking meant that things were moving, that things could be moved in the radiator, she thought. She knew from having an eight-year-old daughter in the house that things could be ripped from walls pretty easily, even seemingly sturdy things like radiators, even more so in a ramshackle cottage that hadn't seen any attention in Christ knows how long. What she needed was some leverage, though. She pushed herself up the wall slightly, as much as her bound hands would allow, and settled down on her knees, her arms still behind her. Her feet were now pressed against the skirting board. She began to lean forward, pushing with her feet against the wall, but as she did so her shoulders started to ache, the force of her body seemingly focussing on wrenching her arms out their sockets. She relaxed. There didn't seem any other way of doing it, though.

She looked around the room for anything that might help. She could see a couple of bits of broken glass over by the window, but too far away to reach, and anyway she couldn't see her wrist bindings, didn't know if they could be cut easily, and wouldn't know how to reach the glass with her tied hands anyway. There was nothing else for it, she was just going to have to push like hell and hope that she didn't dislocate her arms. She steeled herself for the pain and tensed her legs, ready to push against the wall for all she was worth. She took a couple of big, deep breaths, counted slowly to three and then strained, pushing with all her might against the wall. The pain shooting across her collarbone and into her shoulders was immense, and she thought she would pass out from the initial shock of it, but she kept pushing, pushing, pushing, straining every sinew in her body. A brief image flitted across her mind of herself as the figurehead of a pirate ship, straining proudly into harsh northerly winds and stormy seas, and then, just as she was about to be overwhelmed by the pain in her arms, her back, her whole body, the resistance from the wall behind her gave way, there was an explosion of plasterboard and the sound of metal and stone being wrenched apart, and she collapsed face down on the cold, wet floor, the radiator, now free from the wall, landing on top of her in a flurry of rubble and dust. She lay panting for a few seconds on the floor, recovering from the effort. Her shoulders were on fire. She rolled over and kicked the radiator to one side. The noise of it clanking onto the concrete seemed obscenely loud in her ears. She had been tied to the radiator wall mount with some kind of thick blue plastic twine, but there was enough give in it now for it to roll easily off her hands. She rubbed her wrists, then her shoulders. She could still move her arms, so nothing was dislocated or broken. She rubbed her face and shook her head to clear her thoughts, then picked herself off the floor and made for the unboarded window.

Outside it was still daytime, the thick grey skies casting unrelenting rain down on the earth. She had no idea how long she'd been out. She checked her pockets but the car key and mobile were gone. Neil. Where the hell was he taking David? He had mentioned a boat. She ran to the edge of the ravine where she had seen David's car. Now her parents' car had joined it, about thirty yards further down the slope, tangled up in a dense arrangement of thick, spongy weeds and plants.

Just then a movement caught her eye. Down on the shore, at the bottom of the ravine, were two figures. One was lying on the sand, the other, having clearly just dumped the body there, was beginning to head back up the shore towards the bottom of the ravine where Nicola now noticed a tiny, overgrown path that was cut into the hillside, zigzagging its way through the dense grass. He must be coming back to get her, she thought. As she watched, the figure looked up the ravine and stopped in his tracks. She quickly ducked down to lie flat on her chest, feeling the rain soaking through her, but she knew she was too late. Neil had seen her. She tried to work out what that meant. As she was trying to think, Neil seemed to hesitate for a moment, then turned towards a large, dark rock at the bottom of the cliff. From here Nicola could see several tiny, upturned boats behind the rock, sheltered from view from the sea. Neil turned one of the boats over and started dragging it towards the shoreline.

Nicola had to think fast. She had no phone. She had no car. The nearest people were in Auchmithie, and that was at least fifteen minutes of running across muddy fields. There wasn't time. She didn't know where Neil was taking David, but if it was out at sea and she lost sight of them, then it was all over. She made a decision. She waited until she was sure Neil wasn't looking back up the ravine and began searching for the start of the path that led down to the sea, keeping a watchful eye on the figure down below and ready to dodge for cover if he looked her way.

'Fucking hell.'

David heard the sound of swearing over the shush of the sea lapping in on the shore next to him. He was lying on the beach, his hands tied behind his back, his feet bound together. He rolled over onto his side to look in the direction of the voice. Neil was dragging a small wooden boat towards him, muttering under his breath, a large crescent of grass-smothered cliff face looming behind him.

'You never told me she was so resourceful,' said Neil, noticing David was awake.

'What?'

'Your fucking girlfriend. She's escaped. I should've tied her to the fucking bed, not the radiator. What a fucking idiot. Anyway, that means she's off for help, so we'd better get a bend on. Luckily I got rid of her car, so we've got a bit of time.'

Nicola had escaped, fucking good for her, thought David. But then, shit, that left him alone with this fucking maniac. Shit.

'Where are you taking me?'

'You'll find out soon enough.'

'Look, Neil, she's gone, the game's up, surely you can see that? Let me go and we can sort something out.'

'Exactly how can we sort something out?' said Neil, dragging the boat to the edge of the water, so that the prow was being slapped by little waves. 'You know I killed Gary, so how can I possibly let you go? And don't even bother saying you won't tell anyone, if that's what you were going to say next. Was that what you were going to say next?'

'I was thinking about it.'

'Well, don't waste your breath. It wouldn't actually matter whether or not you did ever tell anyone, I wouldn't *know* whether you had told anyone or not, and I would always know that you were out there and I would worry about whether you would tell someone some day. I'm not about to put myself in that position.'

'So what are you going to do?'

'Good question. I don't know. I need time to think. Which is why we should stop talking shite and get in the boat. Now, to make things a little easier, I'm going to untie your legs. I already carried you down that fucking path,' he glanced back up at the ravine behind him, 'which was probably a mistake. You're not a fucking baby, and you can walk from now on. But it goes without saying, don't get any ideas. The first time you try to run off I'll kick seven shades of shite out of you. The second time, I'll probably just kill you, to fucking hang with it. OK?'

David just nodded. He felt barely capable of walking, let alone running anywhere, so he passively lay there as Neil cut through the plastic bindings around his ankles with a dangerous-looking knife he flicked from his pocket.

'What about the wrists?'

218

'You're joking, aren't you? You think I'm a fucking idiot?'

'Just thought I'd ask. You don't ask, you don't get.'

'Got any other stupid questions, before we go?'

'Where are you taking me?'

'You already asked that one.'

'You didn't answer.'

'That's right. I didn't. Now get in.'

David didn't see any alternative. He looked back up the ravine. Nicola was free, he was genuinely thankful for that. She was out of this whole mess. She would surely go for help, but what form would that take? How do you even get in touch with the coastguard, and how long did they take to get their shit together? Or would the police be quicker? In one sense, he was glad it wasn't him having to explain the situation to the locals in the But 'n' Ben, then again to the coastguard, the police or whoever else, but then he realized that was ridiculous. He would much rather be doing that than be here, in the hands of a fucking madman who would probably just push him over the edge of the boat when they got far enough out to sea. But he wouldn't want to swap positions with Nicola – that would put her here. Was that what love was, refusing to swap positions with your lover to place them in the arms of a psychotic killer? It felt like as good a definition as any to him at that moment, although he could see how you might have difficulty working that into a love song.

What if Neil did push him over the side of the boat once they were out at sea? His hands were tied, he wasn't that good a swimmer anyway and, even in summer, the North Sea would freeze you to death in a matter of minutes. He'd heard somewhere that drowning was a particularly calm and peaceful way to die, but he figured that was a lot of bullshit. There was no such thing as a calm way to die if you didn't want to fucking die. And he very definitely didn't want to die. He wanted to live, with Nicola, with Amy, with his memories of Colin and Gary, and his memories of this moment, and all his possible futures ahead of him. He wanted to be able to reminisce one day in the future with Nicola, shaking their heads in disbelief and laughing about the time that nutter Neil had held them both captive, then she'd escaped and gone for help but it had come too late, because he was already dead . . .

Fuck. Fucking fuck. He had to think straight. He was going to die, and he had to do something about that. But what? He had been battered half a dozen times since Neil captured him, and it felt as if he was only a thin stretch of consciousness away from passing out again. He had to try and stay calm. Keep on Neil's right side. Don't rock the boat, so to speak. Part of him couldn't believe he was making bad jokes like that to himself at a time like this. What a fucking idiot. What a fucking waste-of-space idiot. Why had he even come back to this stupid part of the world? Every time he came back, someone else died, only this time it was going to be him. He felt like crying, and then got angry at himself for being so pathetic.

'Hurry the fuck up, will you?' Neil was standing by the boat, toying with that torch again. It hadn't escaped David's notice that he'd used a knife to undo his ankle ties, so there were any number of ways in which Neil could help him become a corpse, nice and simple. With a heart as turbulent as the North Sea in front of him, David climbed into the boat and Neil pushed them off, starting the outboard motor with a putter and a puff of diesel smoke and pointing the boat south-west, heading towards the stretch of cliffs between them and Arbroath.

Nicola watched them take to the sea and increased her speed down the cliff path, taking the rough steps in leaps and scrambles. She was sure they hadn't seen her descent. By the time she made it to the shore they had only been on the water for a few minutes, and were still some way from clearing the headland at the south-west corner of the bay. She headed straight for the large rock from where she'd seen Neil retrieve a boat and sure enough, there were two more small rowing boats hidden there. She could hardly believe he'd left the boats here, knowing that she'd escaped. Maybe he hadn't seen her after all. But surely he would've come back up to get her in that case. Then it clicked – he *had* seen her, but he'd assumed that she would run off for help. It hadn't even occurred to him that she, being a fucking idiot helpless woman, would try and follow them without anyone else as back-up. Typical fucking man, she thought. OK, not all men, just the uber-macho, psychopathic killing machine ones.

Of the two boats in front of her, one didn't have a motor on it. She flipped the other one and it didn't look up to much either – paint almost completely peeled off, the rather flaky wooden planks looking as if they might spring apart given the slightest provocation. It would have to do. She started pulling it down to the sea, struggling at first with the inertia of the sand, but gaining momentum as she went. Out at sea Neil and David were nearing the headland. In a few more minutes they would be round it and out of sight. She ran round the back of the boat, heaved it into the water and jumped in. She had no idea about these outboard motors, but she'd seen them used on television. There was always a cord to pull, wasn't there? She hunted around under the motor and her hand clunked against a built-in storage box, secured with a padlock. She felt around the box and found a thick, oily cord coiled up behind it. She gave it a yank. Nothing. She tried again. Still nothing. Looking up, she could see the other boat almost at the headland. She pushed her feet against the stern of the boat and pulled as hard as she could, jerking backwards and falling over into the boat as the motor sparked into life with a whine like a scooter's engine. A pungent mix of diesel fumes and rotting fish surrounded her.

She sat up and started guiding the boat. Ahead of her she could still see the other boat, slowly edging its way around the next headland. She headed straight out to sea rather than follow it around the bay, giving her a better angle to keep it in her sights. She wondered about David. Was he all right? Was he even still alive? Surely he must be. Why would Neil be taking him anywhere if he was already dead? But then maybe he was just going to dump the body out at sea. The boat was small on the horizon, but it looked as if the two figures in it were sitting upright. She couldn't believe she was thinking as logically and calmly as this about someone's possible death, but then she'd become used to thinking about death since David had come back into her life. If only she hadn't emailed him that day, asking him to that stupid school reunion, she thought. But then if she hadn't, they would never have met up again. And if they hadn't met up again ... She realized that she loved him. Not in the sappy love-song meaning of the word, but she clearly felt strongly enough to be chasing a bloody maniac around the Angus coastline in an effort to save his life. That would do as a definition of love, wouldn't it?

She noticed it was getting a little darker. The skies were still full of grey, drizzling clouds, but whatever sorry excuse for a sun was lurking behind them, it was thinking about giving up on the day. She noticed as well that she was having to navigate between strange little flags bobbing on the surface of the sea. Probably the sites of lobster pots strung out along the seabed, she thought. She momentarily imagined herself as a lobster, scuttling along down there in her big shell without a care in the world, only to find a trapdoor snapping shut behind her. Within twenty-four hours she would be some posh bastard's dinner. What a way to go.

She looked at the boat in front of her, hugging the coastline. Where the hell was Neil heading? She urged the puttering engine on her own crawling vessel to crank itself up and push her onwards through the sluggish mass of indifferent water between her and David.

15

The Cave

David couldn't really believe what he was seeing. He was sitting in the prow of the boat and for the last few minutes had been stealing glances backwards as the small dot on the horizon resolved itself into a boat. They were being followed and Neil hadn't noticed. He could only assume that Nicola had managed to flag down help sooner than Neil imagined, and the thought exhilarated him. He was simultaneously thrilled that Nicola was coming to help him and appalled at the thought of her putting herself in danger again after having escaped. Mostly he was thrilled. He wanted to fucking marry that woman right now. He was trying as hard as possible not to make it obvious he was looking at the distant boat, but the allure of the curved shape on the water behind them transfixed his mind, and he felt even more self-conscious if he didn't look.

They had been on the sea now for something like twenty minutes. He had continued to quiz Neil about their destination, but Neil just navigated onwards stony-faced, steering the boat south-west along the coastline. David tried to distract himself by examining the cliffs and bays as they passed by. He had been along this stretch of coastline only a week ago with Nicola and Amy, but the looming, blood-red sandstone monsters that paraded past now seemed to bear no relation to the relatively benign cliffs of last week. The sky was pressing down on the land, the clouds felt low enough to reach up and touch, and the rain was beating heavily down, spotting the sea around them and draining down in rivulets from the clifftops. The water at the base of the cliffs was swirling, foamy and dangerous-looking, rolling and bashing against the rock face like relentless enemies at the gates of a castle, gradually wearing down the defences to infiltrate their way in and take over. They were closer to the land than they had been last weekend, and now David could see all sorts of detail he hadn't been able to then – precarious nests lodged into cracks in the cliff, dark, tiny, ominous caves lurking around the base, the swell and chop of waves tumbling over a barely-submerged jagged rock, boulders like giant pebbles scattered around inaccessible bays, strange holes, gulleys, stacks and blowholes appearing everywhere, giant slabs of slanting red stone stacked unstably one on top of the other like biscuits on a plate. The cliffs seemed an altogether more sinister, more dangerous and more deadly place than they had a week ago in the gentle sunshine. It was amazing what being kidnapped by an insane killer can do for your mood, thought David as he winced at swirling, dizzying waves crashing against an isolated stack. A few more years of that kind of abuse and the stack would crumble into the sea, yet another slice of seemingly immovable land succumbing to the relentless, torrential and utterly oblivious power of the sea.

David looked out to the open sea and saw the boat was getting bigger on the horizon – they were being gained on. He wasn't sure how many people were on the boat: he could make out at least one, but there surely must be more than that, he thought.

To David's horror, he noticed Neil slowly following his gaze. With his back to David, Neil sat motionless at the stern for a few seconds, taking in the situation in the hardening rain.

'Jesus fucking H Christ.' He turned and gunned the engine a little more, egging the boat on through the roughening waters. 'How the fuck did she get help so quick?'

David was gutted. The other boat was catching up on them, so it wasn't going to remain a secret forever, but he couldn't believe that his gormless gawking had led to Neil noticing Nicola and the rescue party. Fucking idiot. But he was still massively relieved that there even was a boat out there following them.

That changed everything. At least he wasn't on his own, it wasn't just him against Neil, there were others on their way to help, and that gave him renewed strength.

'Surely there's no point in going on with this,' he said.

'Fucking shut the fuck up.'

'But they know. Everyone knows. It's all over.'

'It's over when I say it's over.'

'But they're bound to catch us. And the coastguard will be on their way.'

'Fuck the coastguard, fuck your girlfriend back there and whoever she's roped into this, and fuck you. They're not going to catch us because we're nearly there, and we'll lose them round the next headland.'

'Nearly where?'

'That's about the tenth time you've asked me that. You're an inquisitive little shit, aren't you? Here's an idea – why don't you shut the fuck up?'

David looked beyond Neil at the other boat. It didn't seem to be getting any bigger, but it was impossible to tell in the rain. He still couldn't make out how many people were on it. He wondered if the coastguard really were on their way, and if so, how long they would take to get here. He wondered what Nicola was thinking on the other boat.

Damn it.

She had been gaining on them for a while, but something seemed to have changed, and they were now travelling at about the same speed. Just as she had been confident about catching them up, they seemed to change direction a little, heading right in towards a headland that from here looked a little like a human head in profile. Then suddenly they were round the headland, staying tight to the contour of the coastline, and she'd lost them.

Nicola tried not to panic as she urged the engine forward. She felt frustration at her slow progress through the waves, shouting 'Come on!' to no one, her voice disappearing into the rain all around her. She kept her eye on the last place she had seen their boat; that was all she could do, stay concentrated and focussed and hope that they'd reappear in front of her once she'd made some way round the headland.

Within five minutes she was at the profiled head where she'd lost them, peering keenly into the rain, the sound of gulls squawking from their nests on the cliff in her ears. Two minutes later she rounded the promontory and . . . nothing. Fuck! She couldn't see another boat anywhere. She frantically scanned along the coastline, and out to sea as well, realizing that this latter effort was pointless – they couldn't have headed out to sea without her seeing them. The light was fading fast, and the rain seemed heavier than ever. She gazed intently ahead along the coast but all she could see was the white fuzz of waves breaking over rocks here and there. For several minutes she scanned backwards and forwards, desperate for something to catch her eye. Nothing.

Think, Nicola. If they're not ahead of you, and they're not further out at sea, then they must have landed somewhere. But where? There didn't seem to be anywhere to land at this part of the coastline – no bay or inlet or anything. She slowly steered the boat in close to the land, the waves rocking her as they rebounded from the bottom of the cliff, forcing her to hold on tight to the side of the boat with one hand. To her left was open sea; to her right, looming so close that it felt like it would topple over onto her, was the cliff, a craggy, dark red terrifying expanse. She continued on for a few minutes until she saw what she thought was a fold in the rock, running vertically for about fifteen feet. As she got up close she realized it wasn't a fold but a crack, about ten feet wide, with a kind of overhanging flap that sheltered it, like a natural sea wall, from the abuse of the waves. It was a sea cave, almost undetectable from the water except when you were really close in, and certainly hidden from view from the land. She looked around again, up and down the coast, and could still see nothing, no boat, no sign whatsoever of Neil and David. They must have gone inside the cave. But it would be dark. She wouldn't be able to see a bloody thing in there. Then she remembered the small built-in box nestling under the boat's motor. It was locked, so she had to boot it open with the heel of her shoe. Inside were a basic first-aid kit, a flare gun and a torch. She lifted the torch and tested it, and a strong beam of light pierced the rain in front of her, playing across the rough sandy rock above the cave entrance. Good enough. With one hand holding the torch and the other steering the motor, she guided the boat slowly into the cave mouth, her pounding heart suddenly becoming loud in her ears as the noise of the rain and the waves outside the cave receded into the background.

'You live in a fucking cave?' David was laughing despite himself. 'You live as a fucking hermit, in a cave?'

Even in the torchlight he could see from Neil's face that this was not something to be laughing about, unless he wanted another taste of Mr Torch. Nevertheless, for some reason he found this incredibly funny. He imagined hermits as mad, old grizzly guys, with matted beards and fishbone necklaces, going slowly insane in the darkness of their hovel, eating whelks and drinking rainwater out of an old hat. Now that he looked at Neil again, he could see him fitting that description in a few years' time, although he had clearly already done the going insane part. This all fitted together nicely, thought David. Sitting here in a dark cave, brooding over your life and all the mistakes you'd made, with nothing else to occupy you except the odd echoing splosh and the distant sound of the sea, well that would send anyone fucking mental, wouldn't it? And if you were halfway to being a violent lunatic anyway, as Neil obviously had been, this sort of sensory deprivation environment was pretty much guaranteed to send you tumbling over the edge.

He looked again at Neil's face and abruptly stopped laughing. Gazing into the hollow eyes of his former schoolfriend, he felt sorry for him, as if life had dealt him a particularly shitty hand, and even then he hadn't handled what he'd had dished out to him at all well. Circumstance had been against Neil from the start, thought David, and really he was to be pitied, not feared. Just then Neil produced the knife from his pocket and angled it pointedly towards David. It would probably be easier to feel sympathy for the guy if he wasn't threatening him at knifepoint, with, presumably, a view to killing him at some point in the not too distant future, he thought. Then he reminded himself Neil had pointlessly killed an old schoolfriend, and – even giving him the benefit of the doubt – he'd been present at the death of another friend, and had been at least partly responsible for that. Fuck sympathy, he thought.

'Get out the fucking boat.'

They had puttered into the cave and onwards for about five minutes in almost complete darkness, just the beam of the torch guiding them as the damp, stone ceiling above their heads gradually descended until they had to crouch in the boat, making David shudder with claustrophobia. But then the ceiling seemed to disappear and a quick coolness to the air and the echoing of their boat engine heralded a wide-open space, a cavern of a place, although David couldn't actually glean its dimensions in the dismal light. He noticed that there was some additional light coming in from somewhere, more than there had been when they entered the cave, so presumably there was another way out. David was briefly proud of himself for noting this instinctively, but then was thrown into depression again when he thought of Neil, the knife and his hand ties. Then he thought of the rescue boat coming, and brightened up again. His feelings were all over the fucking place, he realized.

'I said get out the fucking boat.'

Neil gave him a shove and he stumbled out, splashing up to his knees in the water which was lapping at the edge of a clear area of sloping shingle. He slowly trooped up the incline away from the boat. Behind them David could hear nothing. No boat, no engine, nothing. Maybe the other boat hadn't seen them come in here, or they hadn't been able to find the entrance to the cave.

He felt the beginnings of a panic attack creeping up on him, so he tried to breathe deeply as he sat down on the shingle.

'Get up. Fucking move.'

Neil booted him hard in the ribs and, despite the pain and the mounting panic and claustrophobia, David rose and trudged on. Following Neil's directions they walked on to a smaller sheltered area, like an ante-room off the main cave, which was full of crates covered in tarpaulin. A mattress lay in the corner and a pot sat over a rough fireplace in the middle. It looked as if Neil was set for life here, thought David.

'How long have you lived here?'

'About a year, on and off.'

'Jesus Christ.'

Neil headed straight for one of the crates and dug about inside. He emerged with something black and shiny in his hand and David felt sick. It was a gun. Neil made a point of showing it to David, hefting it in his hand to show its weight, its deadly reality.

'Understand?' said Neil. 'Don't get any fucking ideas.'

'What happens when that other boat finds us? Are you going to shoot them all? Then me? There will be others, Neil. Don't you see? This is all over.'

'They might not find us.'

'And if they don't? What exactly are you going to do?'

Neil looked exasperated from all the questions, and from having to keep re-evaluating his situation, thinking on his feet. He looked as if he had made up his mind.

'Well, my old school pal, then I kill you and disappear. I've done it before, and it's amazing how things can blow over if you give them a while.'

'So what, you're just going to shoot me in a cave, is that it? It seems like an awful lot of trouble, when you could've just pushed me in the water out at sea.'

In the dim torchlight, David saw Neil's face glisten with a mixture of rain and sweat. His own brow was slick with moisture. Neil was quietly grinning at him.

'No, I'm not going to shoot you in a cave,' he said. 'I'm going to throw you off a cliff. Now move.'

With that Neil walked quickly towards David, giving him yet another good belt with the torch across the head, the stars in David's vision blending with the swirling torchlight. Neil pointed him out of the alcove and towards the back of the cave. David had no option but to walk towards the darkness.

But just then they heard a sound like a distant lawnmower. Neil stopped. It was the motor of the other boat! David felt elated, but didn't have too long to think as Neil shoved him over behind a slippery, mossy rock.

'Don't make a fucking sound,' said Neil, crouching down next to him and edging a look round the rock. David couldn't see past the rock, but he could see a beam of light from a torch on the boat, dancing around the space of the cavern like a spotlight raking the sky for enemy bombers. Neil's torch was off. David thought he should warn the folk in the other boat that Neil was lying in wait, but just as he was about to shout out his ears exploded as the sound of gunshots next to him ricocheted around the cavern, bouncing off the wet rocks in every direction, echoing backwards and forwards and filling his head with torrents of noise. Shit, Neil was firing on them.

David tried to get up but felt the butt of the gun smash into his temple and stumbled to the ground. Then he felt Neil's hand pulling at his arms behind his back, dragging him upwards and pushing him deeper into the cave. They stumbled on for a distance over the rough rock in almost pitch darkness until Neil was forced to put his torch on to see where they were going. David quickly looked around, wondering forlornly if an escape route would present itself, but he could see nothing. The torch behind them had gone out – did that mean someone had been shot? Not necessarily – they would obviously put their torches off when the firing started, otherwise they were sitting ducks. Surely they could see Neil's torch now? With the sound of gunshot still ringing in his ears, he couldn't hear anything behind them, and couldn't see anyone either. How the hell did he get everyone into this mess? People shooting at other people in a damp sea cave – how had it come to this? All he did was attend a school reunion, for fuck's sake.

'This way,' said Neil, grabbing David and pushing him to the left. David had looked that way but had only seen bare, dripping walls, but as they got closer he saw an opening. As they reached the opening Neil's torchlight fell upon it briefly, and David couldn't believe it – it was a spiral staircase, cut out of the rock, which went up as far as he could see. What the hell?

'Smugglers,' said Neil, as if reading his mind. 'Now up. And get a fucking move on.'

David felt the cool violence of the gun poking into his back and stumbled on. The staircase was narrow and cramped and the steps uneven and crumbling, and with his hands still tied behind his back it was hard going to hoist himself up, but somehow the presence of a gun in the vicinity of his lower back spurred him on. He wondered what was happening back in the cavern. He still hadn't heard anything. He hoped to hell they would find this staircase and that they would catch up with him and his maniac kidnapper soon. With Neil's torchlight swinging past his shoulders and around the spiral space it felt fleetingly like he was at a club with a strobe light on. He stumbled on, as if in a weird nightmare, hoping all this would end soon.

Nicola stayed down in the boat, making sure there were no more bullets heading in her direction. When she poked her head over the prow she couldn't see anything, the place was virtually total blackness. She had reached the shingle landing area when the shooting started. She was about to get out the boat when she remembered the box. She raked about under the outboard motor and felt her hand slip around the handle of the flare gun. She wasn't sure what the hell she was going to do with it in a cave, but instinctively felt it could be useful. She inched out over the side of the boat and scuttled up the shore, keeping her head down. As she looked ahead she saw a torch come on. She couldn't believe her luck. She was stumbling over slippery rocks and ankle-deep pools of stagnant water, but kept her eye firmly on the spotlight of the torch up ahead. In the waving light she was sure she caught a glimpse of two figures. At least David was still alive, then, she thought, although Neil had a gun which obviously put him at an advantage. Where the hell were they headed? As far as she could tell there was nothing but deeper cave back there, and no way out, although she had noticed that a small amount of ambient light was making its way in here from somewhere.

As she watched the two shadowy figures up ahead, the light from the torch suddenly did something funny, not exactly switching off, but diminishing greatly, as if they had gone behind something. She had been travelling sideways for the last couple of minutes until she found the cave wall. From there she felt her way round, the clammy damp of it against her palms. Up ahead of her the torchlight was becoming a faint glow, like a house light on a dimmer switch, but it was still enough to follow. She made her way as quickly as possible along the slimy cave wall, still not willing to switch her own torch on. The faint glow up ahead was getting dimmer but closer, and then the wall under her hand fell away and she was standing at an opening in the cave wall. The torchlight was spilling down from above, and in the glow she could see a set of spiral steps. Another way out. She wondered what the hell Neil was thinking of now as she started up the stairs, three at a time, her torch in one pocket, the flare gun tightly in the grip of her other hand.

David was dizzy from the repetitive turning and climbing, as well as the umpteen blows he'd received. He couldn't think at all. For a while, in the concentration of not falling over or passing out, he was mesmerized by the repeating steps under his feet, and forgot completely where he was and what he was doing. It reminded him of that black monument in Edinburgh's Princes

Street that he'd made the mistake of climbing up once. By the end of it he could hardly squeeze up the cramped space, and then he'd met a large American coming down and had to backtrack dozens and dozens of steps. He came to and almost fell over. How long had they been going up now? It seemed like forever, but in a rare moment of lucidity he realized that his mind was almost certainly playing tricks on him, and that it was probably only a few minutes. As they climbed, the air around them became drier and warmer, and David thought he could smell earth rather than dank dampness all around him. Neil was still coming up close behind him, issuing a reminding prod with the gun in his back every few steps. Just when David again thought he was about to pass out, as a wave of nausea passed over him, the steps stopped abruptly at a landing. He looked up at the low stone ceiling and there was a rough wooden hatch embedded in it. David just stood there exhausted, slouched and panting, his arms still behind his back, the ties cutting into his wrists, his hands numb. He did a quick inventory of how his body felt. His kidneys or liver or whatever it was back there was still aching, and now his thighs burned from the exertion of the climb. His neck and head were throwing out bursting throbs of pain at intermittent intervals, and his jaw felt loose. His forehead was a solid wall of pain, but his brain seemed to be blocking that out. Probably for the best.

As he stood wondering what the hell was going to happen next, Neil started playing with the hatch, jiggling it backwards and forwards. It was stiff but eventually he jerked it downwards. Above it was a small cavity leading upwards, ending in a rough stone slab roof about the size of a manhole cover. He reached in and pulled out a rope ladder. He gave David a sly look, smugly aware that his captive wasn't about to go running off or even try to move, then quickly climbed the ladder and pushed at the stone slab for a few moments before it opened out and the grey skies of evening appeared above them. David could see that the slab had a thick covering of earth and grass; small clumps of mud and turf fell from it, tumbling down as rain came pelting in the opening. Neil descended again, his square face glistening and muddy from fallen debris. He motioned for David to climb.

David tried to indicate his hands tied behind his back, but the motion of lifting his arms sent ripples of pain through his shoulders. 'I can't climb up,' he said. 'Not with my hands tied.'

Neil seemed to consider this for a moment, before quickly whipping out his knife and cutting the ties behind David's back. He immediately stuck the gun in David's back.

'Just remember I've got this,' he said. 'So don't be a clever bastard. Climb.'

The rain was pouring in through the hole above them as David rubbed his wrists, shaking his hands to get the circulation back, then took hold of the rope ladder. As he did so he heard the distinct sound of footsteps on stone from beneath them. As David stood hesitating, not knowing what to do, the footsteps got louder and louder in only a few seconds. They were being caught up, and fast. Neil punched him in the back of the head and poked the gun into his back.

'Fucking move. Now!'

David started up the rope ladder, swinging as he went. He was trying to go as slowly as possible, but there was hardly any length of ladder, so he was soon at the top. He pulled himself up through the opening, the rain pounding against his head and the grass around it, the wet earth feeling fresh on his hands. He rolled over onto his side and as he looked back Neil's hands and head emerged from the hole. As he watched, more of Neil came into view and then, almost without thinking, with a sudden rush of adrenalin he shot his left leg out with all his might towards Neil's right hand holding the gun. His foot collided with Neil's wrist, making Neil lose his grip on the grass, and the gun skittered away across the greasy ground. Neil reached for the gun but was too late, then grabbed David's ankle, hauling him towards him while also using the ballast of his body to pull himself up out the hole completely. David instinctively swung his other leg round and caught Neil on the jaw with an almost perfect connection, something he would've been proud of on the football pitch in other circumstances, and Neil swayed from the contact, briefly loosening his grip on David's ankle. David scrambled towards the gun, which was about five yards away, noticing out of the corner of his eye that they were now on a clifftop and, of course, it dawned on him as he spotted a small memorial stone a few yards away, it was the place where both Colin and Gary had died. As his body scampered and slid across the wet grass his mind whirled with it all – this was Neil's plan all along, for him to meet the same death as the other two. Was it for neatness' sake, or something else? All this passed across his mind in a split second, the same length of time it took for Neil to grab hold of his ankle again before lunging forward and falling on top of David just as he reached the gun with his right hand. The force of Neil landing on him just as he was picking up the gun sent the weapon flying out of his grasp again. They both lay in a heap and watched as the gun, seemingly taking forever, arced its way through the rain-sodden air away from them before disappearing over the edge of the cliff ten feet away.

For a moment they both lay there. Neil came to his senses first, grabbing David with one hand and hauling him up to his feet. With the other hand he pulled the knife out of his pocket and held it to David's stomach.

'Now, hold on there.'

The voice came from behind them, heard clearly above the sound of the rain. They both turned, rainwater spraying off their heads, to see Nicola standing next to the opening in the ground, a gun in her hand.

They stood like that for a second, each of them taking in the situation.

'Was that a gun I saw going over the cliff?' said Nicola calmly.

Neil tightened his grip on David and took two steps backwards, hauling David with him. They were standing about a foot away from the edge of the cliff. He angled the handle of the knife down to show the whole length of the blade to Nicola while still keeping the blade pressed into David's stomach.

'I've still got this,' he said. 'If you do anything, I'll kill your boyfriend right here.'

'Technically, he's not my boyfriend.'

'I don't think this is quite the time for this,' said David.

'Well, we've never really got around to talking about things in those terms, have we?'

'Shut up, you fucking slag,' said Neil.

'Now, that's not very civil, is it?' said Nicola. 'I think we all have to try to stay calm.'

'Don't fucking patronize me.'

Just then David seemed to realize something. 'Nicola, where's the rescue party?'

'You're looking at it,' said Nicola.

'What?'

'Sorry, were you expecting the fucking cavalry? I didn't have time to get anyone else roped into this ridiculous escapade. You should thank your lucky stars you've got me.'

'Jesus,' said David.

'When you two lovebirds have quite finished,' said Neil, 'there's the little matter of David's death to deal with.'

'Fuck off, Neil,' said David, struggling to free himself. Neil jabbed the knife into his stomach, and David felt a sharp, precise pain in his abdomen.

'Jesus fucking Christ, Neil, you stabbed me!'

'Shut the fuck up, it's only an inch yet. Any more struggling and I'll finish the fucking job.'

'You fucking stabbed me!' David's face was going white.

'You're not going to kill him,' said Nicola quietly.

'And why not?'

'Because if you try to, I'm going to shoot you.'

'You wouldn't have the bottle. And besides, you probably don't even know how to fire a fucking gun.'

'I can assure you I do have the bottle, and I know full well how to fire a gun. But if you don't want to take my word for it, well, that's a chance you're going to have to take, isn't it? This is a bit like that scene in *Dirty Harry*, isn't it? Or *Reservoir Dogs*.'

'Shut the fuck up,' said Neil.

'Yeah, maybe a little less of the cinema comparisons, eh?' said David weakly.

'Are you still in the huff I didn't bring a superhero to rescue you?'

'I'm not in a huff,' said David, feeling tears welling up in his eyes despite himself. 'I'm glad you're here.'

'Very touching,' said Neil. 'You pair are fucking pathetic, you know that?'

'And what are you?' said Nicola. 'A cowardly killer who won't even face up to his own psychological problems? Instead you go around murdering your old schoolfriends just because you can.'

'Here we go with the psychiatrist bullshit again,' said Neil.

'You're right,' said Nicola. 'I'm sorry. It's way past that, isn't it?'

There was silence again for a moment. The rain beat down on them. Neil and David were at the cliff edge; Nicola was pointing the flare gun at them from about five yards away. Behind them she could see the blinking of the Bell Rock lighthouse, miles out to sea. She tried to use the quiet to weigh up her options. If Neil tried to kill David, she would have to pull the trigger. She didn't even know if you could shoot someone with a flare gun, let alone whether this particular flare gun actually worked or if it was loaded. And for that matter, she had no idea how to use it, whether there was a safety catch on it or something. But if push came to shove, she would have to use it. She looked at David, who seemed petrified. His face was going a grey colour that matched the sky and the expanse of sea behind them. How accurate were flare guns? If she shot Neil, would she also shoot David? Was that better than having him stabbed to death, or the pair of them tumbling over the cliff? She couldn't even begin to imagine what David was thinking, let alone try to second-guess

Neil. They had both clearly been expecting a rather more impressive rescue party, but, well, they were all just going to have to make the best of the situation, weren't they?

'It seems we're at something of a stalemate,' she said after a while.

'It does, doesn't it?' said Neil.

'Why are you doing this, Neil?'

'It's a bit late in the day to be trying to engage me in dialogue, isn't it?'

'I'm genuinely interested,' said Nicola. 'Tell me.'

'I went through all this bullshit with droopy-drawers here,' said Neil. 'You people and your reasons, your fucking cause and effect, your fucking motivations. It makes it easy for you in your safe little lives if people like me do what we do because of broken homes, or abusive parents, or bullying, or what we've seen while fighting in the army. Well, it doesn't work like that. Sometimes in life the past doesn't affect the present. Sometimes people just do stuff, do bad things, because they can and because they don't see any reason not to, and because they can get away with it. Your past doesn't make you who you are; it doesn't turn people into monsters. It doesn't give people excuses for bad behaviour; you don't *need* an excuse for bad behaviour.'

'Are you saying you admit that morally your behaviour is bad?' said Nicola.

'Fuck's sake,' said Neil, tightening his grip on David's collar. 'I've had enough of this.'

He took another small step backwards, so that both he and David were standing right over the edge of the cliff. David made the mistake of looking down behind him, and felt dizzy at the huge drop to jagged rocks below. He quickly looked back towards Nicola. She seemed calm; her face was pale but beautiful. Her hair was plastered across her face and there were flecks of mud across her cheeks and on her hands. But her face seemed to glow in the downpour, it seemed to David like a beacon in the dark, a lighthouse beaming out a signal that, if he could only follow it, would lead him to safety. He felt blood oozing from the wound in his stomach. He had no way of knowing how deep it was or how much blood he'd lost, but he didn't feel too good, whatever was happening in his gut.

'And what about that?' said Nicola to Neil, pointing the gun at David's wound.

'What about it?'

'I presume you deliberately made the first two deaths look like accidents. Well, if you push David off, it's never going to look like an accident now, he's got a fucking big gash in his stomach.'

Neil seemed to consider this for the first time.

'You're right,' he said, and David felt a surge of relief. 'It makes no difference now if I just stab him properly, *then* push him off the cliff, does it? Like you say, the game's up on the accidental death thing, so it hardly matters how he dies now, does it?'

David looked at Nicola.

'Thanks for that,' he said quietly in her direction. 'Thanks for pointing that out for him.'

'Sorry, love. That line of argument didn't quite work out exactly as I planned.'

'Wait,' said Neil, staring at Nicola's hand with a look of increasing incredulity. 'Is that a flare gun?'

Nicola just stared at him, her mouth a thin line.

'A fucking flare gun?' said Neil. 'You were going to try and kill me with a flare gun? That is fucking hilarious. You can't kill someone with a flare gun, you fucking stupid cow. Jesus Christ. I really have had enough of you pair.'

Neil turned to face David and gripped the knife firmly in his hand.

'David! Look out!'

David felt the blade against his soft belly flesh again, and tried to get his hands in the way, feeling the edges of the blade slide along his hands, cutting his palms as it glided. There was no pain, not yet. He felt unsteady on his feet, felt Neil pushing him towards the cliff edge, felt his feet slipping on the wet grass, on the crumbling edge of the cliff. He watched in slow motion as Nicola moved towards the pair of them, skidding across the damp earth like an ice skater, the flare gun raised and pointing at Neil. He was holding on, something in him was keeping him upright, keeping his feet on the edge of the earth, and he watched in amazement as Nicola grabbed at Neil's arm to try and bring the knife out of his stomach, spinning Neil slightly away from David's body so that he was briefly facing Nicola, and then David's eyes were momentarily blinded by a flash of orange light so bright the force of it almost pushed him over the edge. There was an intense burning smell, like fireworks, and he saw a look of shock on Nicola's face as Neil slowly toppled backwards towards the edge of the cliff, clutching at his stomach which was ablaze, the scorching, luminescent orange flame shedding a trail of frantic, fizzing sparks as he stumbled back. He watched Nicola try to grab for Neil, but she couldn't reach his hands which were scrabbling at his stomach, trying desperately to claw out the distress flare firmly embedded there. He caught a glimpse of Neil's shocked face as his footing finally gave way and he fell from the cliff, down through the rain, his stomach blazing like a furious sunset, all the way down to the sea, where his body jolted horrendously on a jutting sandstone outcrop. He lay there, sprawled on his back at an impossible angle, the glow in his stomach gradually petering out like a used-up sparkler.

Nicola couldn't believe she'd shot him. She couldn't take her eyes off the dead body at the bottom of the cliffs, the glow in Neil's stomach fading like an untended fire in the grate overnight. The flare gun hung hot and limp in her hand, and she could smell the firing mechanism, the acrid taste of it burning her nostrils and throat. She felt a hand touch hers and turned to see David looking at her, a lost look in his eyes. She looked down and saw the knife still sticking out of his guts. She slowly guided him away from the edge of the cliff and sat him down on the wet grass. She wiped his brow gently with her hand, then braced him and pulled the knife out. He squirmed, then passed out. She laid him down, took off her jacket and held the material against the gaping wound in his stomach. With her other hand she pointed the flare gun into the sky and pulled the trigger. A flash of orange arced across the evening, illuminating the two of them, slumped on the drenched clifftop. She settled down to wait for the coast-guard to come, pressing as hard as she could on David's stomach, and wishing the rain would stop.

16

The Last Tombstone

The sunlight glinted off the glistening marble tombstone, making David wince. High above a jet trail puffed lazily across the pure blue, as the heat of the sun created a shimmer at the edge of his vision. David could smell the grass and imagined he felt a thrum of energy under his feet from the sun's rays.

They were about a hundred yards from Gary's grave, a little closer to Colin's, and only a stone's throw from the neat line of marines' graves. Neil was not welcome in the chalky ranks of marines' epitaphs and had no family left, so after the routine post-mortem David and Nicola, surprising themselves, had clubbed together to pay for the funeral.

Here they were, seven days after the three of them had last been together on the edge of Arbroath cliffs in the rain, on the verge of ending each other's lives. The sun was shining, and it struck David once again that sunny weather was wholly inappropriate for a funeral, but he said nothing. As the minister started the brief burial ceremony, he and Nicola exchanged glances. They were the only people here.

Nicola held out her hand and David took it gently, wincing at the pain in his hand. He could feel the sweat underneath the bandages on both his hands, and wanted to scratch them, but held himself back. The itchiness meant they were healing, the nurse had told him. His stomach wound wasn't anywhere near being itchy yet, it was still just brutally sore, but at least he'd weasled some morphine out the doctors for the pain. He looked down and could see the bulge of the bandages under his creased white shirt and tatty suit jacket. He looked at Nicola, who reminded him of Jackie Kennedy in her shades and rather prim-looking suit. It was a good look, and it suited her. She always looked good at funerals, he thought, and he'd seen her at plenty of them. He looked like he felt – shit. Shit, yet ecstatic to be alive, and holding the hand of this beautiful woman.

He owed her his life. After he passed out on the cliff, she told him she'd fired off a distress flare and waited for help. A lifeboat arrived surprisingly quickly and spotted Neil's body sprawled on the rocks. She fired another flare to draw their attention, and within minutes a coastguard helicopter had arrived to pick them up. By the time they got to hospital David had lost a lot of blood – they measured it in pints, which seemed like a hell of a lot of liquid to do without – but they quickly stabilized him and saw to his wounds. He was lucky, the knife in the stomach hadn't damaged any of his main organs. It would hurt like hell for a while yet, but he wasn't in any danger. His hands were the same, badly cut but no severed tendons, so he wouldn't lose the use of any of his fingers.

He had remained unconscious throughout it all, and into the next day. Nicola tried to stay at his bedside but the police took her away for questioning. There was a dead body to account for, after all. She spent several hours in the station, the detectives starting off incredulous, then gradually coming round to her story as they checked it out. They released her by morning. Amy was safe at her friend's house, so she returned to the hospital. By the afternoon the police had finished examining the derelict cottage and the cave, and told her she was no longer needed for their inquiries. The police refused to tell her what they found in Neil's two hiding places, and she didn't push it further. She didn't want to know, didn't need to know anything more about him.

The first David knew of any of this was that evening, but by then Nicola had left to return to Edinburgh and Amy. She phoned that night. He cried down the phone, out of relief more than anything else, and just the sheer joy of hearing her voice. He spent the next three days in hospital being monitored before they released him. Nicola collected him and took him back to her flat, where she and Amy looked after him, one changing dressings and sorting out medication, the other distracting him with silly games and gossip from her school. Still Waters had been at the point of sacking him, but his five-week sick line had bought him a temporary reprieve.

And now they were back in the Western Cemetery in Arbroath, where three of David's old schoolfriends were now buried. He was the last surviving member of that daft little drinking crew of theirs. The thought appalled him as he stood by the graveside, and he felt tears sting his eyes. He gripped Nicola's hand tighter, despite the pain, and swallowed hard.

The minister finished his spiel, and they both threw a handful of dirt onto the coffin as it was lowered into the grave. Neither of them said anything. It didn't seem like there was anything to say. People were dead. And for what?

The minister excused himself and left, and a moment later Nicola and David turned their backs on Neil Cargill's grave as well, and walked slowly out the cemetery with the sun on their backs.

'So, what now?' said Nicola.

They were standing, surrounded by tourists, in what would've once been the nave of Arbroath Abbey, the perfect, stripy turf under their feet looking fake green in the luminous sunshine. Up ahead, Amy was skipping and leaping from pillar stump to pillar stump.

David looked at Nicola. They had changed out of their funeral clothes, and she looked fantastic in a simple tight T-shirt and jeans.

'What do you mean?'

'I mean, what now?'

'Care to be more specific?'

'Not really. I just meant with our lives. With you, with me. With you and me. All that sort of thing.'

'Right,' said David. 'I don't know. What do you think?'

'Well, we could start by going on a proper date. So far there's been a school reunion, a couple of funerals and a kidnapping involving a boat chase and a clifftop stand-off. Now, I'm far from a traditional sort of girl, but maybe we could just go out for dinner and a movie next time.'

'Dinner and a movie sounds great.'

They walked slowly up the expanse of grass, not talking.

'Did I ever tell you,' said Nicola, 'that a David Lindsay was one of the signatories of the Declaration of Arbroath?'

'I don't think so. Is that supposed to mean anything?'

'Not really. Just thought you'd like to know. It's something I thought of from the past. It's not important.'

'The past is important,' said David. 'But so is the future.'

Nicola looked at him with a raised eyebrow, but said nothing. They stood in silence a moment longer before David spoke.

'Did I ever thank you properly for saving my life?'

'I don't think you did,' said Nicola. 'But forget about it. It's all in the past.'

She leaned over, kissed him on the cheek and turned to chase after Amy. David watched her go, and a smile appeared on his face.

Acknowledgements

Immense and heartfelt thanks go to Trish for her love, understanding and support, Judy Moir for her crucial encouragement and boundless enthusiasm and Lucy Luck for her kind words and expert guidance.

He just wanted a decent book to read ...

Not too much to ask, is it? It was in 1935 when Allen Lane, Managing Director of Bodley Head Publishers, stood on a platform at Exeter railway station looking for something good to read on his journey back to London. His choice was limited to popular magazines and poor-quality paperbacks – the same choice faced every day by the vast majority of readers, few of whom could afford hardbacks. Lane's disappointment and subsequent anger at the range of books generally available led him to found a company – and change the world.

'We believed in the existence in this country of a vast reading public for intelligent books at a low price, and staked everything on it'
Sir Allen Lane, 1902–1970, founder of Penguin Books

The quality paperback had arrived – and not just in bookshops. Lane was adamant that his Penguins should appear in chain stores and tobacconists, and should cost no more than a packet of cigarettes.

Reading habits (and cigarette prices) have changed since 1935, but Penguin still believes in publishing the best books for everybody to enjoy. We still believe that good design costs no more than bad design, and we still believe that quality books published passionately and responsibly make the world a better place.

So wherever you see the little bird – whether it's on a piece of prize-winning literary fiction or a celebrity autobiography, political tour de force or historical masterpiece, a serial-killer thriller, reference book, world classic or a piece of pure escapism – you can bet that it represents the very best that the genre has to offer.

Whatever you like to read – trust Penguin.